MW01128809

RED RIVER RIFLES
WILDERNESS DAWNING, THE TEXAS WYLLIE BROTHERS
BOOK 1

ISBN 9781798642696

Red River Rifles is a fictional novel inspired by history, rather than a precise account of history. The characters are entirely fictional and names, places, and incidents either are the product of the author's imagination or are used fictiously. Any resemblance to actual persons, living or dead, businesses, companies, events, or locales is entirely coincidental. Each book in the series can be read independently.

For the sake of understanding, the author used language for her characters for the modern reader rather than strictly reflecting the far more formal speech and writing patterns of the early 19th-century.

Cover Design and Interior Format

© THE KILLION GROUP, INC.

DOROTHY WILEY

WILDERNESS DAWNING

RED RIVER RIFLES

THE
TEXAS WYLLIE BROTHERS

PRAISE FOR DOROTHY WILEY'S BOOKS

"The only thing I don't like about Dorothy Wiley's books is that at some point I finish them." – J. Collis

"I am in LOVE with Dorothy Wiley's novels! Amazingly believable and heartwarming tales. BRAVO, Dorothy!" – L. Ratterman

"This book is so beautifully written it's hard to believe it's actually fiction! Wonderful, heart wrenching, and honest this book is amazing!" – C. Nipper

"I love this series! It's about time to reread them all!!" – T.C. Herrera"

"Dorothy puts it all down on paper—love, sorrow, fighting for your rights. My very favorite author." – J. Bailey

"Wonderful story and series. I LOVE her writing! You can't put it down." – G.P. Lewis

"My FAVORITE author!" – K.S. Williams

"Every single page was packed with great reading. I stayed on the edge of my seat from the first page till the very last. I've read thousands of books in my lifetime, but these rank right up there with the best I've ever read" – J. P. Meeks

"Absolutely the very BEST historical romance series ever— and I've read hundreds of them! I highly recommend this series! Excellent!" – J. Blaylock

"Like stepping into a time machine, this book swept me back to the American wilderness from page one. Beautifully written, well-searched, and riveting." – A. Hughes

"The people in these books are as real to me when I read them as they are on any drama series on TV!"– S. Vestal

"There are a lot of writers out there, but few great ones like Ms. Wiley." – A. Foster

"This author and series deserves 20 stars! The writing and the storyline are outstanding." – PJSM

"I absolutely enjoyed both series! Every free moment and late into the night I read your books because I could not put them down. Your storytelling captivated me and made your characters so real I felt like I personally knew them all." – K. Smith

"Every free moment and late into the night I read your books because I could not put them down. Your storytelling captivated me and made your characters so real I felt like I personally knew them all." – K. Smith

"I just finished reading LOVE'S NEW BEGINNING and abso-lutely loved it. Your characters were perfect and I fell in love with all of them." – N. Copeland

"Wonderful story and series. I LOVE her writing! You can't put it down." – G. M. Lewis

"Another great book in a great series. I'm loving these books. Each one grabs my attention from the beginning and I don't want to put it down until I'm finished." – M.J.

"Dorothy combines history, romance, love, honor, integrity, grit, strength, compassion, forgiveness, faults and strengths to create believable characters in a true period of history. This author also adds a religious aspect without a religious specific bent or being preachy or judgmental just thoughtful and inclusive. Hard to put down, clean reading. Excellent author I will continue to follow." – J. Learning

DEDICATION

To Samuel Wiley
Circa 1805 – December 24, 1890
A veteran of the battles of Goliad and San Jacinto
and
Texas Ranger

CHARACTERS

Stephen Wyllie – One of the first settlers of Texas and father of six, age 52 (hero of WILDERNESS TRAIL OF LOVE)
Stephen Wyllie's sons:
Samuel – owner of Red River Cattle Company, age 21
Thomas – age 19
Cornelius – age 17
Stephen "Steve" Jr. – age 16
Jason 'Baldy' Grant – Ordained minister and physician, age 48 (a major character in LOVE'S GLORY)
Melly Grant – Baldy's wife, age 40
Louisa Pate – age 18
Adam Pate – age 8
John R. Pate – Adam and Louisa's father, age 38
Alex Wetmore – trading Post owner
William Mabbitt – trading Post owner
Mathew Hardin – veteran rifleman Battle of Tippecanoe
Herman H. Long – filibuster and Commander of forces at Camp Freeman at Nacogdoches
William 'Old Bill' Williams – trapper and translator
Kuukuh – Caddo Indian brave
Capitán Tomás Fernández – Spanish Royalist Army officer
Claude O'Neil – drunken fiddle player

Petition to the Senate
and
House of Representatives
of the
State of Texas

"Stephen Wiley came to Texas at a time of imminent peril and he and his family endured great hardships and sufferings, nevertheless he was ever ready to face danger when necessary and a frontier life in a new country for the purpose of securing for himself and his family and those that should come after him the blessings of civil and religious liberty as well as the temporal comforts desired by all...

Remember with grateful emotions the day that they pitched their tents and identified themselves with the then wilderness of Texas."

Daniel Daily, for Samuel and John Wiley,
September 4, 1851

FORWARD

THOSE READERS WHO HAVE READ my previous ten novels, know that although they were entirely fictional, they were "inspired" by my husband's ancestors. This book goes beyond the first two series—American Wilderness Series and Wilderness Hearts Series—and incorporates actual family history into the stories. Although this series is also largely fictional, it is based on the real-life of Stephen Wiley (born about 1758 and died December 1826) and his bold decision to bring his four sons to the Province of Texas. That decision would change our family's history forever.

Noted historian Rex Strickland cites sources verifying that Stephen Wiley (current spelling of the last name) and four sons were indeed on the south side of the Red River in 1818, well before Stephen F. Austin brought colonists to the Province of Texas in 1824. So 2018, the year I researched and wrote most of this novel, was the 200th anniversary of Stephen and his sons' arrival in Texas! I am so honored to celebrate, with my husband and our family, this important anniversary with the publication of this book dedicated to Stephen Wiley's eldest son, Samuel Wiley.

The twenty-one-year-old Samuel in this book was my husband's third great-grandfather (who was actually born about 1805, likely in Kentucky, and died 1890, in Wilson County, Texas, just a couple of miles from our ranch). In real life, Samuel would go on to live an extraordinarily heroic life that included fighting at the first Goliad battle, combat at the Battle of San Jacinto (the battle that brought victory against the Mexican Army and gained Texas), and later service for a period of time as a Texas Ranger against an Indian threat.

For this novel, there was no way of knowing, of course, what these men and women were truly like. From genealogical and historical research we know their names, where they lived, and when. We also have military, land, and tax records. But knowing the strength of their character, the depth of their faith, their dreams, and who they loved is another thing entirely. However, having had the pleasure of knowing my husband's grandfather and father, and my husband for more than forty years, I believe I can safely assume the first Wileys in Texas were men and women of honor and strength. And so, the characters in this book, Stephen, Samuel, and the rest of his family are modeled after the Wiley men I've known and researched. Everything else is simply a story meant to bring history to life—to bring the reader to the edge of the West.

There is perhaps no part of American history that is as enthralling as the dawning of the American West. The men and women who came west were responding to not only a desire to better themselves and their families, they were answering a deep-seated westward call that spoke to their very souls. A call which could not be denied despite the risks to life and family in a new, lonely land.

Here, in the *Wilderness Dawning Series*, in the company of Stephen and his four sons, the reader can experience what it might have been like to be one of the first families to settle in the wild and fresh land that would become Texas!

The following short Prologue will bring readers up to speed on what happened to Samuel and his immediate family in the years between the last book, LOVE'S WHISPER, set in 1811 and this novel, RED RIVER RIFLES, set in 1818. Then, in Chapter 1, the story really begins!

Dorothy Wiley

March 2019

PROLOGUE

THE YEARS IMMEDIATELY AFTER SAMUEL Wyllie left Kentucky were not peaceful ones. With his heart hammering with excitement, Samuel, along with his father, three brothers, and their good friends Baldy and Melly Grant, left Kentucky in the spring of 1812. With heavy hearts, they'd said goodbye to his older sisters and their husbands, their Uncle Sam and Aunt Catherine, and their two sons, Little John and Rory. Goodbyes had already been said to their other uncles—William, Edward, and Bear and their families.

Their horses had barely stepped away when Martha ran after Samuel for one more embrace. Since their mother's death soon after Stephen Jr. was born, when Samuel was about five, Martha had pretty much raised them. She'd held him in her arms and wept aloud as she told him she would never see him again on Earth. Their father had gently scolded her saying he'd already promised they would all return to visit every other Christmas.

Samuel guessed that Martha had been closer to the truth because they had yet to return to Kentucky for a visit. They were still too occupied with trying to get settled and staying alive.

They intended to settle in the new lands of the Province of Texas. Their journey took them first to Louisiana, recently purchased by the United States from France. By the time they'd traveled the long, overland journey of seven hundred miles to get there, the War of 1812 raged. The country's second bloody war with the British lasted nearly three years—June 1812 – February 1815—and delayed their planned move to the Province of Texas.

Many of their family members contributed to the war effort in one way or another. Only fifteen when the war started, Samuel and his father, Stephen, both experienced cattlemen, supplied beef for troops. A graduate of a Virginia medical school, Baldy became a U.S. Army surgeon during the war and served at the Battle of New Orleans. Melly, a nurse, worked alongside him.

Back in Kentucky, Uncle Sam and his oldest son Little John supplied trained horses. Uncle William, Uncle Bear, and his brothers-in-law, Gabe and Liam, all served in the militia, while Uncle Edward became an officer in the army. The Kentucky Militia, with 24,000 Kentuckians serving, played a vital role. Of those Kentuckians, newspapers reported 1,200 casualties, more than any other state. This was likely because Kentucky was the site of continuing warfare between settlers and Indians backed by the British.

Men like his Uncle Bear and Uncle William, well used to using Kentucky longrifles with a range of a hundred to two hundred yards, were effective fighters against the British. The British fought old style, marching in mass and armed with Brown Bess muskets with a range of only fifty yards or so. It was a style of warfare dying fast, and England learned too late the superiority of American rifles and grit.

Liam, the husband of his sister, Polly, and Gabe, the husband of his eldest sister, Martha, paid the highest price in the war effort. Weakened by freezing temperatures and inadequate winter shelter, Liam became ill but recovered in a few months. It took nearly a year for Gabe to fully recover from a severe wound.

When the war ended, his father and Baldy decided to wait a few years in Louisiana until it would be safe to settle in the volatile Province of Texas. His father bought five-hundred acres, seventeen miles above Campti, on the east bank of the Red River, in the Natchitoches Parish. But after enduring both a drought and a flood in the same year, the constant harassment of mosquitos, and the threat of feisty alligators, both of which were the major inhabitants of Natchitoches, his father had had enough. Baldy and Melly wholeheartedly agreed and the seven of them decided it was time to leave a land that produced forty bushels of frogs to the acre.

It was time to relocate to the Province of Texas. All those who had already traveled there told newspaper writers the same thing—it was impossible to exaggerate the pleasant character, the natural beauty, and the fertility of the land called Texas.

And so, on February 6, 1818, a Sunday, the day generally

chosen to commence a journey, Baldy said a prayer asking Providence to bless the second leg of their trek to the Province of Texas. Bundled up in heavy woolens against the cold, they set off with Melly driving their horse-drawn wagon loaded with needed supplies. The rest of them rode fine, sturdy horses and guided their fifty head of cattle.

From Campti, they followed the old road south toward San Augustine, the site of an old Spanish Presidio and the only entryway into the interior of Texas from the east. To the south lay the Big Thicket, a nearly impenetrable densely wooded barrier to travel. To the north, predatory and sometimes hostile tribes held the country.

When they reached the Sabine River, they took Herman Gaines' ferry across. Almost at once, the landscape opened up to rolling hills and valleys. On a luxurious carpet of winter grass, rose magnificent trees—oaks, elms, hickories, and other hardwoods. Clear, cold streams provided all the water they needed and, except for one bad storm, they were blessed with favorable traveling weather.

Between San Augustine and Nacogdoches, John Maximillian made them welcome at his ranch at Lobanillo. But anxious to be on his way, his father insisted they leave the next morning.

At Nacogdoches, one of three Spanish settlements in the Province of Texas, they stopped for the evening at the Old Stone Fort, an impressive two-story structure built from native iron ore. The other two settlements in the Province were at San Antonio de Bexar and Presidio La Bahia at Goliad, far to the west and south. Called La Casa Piedra by the Spanish, the Old Stone Fort was a mercantile house and a seat of civil government for Nacogdoches. At the fort, they were able to find beds and a good Spanish meal made of goat and vegetables.

The next morning Samuel observed that Nacogdoches, situated about sixty miles west of the Sabine River, sat in a small valley surrounded by woodsy bluffs. A branch of the Neches made a semicircle around the scenic settlement. Someday, he hoped the cattle operation he planned would bring him back to the pleasant little town.

Over the next few days, they traveled due north. They forded minor rivers, slogged through mud in creeks, and skirted around canebrakes. Several times they had to use all their horses and ropes to pull the stuck wagon free.

After their journey of nearly three hundred miles, they finally arrived at their destination—a little settlement on the south side of the Red River named Pecan Point. His father and Baldy believed that the remote outpost would one day become the front door to a new land called Texas.

For the first time, Samuel saw land so beautiful it rivaled even the most glorious parts of Kentucky. The grass looked like emerald-green velvet, the air smelled clean and sweet, the river shimmered, and the land south of the Red River was well-watered with springs, creeks, and bayous. Close by, near the Pecan Bayou, grew woods containing fully mature, virgin timber, some greater than three feet in diameter. The old-growth timber of these trees—shortleaf pine, white oak, loblolly pine, red oak, red maple, and hickory—made a cathedral-like canopy that Samuel loved to ride under. And beneath these magnificent trees, grew a lower story of dogwood, beautyberry, mulberry, and farkleberry.

The lush land here was an area claimed by both the United States, through the Louisiana Purchase of 1803, and by Spain, who claimed all the land to the Red River. The settlement was fair distance from Washington and anything official though. And Spain had bigger worries than the exact boundary line for this remote part of the Province. But Spain welcomed foreigners offering some settlers generous land grants, to encourage economic development and to help deter the aggressive and mobile Plains Indians. In other words, the Spaniards wanted the Americans to be the ones to die fighting Indians.

Just who owned this part of the Province remained a matter of debate. It was even rumored that Mexico would soon try to take Spain's territories from her in a revolution. And mixed in with all the conflicting claims and moving boundaries were the Indians who often exercised claims of their own.

Some tribes only recently migrated to the area north of the Red River. Renegade bands came and established themselves without the permission of other Indian tribes or the American or Spanish governments. Lately, one such group of fierce Comanches relocated from the mountains of the northwest to the southern plains. Other tribes, like the Caddos had lived in the area since ancient times until in 1795, they moved a hundred miles to the southeast to the shores of Caddo Lake.

With the departure of the Caddos, Samuel had learned, the area had remained uninhabited until three years ago. It was then that venturesome traders, trappers, hunters, and settlers like his father, who believed this rich land belonged to the United States, started to drift in. They all still considered themselves citizens of the United States. The ill-defined boundary line between Spanish Texas and the American Territory of Arkansas was not something that concerned any of them. They would not be restrained by such details. And apparently, officials in Washington weren't too concerned either, because they failed to make the boundary clear.

To Samuel, it didn't matter who owned the magnificent and mysterious prairies and woods that stretched seemingly without end alongside the Red River's banks. For miles upon miles, it was land lacking in civilization just waiting to be appreciated by somebody.

Somebody like him.

CHAPTER I

Pecan Point, Red River, Province of Texas
September 1818

SAMUEL WYLLIE STARED INTO THE darkness, his instinct telling him that Indians lurked around them like empty-bellied wolves prowling in the night.

He nudged his younger brother with the butt of his rifle. They'd both been sent by their father to stand guard over their homeplace. Their faces darkened by mud, they lay beside each other on the roof of their large horse shed. From there, a tall two-story structure, they could see a threat coming from any direction. Samuel faced north and Thomas, his nineteen-year-old brother, south. Thomas kept nodding off, but Samuel knew better than to disappoint their father, Stephen, by letting their cattle and especially their horses be stolen. The barn below them held their father's prized stallion and six other horses, including Samuel's own fine gelding, Samson.

"Thomas, wake up," Samuel whispered. "Get ready. We're going to do a little shootin'." No one was going to steal their horses. Not on his watch. He and his father shared a sincere love of their horses. And on the frontier, whether a man would live or die often depended upon his horse.

Thomas came instantly awake and snatched up his longrifle. They all used Kentucky longrifles. Longrifles were lightweight, possessed graceful long lines, and economically consumed powder. But most of all, they were fatally accurate.

"What's out there?" Thomas whispered.

"Just listen."

The many desolate miles surrounding them provided a happy hunting ground for thieves. Indians more often stole horses than cattle. In fact, Joseph English of Clear Creek lost several high-value horses. Thirteen horses were also stolen from the Pecan Point settlement not long ago. And last month, upwards of twenty horses were stolen from the other settlements along the Red River. In each case, the horses were taken without alerting the owners.

The Spanish authorities, ill-equipped to do anything about it, could not stop the Indians from robbing the people on the river, not only of their horses and livestock but even occasionally of their household goods. Determining which tribe was responsible was often difficult because many tribes—Caddo, Kiowa, Choctaw, Cherokee, Delaware, Pawnee, Osage, and Comanche—traversed the area even though they didn't live near here.

And the unscrupulous rustler, who would rather steal than purchase his beef, was always a threat too. But not for long. The only authority in the area was their own longrifles. Rustlers were killed where they were found. Samuel witnessed this form of punishment when rustlers stole a dozen of their branded cattle. He'd joined his father and other men from the settlement in pursuit. The rustlers were unable to move quickly because of the cattle they'd stolen and they soon caught up to the two thieves. They'd admitted their guilt and begged for mercy.

"It's God you should ask for mercy," his father had said a moment before the thieves were hanged.

The entire event had been hard for Samuel to watch, but it put other rustlers on notice. His father was not a man to cross. Those who looked with covetous eyes upon Wyllie family cows would pay for it with their lives. Conversely, if a man asked his father for food, without hesitation, he'd give him a hearty meal and a shirt for his back if he needed it. But after that, if he wanted more, he had to work for it.

Samuel cocked his ears and listened to the silence of the night along the Red. It was too quiet. The spotted frogs along the river's edge, normally so loud at night he'd nicknamed them chorus frogs, had gone silent. A strange, threatening silence hung in the air—the kind of stillness that raises the hairs on the back of your neck. And the shadows of the night against the moon's bluish-gray light gave Samuel an eerie sense that violence was coming.

Soon one of the horses below them neighed and another whinnied. That's when his heart quickened because a horse can smell danger.

Too often, danger was commonplace here for they lived in a savage frontier stretching many wild, lonely miles. Life itself was a gamble in this hinterland between two countries—the United States and Spain—inhabited mostly by buffalo, the Indian, wolves, and a few daring settlers. Only those colonists brave enough to carve a home out of a raw land could live here. A place where every day, at every turn, danger lurked like a wicked member of the family.

"Do you want me to go wake Father?" Thomas whispered.

"No, just keep your eyes open."

The rest of their family—their father and their younger brothers Cornelius, age seventeen, and Steve, age sixteen, would be asleep inside their log home, their beds cushioned with buffalo hides. Their only neighbors, their close friends, Dr. Baldy Grant and his wife Melly, lived just twenty-five yards away. Both a preacher and a doctor, Baldy was one of the best and smartest men in this or any other land. He was also a fiercely loyal comrade. Samuel knew he would come running, rifle in hand, at the sound of the first shots. And Melly, who often served as the doctor's nurse, had been like a mother to him and his brothers since they'd first met her in 1811.

For several long moments, they remained motionless atop the barn. Tales of Indian raiders who swept down on the settlers along the Red on dark and bloody quests filled Samuel's mind for a minute. Marauding bands of Indians often menaced their sparsely settled area. And the thought of one threatening his family unnerved him. One poor man, a trader named Pierrier, who had unwisely come alone from Natchitoches, was attacked while he was drying his clothes. They scalped him, cut off his head, and left his body for the scavengers. And that wasn't the only time men around here had their heads removed by Indians. The thought of dying that way made Samuel shudder and he gripped his longrifle even tighter.

He pushed the gory account and others from his mind. He needed to focus. He needed to notice every sound, no matter how small. He needed to detect every movement of brush or tree not caused by the breeze. All of their lives might depend on discerning the slightest aberration.

Then he spotted his enemy through the moonlight. A crouching Osage brave, bent over at the waist, held his bow notched with a dressed-up feathered arrow. As the brave crept toward the barn, another brave followed him, a knife in one hand and a hatchet in the other. They both wore breechcloths and several beaded necklaces. Their eyelids, cheeks, and torso were painted orange-red. The hair on their heads was gone, except for a front-to-back crest, which was dyed a brilliant red. The headdress of the first brave held the withered head and feathers of a small raptor, likely a hawk. The pointed curve of the hawk's beak was perfect for snatching up mice from the prairie. But this Indian raptor wasn't hunting mice. He was hunting horses. Or men.

Not wanting to draw their attention, Samuel slightly nudged his brother and pointed only a finger.

Thomas nodded but was smart enough to wait until Samuel fired before he moved around to face the threat.

Samuel's eyes widened as several more Indians streamed out from the brush. He lined up his rifle sights on the first Indian and fired.

As the Indian fell the other braves hesitated a blink of a moment.

In that instant, Thomas turned and fired his rifle and a second brave tumbled to the ground. Then Samuel and his brother yanked their pistols out and began firing at the other braves, who were now all whirling around to flee. Hitting a sprinting brave with a flintlock pistol was far more difficult and Samuel's first shot missed. Taking a steadying breath and carefully lining up the sights of his second pistol, he fired again and his shot struck a retreating brave. Both of Thomas' shots missed.

Their father and brothers thrust their longrifles through the cabin's portholes and the sound of four other rifles exploded into the night one after the other. Meanwhile, Samuel and Thomas quickly reloaded their flintlocks in silence.

Samuel scrutinized the area, his darting glances searching for signs of other braves. But the threat was now well-hidden in the cover of darkness.

His father and other brothers undoubtedly realized the same

thing. Seeing no further threat, after a few minutes, they slowly filed out of the cabin, their longrifles held at their shoulders and pointed toward the distant brush.

As he predicted, Baldy came running up. "Indians!" Baldy yelled, taking in the three bodies scattered about. "I thought it might be. Everyone all right?"

His father nodded grimly. "My boys made them scatter like a covey of quail. You'd best get back to Melly in case they circle around. But my guess is, they've learned we're not an easy target, thanks to those two." He pointed up at Samuel and Thomas, a look of respect on his face.

Baldy waved to the two of them and turned back toward home. "Save one of those bodies for me," he yelled back at them.

Samuel knew the doctor meant to dissect the brave to help him learn about men's bodies. Although Samuel understood the need for knowledge of what was inside of a man, he still found the practice grisly.

Stephen motioned for them to come down. "Samuel and Thomas, you've earned a rest. Go to bed. Cornelius and Steve will take your place until dawn. I'll check on the horses." With that, while Samuel and Thomas climbed down, his father took long, swift strides toward the horse shed. Always cautious, his pistol was drawn.

Samuel wasn't surprised that his father would send his two youngest up for guard duty. Young men on the frontier grew up fast and Cornelius and Steve were both crack shots. About once a month, the four brothers would have shooting contests. It seemed like every month a different brother would win so Samuel decided they must all be first-rate marksmen.

Six-feet tall and heavily muscular, his father possessed a natural authority. But it was more their respect for him that made Cornelius and Steve both say, "Yes, Sir."

"Wait, keep our pistols for the rest of the night," Samuel said, handing his two to Cornelius. "Stay alert, they might come back."

Thomas handed his pistols to Steve. "Yup, better not fall asleep."

Samuel wanted to snicker, but Thomas' expression was serious, almost somber.

Cornelius and Steve nodded and scurried up the ladder and then hauled it up to the roof to keep anyone from climbing upward.

Thomas turned and strode toward their house, his head bowed.

Samuel glanced at the bodies of the braves and then up at his other brothers. He didn't want to leave them out here alone. Once again, rifle at the ready, his keen eyes surveyed the brush and trees for any sign of danger.

"I checked on George and the other horses. They're all there, thanks to you," his father said walking up.

"And Thomas," Samuel said.

His father's hand rested on one of the two heavy pistols that dangled from his belt. They were always loaded and always on his person or right beside him. "What are you waiting for?"

"I think I should stay out here too," Samuel told him.

"No, your brothers need to learn to carry their weight. Being responsible for the safety of the horses and us is a great way for them to learn it. Besides, I don't think we'll see further trouble tonight. If I did, we'd all stay out here. Those braves will move on to an easier target."

"There aren't many easy targets in this part of the country."

"Agreed. Everyone's been on edge and alert since the last Indian attack."

"What about the bodies?" Samuel asked.

"Leave them until morning. We'll take them closer to the river and bury them there, except the one Baldy wants to examine. The Osage place their dead in a sitting posture on the ground and pile a heap of stones around the body for its protection."

Samuel sighed and swallowed hard. The killing left a sick feeling churning inside of him. "I'll do it. And I'll bury the other one after Baldy is through studying it."

"You did well, son. I know killing isn't easy, but they were here to steal from us or worse. If that wasn't their intention, they would have come peacefully during the day." He strode over to one of the braves and pointed down. "These braves have lethal weapons in their hands that would have been used on one of us without quarter."

Samuel stood beside him and stared down at the sharp blade of a tomahawk. "And they died on our homeplace. We weren't in their territory."

"True. The Osage homelands are far to the north. Gather up

their weapons and then come inside."

Carrying the Osage weapons, Samuel ducked as he entered the cabin. The door didn't quite accommodate his six-foot-three stature. He piled the weapons by the door, and then rinsed the mud from his face. After drying off, he glanced over at Thomas who sat staring into the hearth. He joined his brother, sitting down on a log stool, and gazed into the hearth too. He found the embers of the dying fire consoling.

"Here, drink this," his father said handing them both a couple of fingers worth of whiskey. "It will help you sleep."

"Why did they make us kill them?" Thomas asked, accepting the tin cup. It was the first time his brother had killed a man. He knew Thomas would not let the event pass without some earnest soul-searching.

Their father sat down next to them. "Many Indians are honorable, noble people whom whites greatly misunderstand and often mistreat. Among some natives, however, pride, greed, and other human vices flourish just as surely as they do within some white settlers. Make no mistake, the code of honor and morality held by Indian tribes often differs from Christian values. What is dishonorable to us may be honorable to them."

Samuel took a long sip of whiskey. "A thief is a thief no matter his heritage."

"I agree," said Thomas. "They deserved what they got." He tossed back the rest of the whiskey in one gulp and after he coughed a bit, he stood up. "I'm going to bed."

Despite his brave front and the whiskey, Samuel suspected his brother would have a hard time sleeping tonight. Likely he would too. His mind burned with the image of the two braves he'd killed falling down dead. But that memory was not unexpected. Taking a life should never be easy, even when it deserved to be taken.

Their father stood as well, his knee cracking as he did so. Although still a vigorous and powerful man, at fifty-two, the hard wilderness of Kentucky and now the dangers peculiar to the Province of Texas were just beginning to take a toll on his body. A trailblazer by nature, his father had always ventured into the most remote areas, wherever there were rivers or streams to provide water. Places where other men feared to go. His robust constitution, iron endurance, and his natural courage made him well-suited for braving the edge of the frontier.

Samuel liked to think his father had passed those same qualities on to him. He hoped that someday he could be the man his father was. The older he got the more Samuel appreciated his father's great courage and valor.

And their small community at Pecan Point and the larger Jonesboro, a little further west, could both claim a great proportion of similarly heroic men. Men who came mostly from Kentucky and Tennessee. Like his father, many of their fathers eagerly followed behind Boone over the Wilderness Road or pioneered with Sevier along the Holston River. They were born adventurers, courageous, and skilled, with a knack for wringing sustenance from the wilderness. They were men like Colonel Mabbitt, brothers Adam and Alex Wetmore, Adam Lawrence, and Claiborne Wright—pioneers who knew how to fight for a new life.

In 1818, Samuel's family joined these men at the Red River settlements. They were among the first Americans to venture into the vastness of the Texas Province.

And Samuel was proud to be among them.

CHAPTER 2

⁊❧

North side of the Red River, above Pecan Point

LOUISA PATE'S SWEATY PALMS GRIPPED the stock of her father's heavy rifle.

John R. Pate, her father, was a man of iron will and indomitable force. Once he'd resolved to claim land in the Province of Texas, or maybe it was the Arkansas Territory—no one was sure what this place was called—their destiny was fixed. They'd arrived at the Pecan Point settlement a week ago and her father had purchased, on the other side of the Red River, a log cabin and acreage from a settler who was in a hurry to leave.

And so it was that she found herself hiding in the settler's cornfield with her little brother. Summer rains must have come at the right time for the sweet-smelling corn stalks stood thick and tall. In addition to the corn they would harvest next month, the stalks provided a place to hide. For that she gave thanks.

Beside her crouched her wide-eyed, eight-year-old brother, Adam. They'd heard barking and when she peered out into the darkness, she'd seen their dog's alert stance and movement in the bushes. At once, she'd grabbed the loaded rifle her father had left with her and snuck out the back window with her brother. With Adam's small hand in hers, she'd run with all her might toward the cornfield. Unable to keep up, she'd had to carry him on her side the last few yards.

"Pa should be here," her brother said.

"Hush, Adam!" she whispered into his ear.

Their father had left that morning for Jonesboro, a larger settlement about thirty miles away. He said he planned to buy supplies for their new home and an evening's 'entertainment' as he called it. So, since that morning, she had been left alone with her brother. Louisa's mother and Adam's mother had both died long before they came here.

Her father also wanted to find someone willing to rent a slave. He didn't have the money to buy a slave, but he could rent one for a while from someone else. Apparently renting a slave for labor was a common practice amongst settlers who couldn't afford to buy one to work their farm and fields. She found both owning and renting another human being disgraceful and wanted to tell him so.

But she didn't. The one time she'd stood up to him, by simply calling him old-fashioned, she received a slap to her cheek so hard it knocked her off her feet. Glaring down at her with narrowed, dark eyes, he'd shouted, "I'll teach you to respect me." Then, her father jerked her up by her hair and shoved her across the room. Her punishments were occasionally even more severe. Every so often, he would throw things at her or rip up her clothes. She would sometimes cry out, sometimes silently curse. But most of the time she would just tremble deep inside herself.

She never fought back.

Whenever her father hurt her, it always made Adam cry. And every time her brother cried, her father would whip him with a belt. "Men don't cry," he would yell as he snapped the leather across her brother's small back at least once and, if he were really angry, two or three times.

For her, witnessing Adam's rough treatment was her father's cruelest punishment. The sight wounded her more than anything else he could do to her.

So, for the last several years, to protect her brother, she avoided doing or saying anything to set their father off. She would also feign respect for her father. That helped, but her tenuous harmony with him was as fragile as butterfly wings. Her life was an uneasy charade with only a pretense of happiness.

That morning, her father had made sure she was well armed before he left and told her she was responsible for protecting their home. But when the Indians showed up, her first thought was to protect Adam, so she chose to hide him rather than fight.

She hadn't had time to grab the pistols, shot sack, and powder horn. Only the rifle. And the single shot it held was all that stood between her and her brother's certain captivity if they were discovered. And for her, capture meant...

God be merciful, she prayed.

Her heart beat so hard it hurt as she peered through the corn stalks. By the silver-sheen of the moon, she saw the slinking braves surround her home. They appeared to be Comanche because straight-up eagle feathers and weasel tails decorated their hair worn in two long braids, the style of Comanche braves. She'd read newspaper accounts of Comanche attacks and remembered the writers' frightening descriptions. Comanches would strike without mercy, from infants to old people. They were known to rape, pillage, torture, and even commit frightful butchery of the dead.

These braves were even more fearsome than she had imagined.

When the braves discovered that the house was empty, they whooped and yelped. Their shrill cries made her skin crawl and she snuggled deeper into the earth and rubbed dirt on her brother's face and her cheeks and forehead.

She wanted to run into the night as far away as their legs would carry them. But if she moved, she risked disturbing the corn stalks and alerting the Indians to their presence. Best to stay put.

She tried desperately to push the heartrending stories she'd heard of Indian atrocities from her mind. For Adam's sake, she could not afford to panic. She forbade herself to tremble and clenched her jaw to block the sob that wanted to escape her throat.

For nearly a half-hour she observed the braves loading their horses with her family's belongings. With every minute, she despaired more. They would be left with nothing.

Even when she heard them ride off, she still couldn't move. She kept her hands frozen around the rifle and her body burrowed into the earth.

After Adam saw them leave, he soon fell asleep beside her in the corn row.

She snuggled closer to him and covered his little back with her arm to keep him warm. She loved him so much. Her brother was the only good part of her life.

She would do anything to protect him.

After a sleepless and shivering all-night vigil, dawn finally came, casting an orange glow over the land. But a heavy mist creeping up from the river would soon reach them. She woke Adam and they staggered back to the house, hand in hand, to survey the damage. Her old mare was dead, drilled through with the shaft of a Comanche arrow. Her throat tightened with sorrow. She'd loved that mare. They'd been through many miles together. The horse was an old gal but still a trusty mount. Sadness gripped her, but Louisa would not let herself cry.

"Why did they kill her?" she asked.

"Maybe the Indians knew how much you loved her," Adam said.

Then, in the same spot he'd been standing in the night before, they found Adam's dog, Buddy. His neck was covered in blood. Her brother dropped to his knees beside the dog and wailed.

Louisa's heart broke as she tried to comfort him.

The Indians must have also known how much Adam loved Buddy.

For a long time, they just sat there in the dirt beside each other.

When Adam recovered enough to stop crying, Louisa led him toward the cabin. With her heart beating hard, she took a cautious step inside the dim interior. Their dismal cabin was even gloomier now. All their food was gone. The flour, the smoked wild hog, even their salt. The table with her stew pot, frying pan, and a cooking knife sat empty. Their meager bedding and winter blankets were also taken. Worse, all their clothing and shoes were stolen. She had precious few clothes anyway. Just two threadbare gowns. Now, all she had was the shift she'd slept in. It was the same for Adam. The nightshirt he wore was all he had left. Worst of all, their two pistols, shot, and powder were gone.

Father would be furious.

Frantically, she searched for the family Bible. Everything was in disarray and her eyes darted here and there. She righted a small table and spotted the Bible underneath. Grasping it against her chest, she whispered, "Thank you." The Bible was all she had left of her mother. In the front, in her mother's beautiful hand was Louisa's name and her birthdate. Her father's second wife,

Adam's mother, had also written her brother's name and birth-date under hers. She ran her fingertip over the writing, feeling the love their mothers must have felt as they'd written the names of their babies.

When she glanced up, she saw Adam sitting on the floor silently crying.

"We're goin' to die. We'll starve or freeze to death," he sobbed.

"No, Adam, no," she said as she crouched next to him. "Pa will buy us more food and clothing." At least she hoped he would.

"But he doesn't have much money," Adam wailed.

"Then I'll go to work and make some," she said. She wondered just what she would do, but she didn't wonder about her willingness to do it. She would do anything for her little brother. Well, almost anything. She wouldn't sell herself, although she suspected that for enough money, her father would sell her.

"When will Pa be back?" Adam asked.

"I don't know. It might be a day or two." She couldn't let Adam go that long without eating. He was already far too thin, and they would both grow weak from hunger. "We'll have to cross the river. There are settlers on the other side. We've seen their cabins and cattle in the distance. We can alert the settlers to the Indian threat and maybe they'll be kind enough to give us some food."

"Won't Pa get mad if we're not here? He'll think the Indians carried us off."

"You're right. He will." She thought for a moment. There was a little paper, quill, and ink hidden beneath the floorboard with her father's papers. She pried it up and scribbled a note as best she could. She could read well, but since paper was so scarce she hadn't been able to practice her writing. So her script was crude and her spelling uncertain. She wrote *akros river*, drew an arrow that pointed toward the river, and signed it L & A. She positioned the note on the table so that the arrow pointed toward the Red River. Then she returned the writing materials to the hiding place and put the floorboard back in place.

"Your mare is dead. How will we get over there?" Adam asked.

"We'll walk. After summer, the water level is low and there's a buffalo trail across it." They'd been told that Pecan Point was the only crossing place on the Red River for buffalo for many miles. If buffalo could get across, they could too.

Adam pointed to her thin shift. "You're goin' to go out dressed like that?"

"I have no choice. I don't see any other clothing or even a blanket around here. Do you?"

"Nope. And our boots are gone too."

Louisa snatched up the rifle in one hand and took Adam's hand in the other. Clutching both, she banished the tears that wanted to fall and filled her heart with determination.

She didn't look back as they left. There wasn't much to look at.

Louisa led her brother through the grass-covered fields and under tall trees toward the river. She knew the well-trodden path well. She'd always loved to run and, since her father was a late riser, she'd sprinted to the river every morning since they moved here. Sometimes she ran in the evenings too, but she always made sure she was home before dark when coyotes and other critters came out to hunt.

As she ran down the well-worn path, it always felt healing for her heart to pump hard and fast. The air would lift her long hair and cool her skin as her feet flew over dew-covered grass and leaves. Running gave her a sense of strength and freedom.

But the feeling was always only temporary. As soon as she returned home, she would feel weak and trapped again. If only she could run away from her life. When would her struggles end? Would she ever know happiness? After her father's rages, she would cry out to heaven with all she had left inside her. But her prayers and her faith were wearing as thin as she was.

They stepped down through loose, reddish soil as they descended the steep, tree-lined bank. Fortunately, at the end of summer, the water level in the Red was low and only a foot or so deep where the water still flowed. They could easily wade through it. But there was another problem—quicksand. It had once swallowed a man and a horse in minutes, she'd been told.

She handed the rifle to Adam. She had to find a sturdy stick to use to check for quicksand.

"It's heavy," Adam said. The rifle was as tall as he was.

"I know," Louisa told him, "but I've got to check for quicksand. Just be sure you don't shoot me with that thing. Never point it toward a person unless you intend to defend yourself. Put the barrel on your shoulder and hold it on the butt."

The first time she'd gone to the river to bathe and wash their clothes, her father had warned her to tread cautiously along the river's edge because it was a common location for quicksand. She suspected his warning stemmed more from not wanting to lose his cook and laundress than it did from concern for her.

She eyed the terrain and saw what she thought was the buffalo trail. Although the low morning fog and the mistiness of the river limited visibility and made it difficult to be sure. Water bubbled up in some spots. Those were the most dangerous places because it meant there was air underneath the soil. She spotted a long branch and snatched it up and took them a little further west where patches of the ground appeared drier.

With quiet caution, she thumped the mud in front of her with the pole and started slowly across. "Stay right behind me," she warned Adam.

"Are you sure this is the buffalo crossing?" Adam asked. "What if it's closer to the settlement?"

She wasn't sure. But she had to try. On foot, it would take them too long to reach the settlement. She needed to get Adam to safety now before any more Indians showed up. She took a deep breath, and stepped out onto the sand. When the ground easily gave way under the stick, she quickly took another course.

"What if we fall into the quicksand?" her brother asked as he yanked a bare foot out of the sandy slurry.

"Pa said to lean back and wait for your legs to float up, even if it takes an hour."

"What if they don't? What if my head goes under too?"

"Adam, let me concentrate." Taking slow, measured steps, she couldn't wait to reach the far bank. The distance seemed to stretch forever. From inside the riverbed, the river's width seemed far wider than it had when they were standing on the riverbank. If she'd known it was this far across, she would never have attempted the crossing.

Step by careful step she moved them forward. The river bank seemed close now. She glanced back at Adam whose look of trust and hope made her even more determined to get him to safety.

As the sun rose, the morning air grew humid on the marshy

riverbed and mosquitos started to buzz. First a few, then what seemed like hundreds hummed around them. Wearing only their thin nightclothes, they would soon be covered in bites. In her panic, she swatted at the swarming mosquitos with her stick and accidentally flung it.

"I'll get it," Adam said.

"No," she said, but he'd already stepped toward it.

Her eyes widened in horror as her brother sunk to his calves.

"Oh, Lord, no!" she cried. "Adam, quick, toss me the rifle. Its weight will make you sink further."

He tried to toss the rifle to her, but its weight was too heavy for his small arms, and it landed between them. They both stared down with widened eyes as it sank into the mire.

"Help me!" he cried.

"Raise your knees!"

He tried but his legs, surrounded by heavy sand, didn't budge. "I can't." His sweet little face twisted with fear.

Her mind raced. If she could just reach the rifle, if it hadn't sunk too far, she could use it to tug him out. "Adam, don't be afraid. I'll get you out."

On the verge of tears, Adam merely nodded.

Slowly, she shifted toward him.

CHAPTER 3

SAMUEL STOOD AND WIPED HIS hands on his pants, finished with the grim task of burying two of the braves. He left
some of the rocks, deposited by the Red River over centuries
along the bank when its waters ran high, in a pile. He would use
them later for the third brave who was at the moment advancing
medical science.

The rising sun revealed that the river was now only a peaceful,
shimmering, thin blue ribbon. But heavy spring and fall floods
often made the currents run so strong the river would create
numerous cut banks, oxbow lakes, and bayous. The cut banks, or
river cliffs, formed as the river's strong currents collided with the
soil on the river bank, often exposing tree roots and rocks.

When they'd arrived here in early spring, the river flowed
strong and its sparkling surface soon bewitched him. He yearned
for it to run wild and free again and reflect the color of the sky
and the trees. But not too wild because floods caused the river to
clog with debris and teem with danger. And when overfull, the
river always appeared rusty red, at least that's what the old-tim-
ers told him. The color came from the red soil to the north that
seeped into it as the water snakes south over hundreds of miles.
The river's long path ran south through the high plains and then
east through the valley of north Texas before it turned south again
and headed down through the mossy gloominess of Louisiana.

Here, though, no gray moss hangs like old men's beards from
the trees. Their land was fresh-faced—a land with creation's dew
still on it. Samuel wondered though if it would stay that way for
long. Farmers were trekking to the West from the stony fields

of New England and southern families were drifting in from the crowded lands of Virginia and the two Carolinas. Still other pioneers—English, Scots, Welsh, and German—were newly arrived immigrants from clear across the Atlantic.

Samuel climbed onto the wagon seat and gazed at the landscape, now covered in both shadow and light. The river and the wilderness stretched in both directions as far as he could see. Both were full of allure for a man who sought their bounty. But they were also full of perils and even terror for anyone who plunged into them unprepared or unwary.

His family was more prepared than most. Before they left Kentucky, his father had the foresight to amass considerable savings. And before they left Louisiana for Texas, they also acquired a sizable arsenal of rifles and ammunition as well as building tools.

Before departing Kentucky, his father had gifted his large cattle operation and his land to his two daughters and their husbands, knowing their children would need the land to survive. Land in Kentucky, especially acreage large enough to support cattle operations, had grown expensive and scarce. But Stephen believed he was quite capable of acquiring more land for himself and his four sons. They just had to be willing to go get it.

And they did. On a peninsula formed by a loop of the Red River, they claimed six square miles. To the south, a fork of Pecan Bayou marked their southern boundary. In between these two waterways, monstrous trees stood like stoic giants, taller than any he'd seen in Kentucky or Louisiana.

As soon as they arrived at Pecan Point, the seven of them built a sturdy home for themselves and one for the Grants. Then they'd built a sizable shed for the horses with a room above and a spring house. In this land of dugouts and rickety shacks, their large log cabins with wrapped around porches were actually quite grand.

Some of the settlement's other first arrivals were Indian traders intent on profiting off the steady influx of new settlers and from trading with the Indians. If the traders were not poachers, they were not killed by the Indians. In fact, approved traders were even encouraged by the Indians.

But profiting from trade was not Samuel's intention. He intended to earn a living, as his father had successfully done in Kentucky, from raising and selling cattle. He merely wanted and needed grazing land for their cattle.

There were a lot of reasons behind his father's decision to leave Kentucky with his four sons. The most important one was that everywhere his father turned at their Wyllie Cattle Farm, located north of the Cumberland River, there were reminders of Samuel's mother, Jane. Those reminders were like a millstone hanging from his father's neck. His father still loved Jane deeply and everyone knew he could never be completely happy again until he left and started a new life free of bittersweet remembrances.

His father also wanted to acquire more land for his sons. And the northernmost part of the Province of Texas, with its vast prairies and endless hills, offered land just for the taking. The very fact that it was a favorite grazing spot for buffalo proved that it would make first-rate cow country. The only problem was that where buffalo were, Indians were close on their hides. They'd also read that immense herds of wild cattle and horses roamed the Great Plains and there was a large market for them in the thriving trading centers located at Natchitoches and Nacogdoches.

But there was one more reason for their leaving. And it was the reason his parents had migrated in the first place, before Samuel was even born, from New England to Kentucky. Stephen Wyllie was a man who would always be tempted by the call of adventure. As other men were tempted by women, strong drink, gambling, or other vices, his father was seduced by the unknown. It wasn't merely the land that called to him. It was the quest, the journey, the excitement of a new venture.

As for himself, Samuel needed no other inducement to come to the Province but the urge to go—to see the next prairie, the next mountain, the next river. He liked to think it was the same spirit his parents had as they crossed the Alleghenies. They said he'd been conceived on their thousand-mile journey to Kentucky. Maybe that was the reason he was always eager to see new places. And why he embraced being a cattleman rather than a farmer because he could never be content to plow a few acres. He needed wide open spaces.

He needed the West.

So they had come to the Province on their own initiative and bore their own expenses. When they arrived, there were no agents or Spanish officials authorized to convey titles to put them in legal possession of their land. Each settler simply appropriated the land he preferred by marking his boundary trees, making notes of the waterways and or other landmarks, building a dwelling, and making other improvements. Thus, six months ago, between Pecan Point and Pecan Bayou they had claimed four-thousand acres, the amount normally allotted for a family.

It was his father's intention to give each of his four sons a thousand acres whenever they married. But their life at the settlement left little room for romanticism. It was a life that tended toward realism.

For Samuel, the prospect of marriage held little interest even though he was twenty-one and well past the age most men married. His fathers and brothers needed him, and he intended to stay with them at least until his youngest brother, Steve, put in a few more years and grew a few more inches.

For a minute, he watched a low fog creep into the riverbed. Then he turned the wagon toward home, only about a hundred yards away, to swap it for Samson, his big-hipped gelding. When he arrived at the horse shed, he hurriedly unhitched the wagon team and then let his father know he had finished the burial and was about to go out to join Thomas to watch over their herd.

"Eat breakfast first," his father said glancing up from the letter he was writing to his brothers in Kentucky. "I don't think we'll have any further trouble from the Indians during daylight."

"I'll just check on Thomas first and afterward I'll come back to eat."

His father nodded. "I sent Cornelius and Steve to sharpen the scythes and then to cut grass for a couple hours. We need to stockpile fodder before winter hits us hard."

"It will be our first full winter here," Samuel said. "Wonder how much snow we'll get."

"Less than Kentucky, I believe, but the winds may blow even colder."

Samuel stepped outside where it was still warm in September. Steve, who took care of their horses, had already let them all out to graze on their grassy, hillside paddock next to their shed. Their brood mare foraged while followed by her little long-legged filly. Soon, before winter, the foal would need to be weaned. Sired by their father's stallion, George, the filly would likely become a fine horse. Steve was going to enjoy raising and training her.

He whistled and Samson raised his head. The gelding's red coat glowed in the morning light and he flicked his tail and tossed his mane before walking toward him. More like a good friend than a mere mount, he loved that horse and he grinned as Samson presented his muzzle for a rub.

Samuel hefted a saddle onto Samson's back and within minutes, he rode south toward the pasture behind their home where their cattle would be grazing. Riding helped to empty his mind of his morose morning task. A light wind brushed against his face and stirred the branches of tall pines and the grass on meadows where few, if any, white men had trod before his family settled here. Only deer, buffalo, and natives.

Their cattle, both those they brought with them and the cows they'd caught roaming free, grazed on the abundant grass. They'd purchased some of the cattle, about fifty head, in Louisiana. The sturdy cows were descended from Mayflower stock, or so the man who sold them said. Some of the others were Louisiana breeds of French origin.

The rest of the cows, another two hundred and fifty head, they'd caught running wild. These were likely descended from cattle brought to Mexico by Spaniards and then abandoned to multiply over decades. Unbranded, they were what his father called "slicks." After ensuring that they didn't belong to any of the locals, he and his brothers branded them as their own. A brand was the cattleman's equivalent to a coat of arms. Their distinctive brand, a W with a horseshoe shape in the middle of it, distinguished their cattle and horses from another man's.

Regardless of their origins, the cattle were all fat and fleshy with stomachs as round and curvy as large barrels. The bred cows were often so wide they walked sluggishly with their bellies swaying from side to side. It was no wonder since the calves they carried around in those bellies often weighed about seventy-five pounds at birth. Out of a large, mature cow, calves sometimes even weighed ninety pounds.

Like David in the Bible, one day Samuel hoped his Red River Cattle Company would have cattle upon a thousand hills. Well, perhaps a hundred would be more reasonable, he decided. The grass was good and water plentiful, so he guessed it was possible.

It even seemed likely as he admired some pretty, fat calves playing together in the tall grass.

He rode up to Thomas and joined him.

"About time you got here," Thomas said.

"Had to bury those Indians we killed."

Thomas nodded gloomily. "I should've helped you, but, I
couldn't wake up this morning. I didn't sleep well. When I woke
up, you were already gone, and Father sent me out here."

"Nightmares?"

"Yup. Kept seeing all those Indians sneak up."

"There were only six of them," Samuel pointed out. Raiding
parties tended to be small since their intent was horses, not battle.

"That was six too many as far as I'm concerned."

Samuel pointed toward their herd. The strong rays of the morning sun had already burned off all the fog. Sunrays now lit the
backs of the cows and made the dew-covered grass they munched
on sparkle like thousands of tiny stars.

"Take a look at that," Samuel said, "it will clear your mind."
Like his father, his love for the land and raising cattle was far
more serious than that of most men.

"That may be the greatest pasture known to man," Thomas said.

"Father once called Kentucky 'God's Own Pasture' and it was
a fitting description," Samuel told him and smiled as he gazed
upon their land. "But I think that Texas might be called God's
Own Country."

"Hmm. Maybe it will be a country someday."

"Indeed," Samuel agreed. "Or at least a state."

"Did you eat?" Thomas asked. His man's body still filling out,
it was never long before food crossed Thomas' mind. "I did and
it sure was good."

"No, didn't eat. Got up, got the wagon, got the bodies, and
gathered rocks for an hour. Didn't take long to get the task done
after that. Then I came straight here. After that Indian visit, I
wanted to check on you and the herd."

"There's was no sign that they were stirred up during the night,"
Thomas said, "so I think those braves were only after our horses."

"That's what Father said," Samuel told him.

"Go eat breakfast, you can send Cornelius or Steve back."

"Cornelius and Steve are cutting grass for fodder." Samuel

didn't want to leave but his stomach did.

"Melly's made a batch of her butter biscuits," Thomas told him and licked his lips. "If there are any left after you eat, bring them back here. I'm hungry already."

"All right, I'll go. Are both your pistols loaded? And your rifle?"

"Of course they are," Thomas said, sounding affronted. Although only nineteen, Thomas could handle cattle and horses like a veteran. But could he handle Indians?

"Keep your back to that big tree and keep a sharp watch out. If you see any sign of Indians, don't try to fight them alone. Fire a warning shot and then race that horse back home." Like Samson, Thomas' horse was a tall, fast gelding.

"I will."

"I'll be back soon." Samuel turned his gelding back toward the cabins. Melly always cooked for them and for that Samuel was grateful because her cooking was darn good. And no one could beat her strong coffee.

As he arrived home, he thought he heard something. Samson did too because the gelding's ears flicked forward. Accustomed to paying attention to strange sounds, like the bawl of a lost calf or Indians or wolves on the prowl, he stopped Samson and listened. It sounded like a cry for help. Two voices. A woman's and maybe a boy's? Their desperate cries were coming from the Red.

He nudged Samson's sides and leaned forward in the saddle, taking off at a gallop. He rode to the edge of the river and peered down. Not far from the riverbank, a woman and a boy, wearing only their underclothes, were waving frantically at him. They were filthy but the woman's abundant long blonde hair sparkled in the sun.

"Help!" the woman called. "Quicksand!"

Samuel could see that the quicksand was already up to the boy's thighs and the young woman was in up to her hips.

Speedily, he urged Samson down the buffalo trail and then along the river's edge. He dismounted and snatched his rope off his saddle. A decade or more of working cattle had made him skillful with a rope. First, he made a loop in the end and then with a swirl of his arm he tossed the rope and it landed directly in front of the woman.

He'd sent the rope to her first because she was in deeper. But she snatched it up and tossed it over to the boy. The child put the loop over his head and then chest before he gripped the rope.

"Get him out!" she yelled.

Hand over hand, Samuel began tugging on the rope and the boy was soon out and standing beside him.

"Save my sister," the child cried. "Save her!"

"Don't worry. I'll save her." Samuel untied the loop. She would have to just grasp the rope. Since she was sunk deeper into the sandy mire than her brother had been, he feared that a loop around her chest would put too much pressure on her lungs or heart. He tossed the rope and once again it landed directly in front of her.

She grasped the rope and looped it around her hands. "Hurry!"

Leaning back and using the strength of both his arms and legs, he began to pull. She didn't budge. The pressure on her legs was too great.

Her luminous eyes widened in fear. "Please, pull harder," she cried. He could hear the desperation in her voice.

"Bring my horse over here," Samuel told the boy.

When Samson stood next to him, he looped the rope onto the saddle and tied it securely. Then he made the clucking sound that meant back up to the horse. Samson took a step backward and the gluey mud and sand still didn't release the woman.

The rope grew tauter and from her grimace he could tell it was burning her hands.

"Hold tight to that rope and I'll back him up another step or two. I know it's going to burn your hands, but you have to endure it."

She nodded and he urged Samson back. He saw her grimace as the quicksand sucked at her legs reluctant to release its hold on her. Finally, the pressure on her legs let go and she popped upwards a little and then fully emerged when Samson took a second step backward. Stretched out fully on her stomach, she kept her anxious eyes fixed on him.

"Keep a tight grip on that rope," Samuel yelled as he took hold of the rope himself and slowly pulled her up to the edge of the riverbank.

"Thank God," she muttered as she reached him.

He stepped into the shallow water, bent down, and scooped

her up in his arms. Even wet and covered in mud she was the most beautiful, perfect woman he'd ever seen. Scantily clad in a clinging shift, her woman's curves were readily apparent and voluptuous.

Her blue eyes, filled with gratitude, gazed up at him. "Thank you," she whispered. Her voice was soft and delicate, just like her slight body.

He had about a dozen questions he wanted to ask her. "I'm Samuel. What's your name?" he asked first.

"Louisa."

"And I'm Adam Pate," the boy said. "Her brother." He had a mass of unruly brown hair, but the child's cheeks were sallow, and he looked far too thin. "Our home was attacked by Indians. They killed my dog, Buddy, and Louisa's old horse."

That reminded Samuel that they needed to get out of the river. They were far too vulnerable here. The rest of his questions would have to wait. "Adam, we need to get your sister to safety. Gather up my rope and then lead my gelding up the bank. I'll carry your sister to my home. It's not far."

"I can walk," Louisa said, but her weak voice said otherwise.

"I'll carry you. Something tells me you haven't had a very good morning." Based upon her threadbare shift and how thin she was, Samuel suspected she hadn't had a very good life either.

Fatigue shown in her tired eyes as she nodded. But what concerned him even more, was the shadow of sadness, fear, or something else that shrouded her beautiful face like a veil.

He trudged up the soft earth on the riverbank with Adam leading Samson behind him. It occurred to him that he was carrying a woman in his arms for the first time in his life.

CHAPTER 4

"ADAM, I ASSUME YOU CAN ride?" Samuel asked when they reached the top of the riverbank.

The boy nodded. "Yes, Sir. As long as the horse ain't too wild."

Samuel pointed in the direction of their cabin. "Ride Samson to that house and tell my father what's happened."

"What's your father's name, Sir?"

"Mr. Wyllie. Stephen Wyllie."

"And your name, Sir?" Adam asked. "So I won't have to keep calling you Sir?" The boy was so dirty it would take all the water out of the Red to get him clean again. But Samuel had to admire the lad's confident manner.

"I'm Samuel," he said as he gazed down at Louisa. "I'm Stephen Wyllie's eldest son."

"Thank you, Samuel, for helping us," Adam said before he took off on Samson.

Samuel wanted to ask Louisa what caused her to be out in the middle of the river in only her shift, but he thought she might be too exhausted to talk. Her head rested against his shoulder and her eyes were closed so he started toward home.

As he walked, he watched Adam ride toward their cabin, tie Samson on a porch post and knock on the door. His father listened to the boy talking excitedly for a moment and then Adam pointed toward them.

At once, followed by Adam, his father set off taking long strides and soon joined him. "The boy said Indians attacked their home during the night. Is she injured?"

"No, I don't think so. But she and her brother were both horribly stuck in quicksand. As soon as I got her out of the riverbed, she passed out."

"Apparently, those Osage that came here last night left here, crossed the river and went to their place."

"They weren't Osage, Sir," Adam said, struggling to keep up with Samuel's swift strides. "They were Comanche."

"Are you sure?" his father asked. "Their home range is a little further west."

"Yes, Sir. My sister said they were Comanche because they had long braids and feathers in their hair."

Samuel exchanged looks with his father. Lately, small parties of Comanches made their presence felt by the Red River settlers in an unwelcomed way—by stealing their most valuable possessions—horses. However, so far at least, there had been no significant attacks on homes or people by their mighty warriors. He feared this raid on Louisa's and Adam's home might be the prelude to more hostile coming aggression. But since settlers had yet to move further west and penetrate the tribe's buffalo ranges, so far the Comanches had not posed a direct threat. He hoped it would stay that way because no other tribe came close to their reputation for deadly fighting prowess.

"Want me to take over carrying her?" his father asked.

Samuel shook his head. "I'm fine and we're almost there." Truth be told, he was enjoying the feel of a woman against his chest.

They soon stepped onto the porch and then went inside. Samuel gently laid the young woman down on his bed. He unfolded a blanket and lightly spread it over her.

"It was bad enough having the Osage raid. Now the Comanche are raiding as well," Samuel said.

"You were lucky you weren't killed," his father told the boy.

"Luck had nothin' to do with it," Adam said, raising his chin. "My sister was brave. She had me jump out the window and we ran to the corn patch and hid in the rows. I fell asleep, but she stayed awake all night guarding us."

"That explains why she's asleep," Samuel said. "She's exhausted."

"That and shock," his father said. "She's been through a lot in the last few hours. More than any young lady should have to endure."

"The Indians killed her mare and my dog. Then they took all our things. Even our food and clothes," Adam said, his voice wavering.

"Where were your parents?" Samuel asked.

Adam glanced down. "Louisa's Ma died a long time ago and my Ma died soon after I was born. Our Pa went to Jonesboro to rent a slave. Louisa doesn't like slaves."

Samuel frowned at the mention of slavery. "I'm sure you mean that Louisa doesn't like *slavery*. There's a big difference."

"Yup, that's what I meant."

"What was the fool thinking leaving you two alone at night in a country this wild?" his father asked heatedly. "You might have been captured and your sister…and you both might have been swallowed alive in that riverbed."

Adam's defiant attitude disappeared, and tears welled in eyes the same blue color as his sister's. "I thought I was gonna die. And I ain't even started really living yet."

"Easy, Father," Samuel said. "The boy's been through a lot. You're safe now, Adam," he soothed, with a pat to the top of the child's head. "And you're right, you have a lot of living yet to do."

His father pulled one of Steve's shirts out of a drawer. "It's just that I hate what might have happened to these two." Stephen turned toward Adam. "Take off that nightshirt and come over here where we can wash you up." He put the washbowl on their dining table's bench where Adam could easily reach it.

The boy tugged the muddied nightshirt off and dropped it on the floor. His small naked body looked dreadfully thin.

Samuel's father handed the child a wet cloth. "Wash your face and hands first. Then your legs and body."

Adam did a reasonable job of getting the mud off. When he finished, he said, "Wasn't my sister brave? I think she was."

His father dropped the clean shirt over the boy's head before he answered. The shirt came to Adam's knees but at least it was clean. They would have to get pants for him later. "For certain, your sister's courage saved you from a horrible fate. But why did you cross the river after the Indians left?"

"Louisa wanted to warn the other settlers. And we didn't have any food at all. We took the buffalo path down. Some of it looked soggy, so she went upstream a bit. She got a stick and she checked for quicksand with it. Then a swarm of mosquitos attacked us, and she dropped it."

Now that the mud was off of the boy, Samuel did notice a large number of red bites swelling on him. Perhaps Baldy would have something that would stop the itching.

Adam continued, "When I tried to pick the stick up, I sank. Then our rifle sank. Then she sank when she tried to help me. It felt like the devil his self was tryin' to pull us down to hell," the boy concluded, breathless.

"You're safe now," his father said, kneeling to face Adam eye to eye. "You can feel safe here. We are all well used to fighting when needed. And so are the other men on this side of the river."

On the south side of the Red, the settlers were left to their own defenses—their rifles, each other, and an abundance of courage. Being on the frontier required certain essential skills—marksmanship, horsemanship, a mastery of surviving outdoors, and knowledge of one's foes. This need for understanding their enemies was one reason they were all avid newspaper readers and gulped up news carried by travelers.

Greener settlers tended to settle on the north side of the Red because it was more certain that it was part of the Arkansas Territory and part of the United States. Sometimes they even received protection from the Army.

Understandably, for all settlers in the West, apprehension became a daily part of their lives. For they knew that no new land could be gained without facing danger. That fact made some of them uneasy, and some of them afraid at times, but for the most part, they were also courageous and resilient.

"Did you leave a note for your father?" Samuel asked.

Adam nodded. "Louisa drew an arrow that pointed here."

His father stood. "Then the man will be coming here."

"Would you like some food, Adam?" Samuel asked.

"Yes, Sir, I surely would. And some water would be real good."

Samuel handed a cup of water to the boy and he gulped it down.

"I'll go to Baldy and Melly's and bring the two of them here and some food," his father volunteered.

"I'm sure the rope burned her hands when I pulled her out.

Have Baldy bring some salve for her hands and for their mosquito bites," Samuel told him.

Adam scratched his arms. "Those 'squitos had some of me for breakfast."

Situated well out of the Red's floodplain, their homeplace was relatively free of mosquitos. The abundance of birds—including Mockingbirds, Scissor Tailed, Meadowlarks, and Blue Jays among others—kept the pesky insect at bay and filled the surrounding forests with song.

Father put a hand on Adam's shoulder. "Want to come with me, Adam? Melly makes a respectable biscuit."

"Sure!" the boy said and dashed to the door.

"Grab your dirty nightshirt and bring it with you. Maybe Melly knows a trick that will get it clean again," Samuel told him.

After they left, Samuel remembered too late that Baldy might be dissecting the brave.

Samuel hauled a stool next to his bed and gazed down at Louisa. She seemed so small and fragile but based on what her brother had said she possessed a good deal of courage and grit. He wondered how old she was. What she liked to do. How long she had lived across the river. Most of all, he wondered when she would wake up.

When she did wake up, Louisa would need to wash the mud off and don some fresh clothes. That was for sure. Perhaps Melly could help with that.

Samuel knew that Baldy's wife, every inch a lady, would welcome Louisa with as much cordiality as if she were mistress of a mansion in Louisville, not a cabin in the remote wilderness of Texas. The woman had managed, with the few things she'd been able to bring with her in their wagon, to create a comfortable home for her husband and a kitchen that produced some of the best food Samuel had ever eaten. In fact, they ate most of their evening meals with Baldy and Melly. And sometimes, she would bring their food here.

For their journey to Texas, they'd loaded the wagon with a good assortment of building tools, chickens and coops, barrels of spring water, flour and sugar stored in watertight barrels, ammunition, extra weapons, seed and seedlings for planting, and a keg of whiskey to use in case of illness or a special occasion. They'd also hidden money in $5 and $50 dollar amounts in the bottom of the barrels and they each wore a money belt that carried $500. His father even made Melly wear such a belt.

In the six months that they'd lived at Pecan Point, having enough to eat had never been a problem for them. The wilderness was swarming with food—deer, turkey, small game of every kind, coveys of game birds, even black bears for fat. The river held all the fish they could ever want, and wild berries and nuts were plentiful. Most of the settlers had corn patches and gardens and a few grew cotton. Baldy had helped Melly start a garden soon after they all got here, and she'd managed to grow some fresh vegetables. The fertile soil here produced abundantly— wheat about eighty bushels to the acre and the cornfield looked like it would yield even more. Samuel hoped their newly planted orchard would prove just as productive.

Louisa was so thin he doubted that she'd eaten well on her family's journey here. Perhaps he could do some hunting for them and Melly could spare some fresh vegetables.

The door flew open and Adam was the first to enter. "Did she wake up?"

"She's still asleep," Samuel said as his father, Baldy, and Melly joined them.

"Let me have a look," Baldy said.

Samuel stood and gave the doctor, and sometimes preacher, the stool.

Baldy checked her pulse and forehead. "Was she injured at all?" he asked Adam.

"No, Dr. Grant."

"That's good. You said she was up all night guarding you?" Baldy asked.

"Yes, she held the rifle toward the house all night while we hid in the corn patch. Will she be all right, Dr. Grant?"

"Yes. Yes. She's just exhausted. Let me see if I can wake her. She needs to get out of that wet shift and into some dry, warm clothes before she takes a chill. And she needs to eat something. She obviously needs nourishment," Baldy said. He reached into the bag he'd brought.

"I'll help her bathe and dress," Melly offered.

Baldy withdrew a leather-covered flask with his smelling salts, made from a solution from shavings of deer horns and hooves. Samuel had seen the doctor use it once before to revive a patient. After he held it to her nose for a moment, Louisa coughed and her eyes flew open.

She coughed again and then asked in a frightened voice, "Where's Adam? Is he all right?"

Adam went to her bedside. "I'm here, Louisa. I'm fine. These people took care of us." He leaned against the bed and patted her shoulder.

"Oh Adam," she said, raising on her elbows. "I'm sorry I got us stuck in the river. I'm sorry for not protecting you. It was all my fault. I should have protected you."

"You tried," Adam said.

Louisa's expression was one of self-loathing. "But I failed. It's my job to keep you safe. You could have died!"

"But I ain't dead. And you didn't die. Nothin' else matters," Adam said, surprising them all with his child's wisdom.

"It does matter. I failed. I nearly got you killed," she cried heatedly. "I let you down. I let myself down."

Samuel knew her anger was directed at herself. "Louisa, don't be so hard on yourself," he said.

She sighed heavily. "My father will be even harder," she said, her expression grim and she laid her head back.

Adam frowned and nodded as he stared down. "She's right. He will be."

Samuel and his father exchanged puzzled looks.

Baldy gave her a cup of water and then stood at the foot of the bed. "She'll be fine. Just needs some rest, food, and warm clothes."

"Where am I?" she asked.

"Louisa, you're in our home. This is Dr. Grant and his wife Melly, our good friends. And this is my father Stephen Wyllie."

"You're Samuel," she said, pointing a finger at him. She glanced briefly at the others and then back up at him admiringly. "You're the one who saved us!"

"My other three sons are watching over our cattle herd," Stephen told her. "You'll meet them later."

"I'm pleased to meet all of you." She winced when she rubbed her hand against her forehead. "I don't remember how I got here."

Samuel nearly gasped when he saw the raw skin on her hands. Then he explained what happened after he took her out of the riverbed.

"Your hands have rope burns," Baldy said. "Let me see them. I have a salve that will make them heal fast."

Keeping the blanket across her body, she swung her legs to the side of the bed and extended a hand toward Baldy.

The doctor examined the palm a minute and then looked at her other hand, equally burned by the rope. "I'll need to wash your burns, put some salve on them, and wrap your hands."

"I'll get a bowl and water," Melly said and soon returned with a wooden bowl and clean water. "At Stephen's suggestion, I brought you a clean shift and a gown. It might be a little big on you, but it will do until you can change into your own clothes," Melly told her. "And if you'd like, I'll help you bathe and put a salve on those mosquito bites before you dress. Afterward, you can eat before you rest."

Louisa nodded at Melly and gave her a small smile which was followed at once by a grimace as Baldy dunked her hands in the warm water.

While Baldy doctored Louisa's rope burns, Melly spread food out on their pine board table. Obviously remembering that Samuel hadn't yet eaten breakfast, she set out three plates.

Adam took a seat at once and gazed with wide-eyes as Melly stacked several buttered biscuits on his platter, piled up eggs, and poured sweet milk. The child devoured the food with the enthusiasm of a growing boy.

"You should eat," his father told Samuel. "You never had breakfast."

"I'll wait for Louisa."

She glanced over at him and gave him a smile that made a different kind of hunger well up inside of him.

CHAPTER 5

LOUISA COULD HEAR THEIR MUFFLED voices on the front porch. The men and Adam waited outside. For some reason, it comforted her to hear Samuel's voice, with its strong, yet compassionate tone. Mr. Wyllie's voice held depth and authority while there was a trace of humor and kindheartedness in Baldy's voice.

Since her hands were bandaged, she had bathed and dressed with the assistance of a very considerate Mrs. Grant. When Louisa was done, she felt much better.

Soothed by Dr. Grant's ointment, a mixture that smelled of healing herbs, her bandaged hands didn't burn nearly as much. The Wyllies and Melly all called the middle-aged doctor Baldy, and for good reason. He didn't have a single strand of hair on his head. His eyes were dark, and she'd noticed that his sun-weathered face carried the imprint of a man who had overcome adversity in his life. Louisa also sensed he was a man equally comfortable with shooting lead as he was with removing it from a wounded man.

While Louisa drank a restoring cup of whiskey-fortified tea in front of the hearth, Melly got the tangles out of Louisa's freshly washed hair. Melly's hair was a rich, glowing auburn with a few strands of white at her temples that revealed that she was in her middle years. The green-eyed woman seemed serenely wise and, if Louisa wasn't wrong, both heartbreak and strength etched her still lovely face.

As Melly combed, Louisa took in the remarkably neat and large cabin. It seemed more like a small fort. The sturdy walls were made of unusually large logs interlocked on the ends with notches. On the north wall, four portholes were cut into the logs and covered with doeskin that could be peeled back. On the south wall, there were only two portals.

On both sides of the front door hung a large assortment of weapons—several rifles, pistols, knives of various sizes, hatchets, and two swords. Even some weapons that must have once belonged to Indians hung on the wall. Winter coats, woolen scarves, and hats, that they would soon need, hung from antler wall racks.

On this end of the home, next to the stone hearth, a table held several cast-iron frying pans, a Dutch oven, and dishes that sat on a shelf. On another shelf, she could see coffee, tea, flour, and spices. On the other side of the home, five made-up beds stood next to each other, and above them, rough boards across the beams made a loft that held a desk, chair, and bookcase. And in the middle of the cabin, was a huge pine table that could seat ten or more. The thick door had a heavy bar that could be dropped into place and locked with two substantial bolts.

This well-constructed home made her own cabin look like a flimsy hut. Which it was.

Her thoughts turned to what had happened. What a night of horror! And the morning that followed wasn't much better. But the horrible night and trying morning were over with and it was time to eat and then get back to their home—or what was left of it—if she could figure out a way to get back safely. Perhaps Samuel could help them again.

She couldn't wait to see Samuel's handsome, tanned face again and she pictured him in her mind. The man was downright close to male perfection. When he'd carried her, it was the first time a man other than her father had touched her body. The heart-jolting feel of his strong arms and muscled chest had caused her to swoon. Dr. Grant had blamed it on exhaustion. That was perhaps true, but she thought it might have been more than that.

Samuel's deep voice and kindness had soothed the raw places inside of her. An inside made raw by her father's unpredictable anger and by intense loneliness.

His strong arms had made her feel safe and protected. His dark and slightly wavy hair framed kind, deep blue eyes that sparkled with keen intelligence. He stood well over six feet and his broad shoulders strained the fabric of his coffee-colored cotton hunting shirt. He also wore buckskin breeches and tall brown leather boots. At his waist, free of fat, hung two long-barreled pistols and an exceedingly long knife. The mere sight of the blade would give someone with a weak stomach the colic. She'd also noticed that his hands felt hardened.

She suspected, though, that his heart was soft.

She wanted to see if he would have the same effect on her when she wasn't being rescued from certain death. She wasn't in any danger of swooning again, but she hoped he could once again ease the hurt inside her, if only for a few moments before she had to go back to her own lonely life.

"There now, you're looking far better," Melly said giving her an admiring look. "You are truly a lovely young lady when not covered in mud and a tangled mop of hair."

"Thank you," Louisa said and stood, wearing a borrowed light-blue gown. Fortunately, the too big waist could be tightened, with a sash. However, when she glanced down at the hem it dragged against the wooden floor.

Mrs. Grant chuckled. "We'll have to hem that."

"I'm grateful for the loan of it," Louisa told her. "Will you show me how to hem it up? I've never sewn anything."

"Of course I will. How do those boots fit? I'm tall, but I have small feet."

"With these stockings, they're fine. They're the best boots I've ever worn."

"She's finished, you can come in," Mrs. Grant called to the men.

Louisa stared at the door as a shiver of excitement rippled through her.

Samuel, followed by Adam, stepped inside and he couldn't help but smile at the sight of Louisa. It didn't seem possible, but she was even more beautiful than he'd thought. Her still damp hair hung to her waist and the borrowed gown made her eyes look even bluer. Her fair face blushed as he gazed at her and she shyly glanced down.

He cleared his throat and said, "My father and Dr. Grant just left for the settlement to spread word of both raids, the one here by the Osage and the one on your place by Comanches. They assume your father will spread the word on the north side of the river."

"What about your brothers?" Melly asked Samuel. "Are they safe out there in the pasture?"

"I surely hope so," Samuel said and raked his fingers through his hair. "After last night they'll be particularly vigilant and stay together. My father wants me to go check on them and our prize bull just as soon as Louisa's and Adam's father shows up."

As he and Louisa ate their breakfast, his eyes kept darting to her. He felt a certain disappointment that their time together would soon be ending. He wanted to get to know her better. He tried to assess her beautiful features. She had perfect pink lips and sparkling eyes, but she seemed troubled and edgy about something.

He was too—worried about his brothers encountering more bands of braves. Years ago, when Father first told them that he wanted to move to the Province of Texas, Samuel made a promise to his sisters to keep their father and brothers safe in their new home on the frontier. And a man doesn't make promises he can't keep. So he'd made himself their protector—a self-appointed guardian angel. He was still working on the angel part, but he was a confident fighter, ready to take on any threat to those he cared about. He'd been in more than a few scrapes with those who dared to pick on his brothers, especially when they were all younger.

Thomas, however, was a more cautious type, often quiet and thoughtful, sometimes even pensive. Carefree Cornelius was the family's boisterous frolicker who found a way to say something funny nearly every day. Sometimes that got him in trouble. Their youngest brother, Steve, was Cornelius' opposite, taking everything seriously and more prone to want to work with the horses than cattle.

All three could shoot well, but up until last night, they'd never had to fight Indians. Only he and his father had joined other men from the settlement in several skirmishes with hostiles.

"You and your brother need to stay here until your father comes for you," Samuel told Louisa. Already, his protective instincts made him want to keep Louisa and Adam safe. "If he doesn't arrive today, we'll find places for you to sleep."

"Louisa, you and Adam can stay with my husband and me," Melly said. "We have extra beds we sometimes use when we have more than one patient."

"Or Adam could sleep on a pallet in front of our hearth," Samuel said.

"Staying here until Pa returns would be wise. But he should be back soon. Tomorrow at the latest," Louisa told him. Unlike her brother, she ate slowly, taking only small bites. "Your cooking is marvelous," she told Melly. "Thank you for making it for us."

"It is my pleasure, dear," Melly said. She poured some coffee and took a seat. "It's good to have the company of a woman for a change. I am severely outnumbered here—six to one."

Louisa chuckled and her face lit with warmth. "It's been a long time since I've been around another woman for any length of time too."

"How long have you been here at the Pecan Point settlement?" Melly asked.

"Just a week," Louisa said.

"You must still be weary from your journey then," Melly told her.

"I confess, I was completely spent when we arrived. I thought we would never get here."

"I wasn't tired," Adam said. "Men are supposed to stay strong. 'Cause women ain't strong. Except my sister. I think she's strong."

Samuel had to agree about Louisa. Escaping Comanches took remarkable courage. "Your sister needs you to stay strong. However, all the women I've ever known were often stronger than men." By the expression on Adam's face, he could tell that was the first time the boy had heard such a thing.

Samuel wiped his mouth and stood. "Time for me to get out and stand guard."

"You'll stay here until my father comes?" Louisa asked.

Samuel saw fear in her eyes and something else that she wasn't saying. "Yes, until you go back with your father."

They heard a rider coming and Samuel grabbed his rifle and peered out before he opened the door.

"Louisa! Adam!" the rider shouted.

"Pa's here," Adam said.

Samuel wondered why the boy sounded disappointed and why Louisa tensed at the news of her father's arrival. He frowned as he opened the front door for Louisa.

"What the devil happened?" the man shouted to Louisa as soon as he saw her.

Their scowling father, who appeared to be in his late thirties, was dark-haired and rawboned. His sharp features gave his face a stubborn arrogance. Stained, dirty, well-worn clothes hung on his tall frame. He rode a horse that obviously hadn't been groomed before it was saddled, although it appeared to be of good breeding.

Samuel hoped the man's glowering demeanor was due to worry over his children. He stepped off the porch and extended his hand. "I'm Samuel Wyllie, Sir."

Mr. Pate didn't take his hand. "Have you touched my daughter? If you have, you'll both pay dearly." His voice was accusing and hard.

Samuel lowered his hand and stepped back. He clenched his jaw as he said, "I shouldn't even respond to that absurd question. But I will for Louisa's sake. I carried her here to get her help. She was too weak to walk."

"Father," Louisa said, "Mr. Wyllie and his family have shown us only the greatest kindnesses. And Samuel behaved only honorably."

Pate glared at Samuel and then Louisa. "I asked you a question. What the devil happened?"

Louisa took a few tentative steps toward him. "Comanches attacked last night. About seven or eight of them." She explained how she and Adam hid all night and then crossed the river early that morning. And how Samuel had saved them from certain death in quicksand.

"You should have stayed put," he said. He finally noticed her bandaged hands. "Why are your hands bandaged?"

"The rope burned them when I pulled her out of the quicksand," Samuel answered.

Once again, Pate ignored him and said, "You ought to have stuck to the buffalo trail, you foolish girl. Where are my pistols and rifle?"

Considerable embarrassment shown on Louisa's face.

Samuel detested this man already. He hadn't even dismounted, much less hugged his two children who'd barely escaped death twice. How could a man be so calloused toward his own children?

Louisa took a deep breath. "The Indians stole the pistols and powder. And we lost the rifle in the river."

"It sunk in the quicksand," Adam said in a meek voice.

Pate's florid face grew even redder. "I might have known better than to leave my weapons and home to be safeguarded by a weak, simple-minded female and a scamp of a boy."

Samuel turned to Louisa expecting her to dissolve in tears. Instead, only hurt flashed in her beautiful eyes and she was clenching her lips. Right now, she wasn't drowning in quicksand, she was drowning in her father's meanness.

The man's cruelty made outrage swell in Samuel's chest. He straightened his back and said, "That is uncalled for, Mr. Pate. She's far from simple-minded. Your daughter showed incredible bravery in the face of serious danger. Both at her home and at the river."

"If that's so, why are all my possessions gone? Why is my home ransacked? Why have I lost my pistols and my rifle? Women on the frontier are expected to guard their homes with their lives. Clearly, my daughter failed."

"She didn't fail! She kept her young brother and herself from being taken captive," Samuel argued.

"You shouldn't have left them alone! Especially at night," Melly said. The tone of her voice held obvious disapproval. "If she hadn't hidden, I don't have to tell you what would have happened to her."

"She's eighteen! Many women her age defend their homes and their children on the frontier. But now, what kind of life will she and her brother have?" Pate spat. "We've lost everything. Everything!"

"You have your children alive! And I see a pistol on your side and a rifle sheathed in a saddle, which sits on a quality horse," Samuel said. "Be thankful you have those."

"Who are you to be telling me what to be thankful for?" Pate growled. "I'll be thankful when I kill those savages!"

"I'd strongly advise caution, Mr. Pate," Samuel told him firmly.

"A man must protect his property at all costs," Pate said. "Damn any man to hell who sympathizes with Indians, including you! They robbed me."

"I know they did. And another tribe attempted to steal our horses last night. We killed three braves. I'm not sympathetic to thieves. But not all Indians are thieves or hostile. Some are peaceful traders and honorable men."

Condemnation and hatred skewered Pate's features. "I'll kill any Indian I can find, big and little. Nits make lice."

Samuel took a step toward the man. "Listen to me. There are both Comanche and Osage conducting raids. My father and friend have gone to warn the other settlers on this side of the river. If you are wise, you should go and join them at the settlement to see what they plan. Then you should warn all the settlers on your side of the Red."

"I'll go, but it will be to gather up men north of the Red. They'll help me retrieve my belongings. We can take care of a few renegades. We'll kill and scalp all we find. By God's heaven, it's honorable and right to kill Indians."

Samuel rolled his eyes at the man's hard line against hostiles. Wholesale killing of any Indian Pate found could touch off a full-fledged war with more than one tribe. "No possessions are worth your life, Sir. Unless you are an experienced Indian fighter and know this country well, you will only be putting your head at risk if you encounter Osages. And if you lose a battle to the Comanche, you'll wish you were dead before they finish with you."

"So, you'd expect me to just let them rob me of everything I own?" Pate nearly shouted.

"No, of course not. But only the guilty deserve punishment. And there's a time and place to make a stand. We have to be smart about this," Samuel insisted. "The Comanche are tactical fighters. They will send a few braves ahead to lure their enemies into an ambush. They'll wait, concealed, until you're within range. Then they'll strike, raining arrows down upon you. Meanwhile, you will have already taken your single shot with your flintlocks and will have nothing but your knife to protect you from deadly arrows."

Samuel knew that inexperienced fighters often made this mistake. They would fire their weapons too soon. Then the warriors would swoop in on them before they could reload.

"Let's go. We're leaving this coward. Climb up here behind me," he ordered Louisa. "Adam, you can walk."

Louisa glanced down at her brother's bare feet. They were already scratched and blistered. "I'll walk. Adam can ride behind you, Father."

Samuel glanced at Adam. The boy's saddened face broke his heart. "Leave them here, please," he urged. "Since you intend to go after the thieves who robbed your home, they'll be safer here until you are able to stay home with them. There are six men here and we are all well-armed. They will be safe here until this Indian threat has died down."

Pate sneered. "What? You think I'd leave my eighteen-year-old daughter with six men—all strangers to me? For all I know, you're an unholy bunch."

"Sir, I assure you, we are all honorable, men of God. My father is a respected cattleman. Our friend, Dr. Grant is even a preacher."

Pate grunted. "I can just imagine the sermons he'd preach. And I don't intend to listen to them. Any preacher who'd settle in a Catholic Province is not a man of God—unfit to even sing a hymn to a dead horse. All of you must be doing the devil's bidding."

Samuel heard Melly gasp.

"Keep talking like that *if* you're tired of living," Samuel warned. He would hate to challenge this man in front of his children, but the irrational fool was testing the limits of Samuel's patience. "And we live within the boundary of the Louisiana Purchase, not in a Catholic Province."

"That's a matter of opinion," Pate shot back. "At the very least you've struck your claim on the doorstep of the devil's own domain."

Pate's loathing of Catholics stemmed from a Spanish law that required men living in the Province to conform to the Roman Catholic Church. No other religious worship was tolerated. So far, though, Baldy a devout Protestant and those who listened to him had ignored the dictate without consequence. Among the settlers who were their neighbors, there were many families including Samuel's of deep religious convictions. He would not tolerate a man saying Baldy was not a man of God. He was a breath away from beating the snot out of the man.

"Pa," Louisa intervened. "We're going to need a good many supplies, food, blankets, and clothing. Let me stay here in the settlement. I'll find a job and work to earn money to buy back what we lost."

Pate scoffed. "What do you think you can do? You're just a girl. Not even a real woman yet. You can't cook worth a squat. You can't sew much more than a button. And you can barely scribble your name. That's why I have to find you a rich husband."

Louisa glanced down and sighed, appearing defeated by her father's ridicule.

"I'll hire her!" Melly said and marched over to stand beside Samuel.

Pate cocked a suspicious eye. "To do what?"

Melly looked at Louisa and put a motherly arm on her shoulder. "If it's alright with you, Louisa, I could sure use your help with chores like the laundry and gardening. I take care of the cooking for six men. And I don't have time to keep up with all the dirty clothes that come from men who work hard. And we need to get busy planting a fall garden."

"I would be honored to work with you," Louisa told Melly, keeping her back to her father. Then she lowered her voice and said, "But my brother must stay with me."

Melly stared up at Louisa's father. "I'll pay her a fair wage and provide her with meals and a place to sleep too. And, I'm sure my husband would employ the boy to help him with such things as keeping his clinic clean."

"Only if I get their pay. Not them," Pate said. "They belong to me."

"We can pay them once a week. But for this week, I'll pay you in advance so you'll be able to purchase what supplies you need to get by," Melly said, sweetening her proposal to him.

Pate cocked his head to the side and regarded her with suspicious eyes. "Why do you want to hire them?"

"Because I need the help," Melly said. "And because I like Louisa and her brother. She's a fine, brave young woman and I would be proud to call her my friend. And young Adam here appears to be a lad who would work hard."

"I am," Adam blurted out. "I promise I'll work real hard, Mrs.

Grant."

Their sad excuse for a father nodded. "Hmm. All right, but I'll expect payment every Friday."

Melly withdrew two silver coins from the pouch that hung on her belt and handed them to Pate. "I'll give you that much every Friday."

Without so much as a wave to his children, the man pocketed the money, turned, and left.

CHAPTER 6

WITH BALDY RIDING BESIDE HIM, Stephen rode into the Pecan Point settlement. A jumble of rough log cabins and sod houses called soddies, the settlement was little more than an infant of a town although mature principles guided its residents. First, the belief that men have the right to govern themselves as free men. And secondly, the right to worship God as their conscience leads them.

Until they could build something better, many of the settlers near the settlement were forced to construct homes out of what was called rawhide lumber—cottonwood slabs with rough bark on the outside—and they made their roofs out of limbs and thatch. The sight of these rugged shelters made Stephen wonder how they would survive the coming hard freezes during winter.

Circles of men congregated around one of the two trading posts at Pecan Point, this one operated by William Mabbitt. Some men sat on barrels, others stood or leaned on posts. Even one of Mabbitt's competitors, Alex Wetmore, was there as well, and several Indian traders. Besides selling goods to the settlers, Wetmore and Mabbitt would occasionally trade with friendly Indians to buy furs, bowls, baskets, and other items they could then trade here and in Nacogdoches or Natchitoches for flour and other necessities.

The Indian traders dealt mostly with the Choctaws who would come in peace from across the river to trade the number one cash crop, the skin of beavers. They also traded deer hides, venison, snakeroot, and pinkroot for merchandise and whiskey. Snakeroot and pinkroot where both used by drug companies in the east to make medicines. Snakeroot for insanity, fever, and snake bites, and pinkroot to get rid of intestinal worms.

Next to Mabbitt's place, he saw a poorly clad woman named Rose, with a warm heart and a cold, lacerated face. She sat on the porch of the settlement's only tavern, the Red Buffalo, watching the happenings. She was as much a slave as any of the dark-skins at Pecan Point, Stephen thought. But her body was sold for purposes other than labor. The local men who were her customers had given her the name The Queen of Love. Others, mostly the settlement's women, called her Hell-Bound Rose.

The settlement's men arrived at Pecan Point thirsty and, especially in summer, stayed thirsty. So the tavern, with its pictorial sign of a buffalo painted rusty Red River red, was always one of the busiest establishments. The Red Buffalo's regular customers affectionately called the place their watering well. They drank mostly whiskey, sometimes called tarantula juice, because no one at the settlement could brew ale as of yet. And if a man wanted something to drink besides whiskey, it was coffee he ordered. For food, the tavern served chiefly beans, biscuits, beef, and bacon. Occasionally, the fare included Red River catfish, rattlesnake, or another unlucky critter.

Flies hummed around a cart heavily loaded with skins of all kinds and dogs lounged under the shade of the tavern's porch. A beautiful mulatto woman, her face veiled with sadness, worked on a deer hide. A few feet away, two muscled male slaves labored chopping firewood. The cadence of their swings filled the air with an ominous rhythm.

As Stephen rode closer, he observed that the men, who normally shared the comradery of the frontier, all appeared tense and troubled.

The tents and cook fires of new arrivals were scattered nearby with women huddled around them as well. Many watchfully clutched small children or babes in their arms. Some of the older children leaned into their mothers, their faces wary.

None of the men were gambling as was often the case. Gambling, except on horse races, was a practice Stephen detested because he thought card games the ultimate waste of a man's time. Baldy, however, found a poker game entertaining and often joined the gamblers, keeping a rifle across his lap in case Indians or anyone else decided to interfere with their card game. The rifle also had the advantage of discouraging cheating. Gambling gave Baldy an opportunity to sprinkle a little of God's word into the conversation, words that these slippery gamblers might otherwise never hear. Ancient words that resounded with life, hope, and undeniable wisdom.

Back in Kentucky, Baldy preached openly. Those that mocked him or wouldn't listen attentively ran the risk of getting the hell beaten out of them. But here, he was careful to weave his sermons into the life he led as a physician. Still, his closest friend was a mighty warrior of the gospel who also used common sense and stories from his own life to lead others to the narrow gate. And when needed, Baldy would put down his Bible or medical bag and pick up his weapons to ride beside him. He couldn't ask for a finer friend.

The men at the settlement, their clothing dust-blown and stained, glanced up as he and Baldy rode up. Stephen knew at once that something was wrong. Normally, they were a brash bunch who wouldn't hesitate to give a man who deserved it a full fist to his jaw or worse. On the other hand, they'd help any man who asked them for aid.

"Get down from them horses and rest your saddle," Mabbitt said through his soup-strainer mustache. The man was rough-hewn, as if God had carved him out of a tough log with a broad axe.

"What's wrong? I can see something has all of you bothered," Stephen said.

Wetmore regarded Stephen and Baldy with a hard gaze. "Indians attacked the Roberts family in their home last night. An arrow killed Billy's young, breeding wife. Billy must have gone after them. He was killed nearby."

John Tweedy cleared his throat. "This morning, I found Billy's body and lopped off head about a mile from their place. We'll need a wagon for both their bodies."

"Good God," Baldy said. "She was due to deliver her babe next month."

"Where should we bury them?" Tweedy asked.

"We'll worry about burying the dead later. For now, we need to take care of the living," Stephen said. He swore beneath his

pursed mouth as rage twisted his gut. How many more green settlers would set off on a fool's errand against an enemy far more
ruthless than they? He squared his shoulders and he told them
about the Osage and Comanche raids at the Pate's cabin and at
his place, where three braves met their end.

"We should organize a militia company," Tweedy said. "I never
want to see a sight like that again."

Ranging militia companies were often organized in response to
an immediate need and afterward promptly disbanded so the men
could return to their homes as quickly as possible. Fiercely independent free men, these citizen soldiers rarely formed up into a
cohesive team. Stephen knew they could be guided, but not commanded, and then only by elected leaders.

Stephen sensed that they were all waiting for a leader to emerge
from among them. Because he was the most educated among
those living at the settlement, except for Baldy who held several
degrees, the men seemed to hold him in high regard. He dreaded
the prospect of being asked to lead this mulish bunch. But for the
sake of young Billy, his wife, and their unborn child, he would do
what he had to. Their murders could not go unanswered and Billy
had been a good friend of Samuel's. He knew this would hit his
oldest son hard. Maybe it would help Samuel to deal with it if he
knew their murderers had been punished.

"We have to determine which Indians deserve retaliation," Stephen told the gathered men.

Never content to stay in the background, Cloudy Bowers stepped
forward. "You said yourself they were Osages and Comanches."

"Yes, but which one? The other problem we have is that we
don't know if it's a few dishonored renegades who have been
evicted from their tribes or if it's the tribes' chiefs that are behind
these raids. Both are possible. One is a lesser problem. The other
is a major problem."

"What difference does it make? An Indian is an Indian. Like a
wolf is a wolf. We need to rid the frontier of all Indians, just like
we did in Kentucky and Indiana," Mathew Hardin said.

Stephen knew the man was a veteran rifleman of the 1811 Battle of Tippecanoe. Hardin, a hawkish-looking man with a high
temper, was always greased for a fight. His father had been killed
by Indian treachery. The experience warped his mind and twenty

years later he still sought vengeance.

Baldy pushed his mount closer to Hardin. "It's the same difference there is between a good, honorable man and a lying, thieving, no good of a white man," Baldy told them. "I know because I've met a lot of scalawags, shysters, and opportunists in my lifetime."

Baldy was right, of course, but Hardin wasn't the only man there who held all Indians in contempt. At least half of them regarded any Indian who was seen near the boundaries of the settlements to be a fair target. In fairness, even though tribal leaders spoke of peace, they could not restrain their young men from straying into the settlements to plunder, rape, and sometimes murder to attain wealth and war honors. Stephen suspected that this was the case with the unfortunate attack on the Roberts.

And so, once again, the settlers would be forced to push back, and the frontier would remain a dangerous place—a place where death and life held equal strongholds.

"I want justice for the Roberts as much as all of you," Stephen said. "But we have everything to be gained by peace and nothing to be gained by war with entire tribes. I suggest we follow the tracks from the Roberts' place and see where they lead. Then we'll deal with the culprits. Nothing more. Agreed?"

The group of about thirty men nodded their consent.

All but Hardin. The blowhard of the settlement, though outvoted, decided not to stay whipped. "If we're going to go after Indians, I say we kill all we see and then some."

"I say we put Stephen Wyllie in charge," Wetmore suggested.

Everyone said yes or aye, and it was settled. Everyone but Hardin.

And Stephen. Without a say in the matter, he was now the leader of these men. "All right, we leave in fifteen minutes. Use that time to get your weapons, powder, canteen, and your horse and yourself ready. Once we start, there will no stopping."

"I don't have a horse," one young man said.

"Then you can stay behind and help guard the settlement," Stephen told him. "Be sure all the women are armed and their weapons ready to shoot. Tell them to keep their children inside until we return." With the brutal murders of the Roberts, the present Indian threat was now far more serious.

"Yes, Sir," the young man said.

With Stephen and Baldy at the head, the men from the settlement soon stormed toward the Roberts' home in a jumble of rough woolens, buckskins, and misshapen hats. Some carried only a rifle, others only a pistol or a long knife. But glinting, steel-like courage shown on all their faces and buttressed their hearts.

When they arrived at the Roberts' place, Stephen recognized the arrows left behind as those used by Comanche.

As expected, all of Billy's horses were gone. Over the last two years, the young man had collected wild horses and spent endless hours training them. Billy must have heard the Indians leaving with his horses and gone after them. It was a decision that cost him dearly. After killing Billy, the braves snuck back to kill his wife and rob his home.

Stephen's face hardened at the sight of Billy's brutalized body. That could have been one of his own sons. But unlike his sons, the poor young man didn't have a family around to help protect him. He had been all alone.

And the West was no place to be alone.

Stephen soon found the tracks of six braves leading away from Billy's body. They followed their trail upriver. Occasionally, they would lose their trail and have to scour the riverbanks along the waters of the Red until they found them again. Their tracks continued following the river.

After an hour or so, they encountered the camp of the band of six. Their tied horses all carried packs stuffed to overflowing, no doubt crammed with stolen belongings. Billy's horses were clustered nearby and watched over by two of the braves.

On Stephen's signal, they attacked, riding toward the braves in a cloud of brown dust. Their horses' hooves beat thunderously upon the hard ground. Stephen felt his chest tighten as he anticipated having to kill.

When he was within range, he slowed and then settled George as he unsheathed his longrifle. His well-trained, exceptionally intelligent horse stood motionless.

The braves heard the storm coming and remounted swiftly. All lean, hard, and full of fight, the six bristled with weapons—

shields, lances, bows, knives, and, worst of all, rifles. French and English traders had introduced firearms to the Indians in order to trade for pelts and win them as allies in both trade and war. And Spain's failure to regularly supply the Indians with trade goods, especially firearms and ammunition, caused peaceful relations with the Comanche to end. This left American settlers to receive the brunt of Indian resentment.

The warriors Stephen saw before him trained and lived for fighting such as this. They would be aggressive, quick, and fierce. Often called the 'Lords of the Plains,' they presided over a large area called Comancheria. They'd moved south in successive stages, attacking and displacing other tribes, even the Apache, whom they drove from the southern Plains. The area they claimed continually expanded as, one or two tribal groups at a time, they would move further south and east. Pecan Point was a little east of their territory, so this raid made him worry that they planned to continue their nomadic migration.

Stephen leveled his sights on a brave who was just then raising a rifle to take aim at one of the settlers. A blink later, through the smoke of the flintlock's black powder, he saw the brave slide off his pony. The settler would never know how close he had come to death.

The other men from the settlement, their rage fueled by the killings, were full of fire and mettle. The fray lasted mere minutes. When the fighting ended, they had killed three braves. One of them from Stephen's rifle.

Greatly outnumbered, the other three braves rode away from the Red and turned south. Unwilling to relinquish their plunder, they each tugged along the other three horses that had belonged to their dead companions.

Two of the settlers had taken arrows in their arms. While Baldy swiftly removed the arrows and temporarily dressed their wounds, the others quickly searched the three dead braves. They found young Roberts' hat on one of the braves and two men recognized his wife's locket on another. Worse, the third brave wore a large copper bracelet on his upper arm from which hung a collection of scalps.

Hardin removed it and held it up for all to see. Blood still moistened one of the scalps.

Billy's.

Stephen dismounted, unsheathed his knife, and marched over to Hardin. Swallowing the sour bile in his mouth, he removed the bloody scalp as Hardin and the other men watched silently. Then he carefully wrapped it in his handkerchief and stored it in his saddlebag before remounting.

Hardin tossed the other scalps aside. "Savages!" he swore.

The men swiftly remounted and they chased the braves at a thunderous gallop. Soon, though, about half their horses gave out and those riders were forced to slow. Only Stephen, Baldy, and four others were able to stay close enough to give serious chase.

The Comanches differed from other Plains tribes in several ways. Perhaps the most important difference was that they were the finest horsemen of all Indians. It was their one trait Stephen admired. They sat their horses so gracefully and exercised such complete control that they seemed to be part of the animal.

Widely dispersed in family bands, the Comanche ranged in a wide swath from the Arkansas River to the southernmost part of Texas. They were so ruthless, no tribe and few white men dared to challenge them. Stephen began to wonder at the wisdom of further pursuit.

Stephen soon neared the mouth of a u-shaped valley. Shadowy, dark woods encircled the openness like the steel jaws of a giant trap. Sensing imminent danger, Stephen called a halt at once. "If we keep going, we're likely to be caught in an ambush," he told Baldy and the remaining four men.

"They can't be more than a few minutes ahead of us," Hardin said. "Let's finish this!"

"The men elected me the leader," Stephen said, making his voice firm. "And I say we stop here."

"Why?" demanded Wetmore.

"The Comanche are masterful horsemen and mighty warriors, skilled with bow, lance, and tomahawk. They are known for their brutal treatment of captives and butchery of the dead. Do you truly want to risk falling victim to that if there are more of them hiding in those woods far enough back to escape our notice?"

Hardin's face reddened. "I still want to go after them. It's the courageous thing to do."

"Sometimes men mistake stupidity for courage," Stephen told

him bluntly. "You could be riding into a storm raining arrows. I think those six weren't just renegades. They're part of a larger party. That's why they were so well-armed. It's why they camped until we caught up to them. They were baiting us."

Hardin bristled. "Who's with me?"

Except for Baldy, Stephen sensed the indecision among the others, but no one volunteered to go with Hardin.

"Let's get back to the others, while our tired horses can still gallop," he said. Before anyone could object, he turned George and took the stallion to a run.

When they reached the other settlers, Stephen halted and motioned for everyone to gather close. He glanced from man to man as he said, "Fearing a trap, we decided not to pursue any further. We killed half their number and in doing so we achieved some measure of justice. They've received our message that they cannot kill among us without paying a price. Further justice will have to wait until we have a fighting chance. Until we can stand against them on our own ground."

Wetmore eyed the men. "I say we go back to our homes with our lives and bury the dead. Afterward, I will extend credit to any man who needs additional weapons or ammunition."

"I will do the same," Mabbitt said with a sideways glance at Wetmore. "With no interest charged."

Not to be outdone, Wetmore nodded and said, "I'll agree to the same terms. And with the purchase of every rifle, I'll throw in a pound of black powder."

Anticipating the arrival of more settlers to the settlement and the continued threat from Indians, both traders had laid up a good supply of weapons of all kinds, along with powder and ball. It was to their benefit to ensure that all the settlers were well armed.

Mabbit started to sweeten his offer again, but Stephen held up a hand. "Those are generous offers, Sirs," Stephen told the two traders. "But we now need to hurry back and get prepared to fight another day. It may be tomorrow, or the next day, or even the next month. But we *will* have to fight for our land and our homes someday. Each man and woman should have at least one straight-shooting rifle and two good pistols. Fortify your homes, take turns standing guard, and bring your horses and cows in close. Especially at night. Most of all, don't go out alone or in the darkness as Billy did."

"That there is good advice," Wetmore said. "Especially the part about rifles."

Stephen had one more thing to say. "We've claimed this part of the province for American citizens. We must all dig in our heels on our land and trust to our weapons. We can't let Indians or even Spanish soldiers bait us into taking foolish chances. We're all Americans on American soil. But now…we're also all Texians!"

"Hear! Hear!" one man shouted, and the others enthusiastically nodded their agreement.

"I swear, Stephen, sometimes I think you're smarter than the lot of them combined," Baldy whispered to him.

He leaned over toward Baldy. "No, just common sense."

Baldy frowned. "Well, common sense isn't all that common."

CHAPTER 7

꒦꒷

T HAT MAN WOULD SCARE GRIZZLY bears, Samuel thought as he watched Pate ride off. He could hardly find words to describe the man's incivility and ruthless disregard for his children. But that man certainly knew how to find the words to draw blood. Pate couldn't have wounded Louisa more if he'd tried. On top of that, he'd questioned Samuel's honor.

Foul-tempered and uncivil, Pate had chafed him worse than a new pair of boots. How could that tyrant have raised such a charming daughter and an agreeable boy when he was so perfectly heartless? He guessed Louisa and Adam must have both taken after their mothers.

Samuel turned to Louisa. "I'm sorry if we've come between you and your father. My only intention was to help you. And Melly aimed to help too."

"I know, and I'm grateful," she said. "It's just the way he is."

Samuel wanted to learn more but didn't want to say much about their father in front of the boy.

"Louisa, I'll take Adam to my house," Melly said, reading his mind. "I'll start showing him around Baldy's apothecary and clinic. Whenever you're ready, join us. But there's no hurry."

"I'll be along shortly," Louisa said. "And thank you again for giving us jobs. I don't know what we would have done if you hadn't."

Likely they would have starved, Samuel thought.

Melly placed a reassuring arm on Adam's little shoulder. "I bet you'd like a big piece of pecan pie and a glass of milk," she told the boy as they started to walk away.

Adam glanced up at Melly with a beaming grin. "Boy would I!"

"Mrs. Grant seems like such a kind woman," Louisa said. "I'm so grateful to her for taking us in. I truly don't know what my father would have done or how he would have cared for us if she hadn't offered to employ us."

"She's been like a mother to me and my brothers for years."

"What happened to your mother?" she asked.

"She died when my youngest brother, Stephen, Jr., was born. We call him Steve."

"I'm so sorry. My mother died when I was young too."

"That's sad. Unfortunately, I need to go find my brothers. I'll be back as soon as I can. Melly will have a good supply of pistols. Do you know how to use one?"

She nodded. "I do."

"Keep one close by, maybe in your apron, no matter what you're doing or where you are."

"All right. I had better get to work. I'm employed now," she said with a tinge of wonder and a grin. "It's my first job and I intend to do it well."

"Louisa, what made your father like that?"

"Like what?"

"Well, disagreeable, to put it nicely."

"He's always been like that. He's not like my mother was or my stepmother. They were both kind and sweet and loved us. But Pa has always been harsh and thinks first of himself." She stared down at the ground. "I think we have always just been burdens for him to carry around."

"What did he plan for your family here on the frontier? How will he make a living?"

"My father buys and sells land and homesteads. He only bought our place because he got it for next to nothing. The man appeared desperate to sell. Pa will sell it soon."

"Seems like a poor way to make a decent living," Samuel said. "Can't put down roots living that way."

"We've moved a dozen times since I've been able to count without ever clearing timber or fencing a single field. He says he likes living that way because all he has to do to move is put out the fire and saddle his horse."

It was so contrary to the way he'd been raised, Samuel couldn't believe what he was hearing.

"He also plans to arrange a marriage for me at the first opportunity. He said he wanted to hurry up and marry me off before I lost my good looks."

She couldn't possibly lose her looks. He'd bet she'd be beautiful even when she was old and wrinkled. "Marry you off?" he asked.

"Since there are few women on the frontier, he dreams of arranging a favorable marriage contract with someone of considerable means. One of the men who own the profitable trading posts here at Pecan Point or in Jonesboro. Or perhaps a lawyer in Nacogdoches. If he doesn't find a suitable match here, we'll be moving to Louisiana soon."

Stunned and outraged, Samuel said, "To me, that sounds a lot like selling you."

Louisa cast her eyes to the ground. "I've known that was my fate for a long time. Ever since I can remember, he's made me read newspapers and such to be sure I would appear knowledgeable and sound cultured to a potential husband."

Samuel had wondered how someone so deprived could sound so learned.

"A young woman on the frontier is merely a valuable commodity to my Pa."

Well, not to him. He'd saved her from the quicksand. But could he save her from a smothering father? Somehow, he would find a way.

"He also wants to hire Adam out to a farmer for field work. He would in effect become an indentured slave." She raised her head and a swift spark of anger swept across her face.

Samuel shook his head. "I can't believe a father would do that to his own children. And in the meantime, he expects you to manage and defend your home, care for a little boy, and fight off Indians?"

"I haven't been good at any of those things," she said, her voice near breaking. "I don't think I'm suited for the frontier. Life is too hard here. Too unpredictable. Too lonely…" Her voice faded to a whisper.

"Life in the West can be hard. The wilderness is an unpredictable and untamed place as dangerous as it is breathtakingly beautiful. A place as beautiful as heaven must be. It is also an almost sacred place where the bravest can be blessed with life and happiness."

"Happiness. I'm not sure I even know what that is anymore."

Samuel wanted to wrap his arms around her and hug her to him. But afraid she would consider that too forward or improper, he simply said, "Don't give up on happiness just yet. Things should get easier for you. All of us will help you. You are smart and brave and saved your brother and yourself. Don't ever let your father make you think otherwise."

She glanced up at him with a look of gratitude. "You're the one who saved us. Thank you again. I owe you our lives."

"You only owe me your friendship."

For a long moment, they gazed into each other's eyes. The warm look in those blue eyes of hers touched a place deep inside his heart.

"Unfortunately, I've got to go. But I won't be far off. Our cattle are just south of here. About a mile. My father and Baldy should be back soon. Melly will tell them what happened with your father."

"Be safe," she said and marched toward the Grant's home.

As she walked away, his heart wanted to pull her back to him.

With clods of dirt flinging from his gelding's hooves, Samuel galloped Samson toward the pasture where their cattle normally grazed in the mornings as the herd worked their way toward Pecan Bayou for water. He could see his mounted brothers in the distance. Wisely, they had stayed together as they watched over the cattle. A few moments later, he tugged Samson to a gentle stop.

Quickly, he told them about the attack on the Pate place, how he'd pulled the two from the quicksand, and how ungrateful and uncivil their father was. Then he told them that Melly had offered them both jobs.

Thomas wisely focused on the most disturbing news. "So that means that there were raids by both the Osages and the Comanche last night."

"Yes. Father and Baldy rode into the settlement to alert the others."

"No telling what they will find there," Cornelius said. "Others might have been attacked too."

"What does Father want us to do?" Steve asked.

"He didn't say, but I think we should bring Rusty up to the lot next to the barn and then move the rest of the herd closer in," Samuel told them.

They'd brought their best bull with them from Louisiana to Pecan Point. Samuel had crossed one of the English bulls their father had brought from Kentucky with a fine Spanish Criollo cow he'd purchased at a cattle auction in Louisiana. The cow had once roamed free in Texas and she was still a part of their herd. He'd raised their calf and named him Rusty since he was largely cinnamon color with few white splashes on his back half and on his legs. Now, four years later, with his impressive long horns, thick neck, and stout conformation, Rusty was Samuel's most valuable possession.

The three nodded their agreement and they set to work. With his gentle disposition, herding Rusty proved to be a relatively easy task with the four of them to guide him along. Within the half hour, they had the big longhorn inside the lot. He bellowed for his herd a few times, but they heard no further complaints from the bull, and he soon wandered over to the rain barrel up next to the barn and had himself a long drink.

Next, they went back for the rest of the cattle and slowly pushed them closer to their cabin. Fortunately, the pond near the house they used for the cattle was still half full and Melly's garden and the corn patch were fenced off.

"Cornelius and Steve, keep a close watch on the herd. Be sure they stay where we put them," Samuel told them. "Thomas, I want you to guard the houses. Melly is in her house with Louisa and Adam. I'm going to go after Father and Baldy. They may have encountered trouble. They should have been back by now."

❦

"They made your father their leader," Rose told Samuel after she'd told him what happened to the Roberts. "About thirty of them left about two hours ago. I'm surprised they're not back yet.

Want to wait inside with me?"

It didn't surprise Samuel that the militia made his father their leader. He was worth a dozen common men in a fight and his father possessed a heart of honor and a certain natural confidence that made men respect him. That respect was enhanced, no doubt, by the two .69 caliber smoothbore flintlock pistols with nine-inch barrels that always hung from his wide leather belt.

With thirty men chasing six Indians, Samuel decided his father likely didn't need his help. But his friend did. The news of Billy's gruesome death left him stunned. He had to clear this throat before he could speak. "Thank you, Rose, but I must decline. I have to ride out to Billy's place and start digging two graves."

She nodded woodenly. "Poor souls. And so young too."

What a strange day. It started with his burying the two Indians he'd killed last night. Now, he would have to bury his closest friend and his wife, killed by Indians on the exact same night. It was the worst kind of trade. Lives for lives.

He dreaded the task ahead of him but digging Billy's grave, and one for his friend's wife was the least Samuel could do. What else could he do for them now? Absolutely nothing.

He borrowed a shovel from Wetmore's store and headed toward Billy's place, about a mile and a half from the settlement. When he arrived, the door to the cabin hung open. He tied Samson outside and stepped inside the meager house. Everything was in disarray in the normally tidy front room. He headed to their bedroom, fearing what he would find.

Billy's wife, Linda, lay on their bed, an arrow protruding from her chest. Her blank eyes stared at something that wasn't there. The swell in her belly brought tears to his eyes and a lump to his throat. The terror she must have faced and her fear for her unborn child were unimaginable.

"God, why?"

He closed her eyes and took a firm grip on the arrow. Anger tightened his jaw as he gripped the shaft and wrenched it out. He flung the deadly arrow against the wall. "Damn them!"

Samuel took a deep breath and let it out slowly. He wrapped the body in her bed quilt and carried her to the porch. After he gently laid her down, he found another blanket and then set off on Samson toward where Rose had said he would find his friend's body.

As he neared the end of the mile, he worried about what he would find. But he had to take care of Billy. His friend didn't have any family here and few friends. It's just his body anyway because he's in heaven now, he tried to tell himself. But his blood froze in revulsion and his breath hitched when he spotted his friend and nearby Billy's severed, scalped head.

Although he had tried to prepare himself, the ghastly sight sickened him and sweat broke out on his face. He swallowed his choking emotions and the bitter bile in his mouth. But it came back up and he quickly dismounted and leaned over while he retched violently.

It was several minutes before he could straighten up and face the horror again. When he did, his heart beat hard in his chest. Could he do this? He had to. He urged Samson forward. But the horse only took a few steps before he stopped again. Smelling blood, the gelding hesitated so Samuel tied him, grabbed the blanket and rope, and staggered up to Billy. His mind reeled at the shocking sight.

Staring down at the arrow-riddled body, his hand flew to his chest as his mind tried to grasp the ghastliness before him. With halting words, he said, "I'm so sorry, my friend. This is wrong. So dreadfully wrong. You didn't deserve this." He knelt and wrenched each of the arrows free and angrily stabbed them into the ground. Secured with sinew, the turkey wing and tail feathers at the ends of the arrow shafts blurred in his vision, like some sort of ugly, noxious weed.

"You deserved a good life, Billy. Not this. Surely not this..." his voice broke.

He tried to keep his watering eyes off of Billy's face as he worked. He wrapped the blanket around the body and head and then tied a rope tightly around the blanket before loading Billy on Samson, who was none too happy about it.

"Easy boy," Samuel cooed into the gelding's ear. "We have to do this. Let's find Billy and his wife a nice place to rest."

He led Samson the mile back thinking about all the good times he and Billy shared. He didn't want to think about how his friend had died. He wanted to think about how he had lived.

He stopped at a copse of oak trees near their cabin. Billy's favorite tree grew there. The last time Samuel had visited, they'd shared a shot of whiskey under that tree. As they'd leaned against its massive trunk, they talked about their futures. Samuel told him about his plans for Red River Cattle Company. Billy wanted to be the best horse trainer in these parts and sell his horses to the army. They even talked about Billy taking horses along with Samuel's cows and going to various forts together to sell them. Samuel and his brothers would help protect Billy and his horses from thieves. It could have worked. It could have...

Now, Billy and his horses were gone.

At first, he found the digging hard. Not because of the soil's hardness, but because he didn't want to dig his friend's grave. He forced himself to put some guts into it, and soon the loathsome task was done, and he stood before two empty graves. He heaved the shovel aside.

He steeled himself because, now, the truly hard part would begin.

He laid Billy in one of the graves—the exact same spot where his friend had sat while they companionably shared the drink and made their plans for the future.

If only they were doing the same today. If only...choking back his emotions, his thoughts faltered in the grief that engulfed him.

Leaving Samson tied there, he went back for Billy's wife. He carried her himself, not wanting to disturb the baby by putting the body on Samson. Each step toward the grave grew harder—not physically, but emotionally and he found himself taking slower and slower steps. He was growing numb with increasing shock and disbelief.

When he finally reached the burial place, he knelt and gently lowered Linda into the grave. As he had carried her, the blanket had slipped off the top of her body. Unlike Billy, her pale face seemed peaceful. He reached in, rested her hands against her babe, and then used the quilt to cover her head again.

A tumble of confused thoughts assailed him. Right now, he hated Indians. Before this happened, he had respected them. Except for a few ruthless braves, he had thought they were fighting for land too. They fought to the death, whether it was against other tribes or the white man, expecting no quarter for themselves. He could even see nobility in them. But now...now hatred made his jaw clench. It was one thing for a courageous man—Indian or white—to kill in battle. But the braves who had killed Billy and his wife were nothing but thieves and murderers. They'd lured a man from his home in the dead of night, butchered him, and then snuck back and massacred a defenseless woman heavy with child. It was beyond the pale—the absolute opposite of nobility—deplorable and disgraceful.

Even if Indians were fighting for what they perceived to be theirs, what gave them the right to all this land? The West held millions and millions of acres. Tribes constantly moved across it from one spot to another, always shifting and warring among each other for the best hunting grounds. Just as Europeans had done for centuries. American settlers were just another tribe of humanity, trying to claim land to survive. The white man wasn't native, but he was human. And humans need land to survive. A place to raise cattle and grow crops. A place to call home.

Whether they liked it or not, Indians would have to share this vast land.

Samuel knew this was a moment he would remember for a long time. Because in that moment, his youthful, idealistic opinion of the Indian vanished, replaced by the reality of the West. His anger grew to a scalding fury hot enough to burn away the tears he wanted to shed for his friend.

With a brooding intensity, he stared into the holes in the ground. Holes that held all there ever would be of Billy and his family. All that could have been. And all that never would be.

Seeing them down there in the dirt made his heart hurt. With an agony that cried out to heaven, he raised his gaze toward God. But the glare of the sun was blindingly harsh. Although his knees were not by any means calloused from prayer, he knew the only comfort for his grief would come from God. This time, he lowered his head and began to pray for his friend. "I pray the two of you are together now with your baby," he started. But then he had to stop as he stood there wondering if the baby was the son Billy had wanted or if it might have been a pretty baby girl. No one but God would ever know.

The sound of riders interrupted his prayer and he quickly glanced up, fearing it might mean Indians returning for more plunder. Thankfully, it wasn't.

The sight of his father and Baldy at the front of the militia gladdened his distraught heart. Baldy could now lead them in a burial service fitting for a good man, his wife, and babe.

CHAPTER 8

SINCE SHE COULDN'T SCRUB CLOTHES with bandaged hands, Louisa spent the day by Mrs. Grant's side helping her with everything. The woman never stopped. After a while, though, Mrs. Grant insisted Louisa rest for a bit since she hadn't slept last night. In the meantime, Melly would tutor Adam. As Louisa left to go rest, Mrs. Grant gave her brother a slate board to practice his letters on.

She slept for a couple of hours on a bed in Baldy's apothecary. However, after that, she was too excited to sleep, and she wanted to make a good first impression. She found Mrs. Grant and stayed by her side the rest of the day helping her any way she could.

After promising not to touch any of the bottles or jars in the apothecary containing herbal concoctions and tinctures, Mrs. Grant assigned Adam his first duties—sweeping, mopping, and dusting the doctor's surgery and examination rooms attached to the Grant's house. They gathered up a number of cleaning supplies and stood together looking at the doctor's clinic.

Melly glanced down at Adam. "My husband has been so busy with patients, both human and animal, that he hasn't had time to keep his apothecary and surgery as clean as he likes. He insists that cleanliness is indeed next to Godliness."

"Then I'll try to get close to God," Adam said.

Mrs. Grant smiled broadly and showed him how to use a broom, the mop and bucket full of water, and a pile of dry and wet rags for dusting and cleaning. She carefully explained the use of each and showed him the difference between clean and dirty. "Do your best," she told him. "It doesn't have to be perfect, just your best."

Adam had listened attentively, but Louisa wondered how much he could get done. "Mrs. Grant, I'm not sure Adam is capable of doing all that," she told the woman as they walked back to the other side of the Grant's cabin. "He's never been asked to do anything like that and he's just eight."

"Please, just call me Melly. You'd be surprised what children are capable of doing if asked. Samuel's brothers have been helping with chores around the house since they were four or five. Stephen insisted they contribute, and it's been good for them. Adam's work doesn't have to be just right. It just has to be his best, whatever that is. He'll become more skilled with practice and as he grows."

Meanwhile, they ground cornmeal, picked berries for pie, changed bed linens, harvested and washed vegetables, collected chicken eggs, and a dozen other tasks. All the while, the two chatted like close friends. Louisa learned that the Grant's only child, a daughter, had died when she was a young woman. No wonder Mrs. Grant seemed so hungry for Louisa's companionship.

Sometime later, when she and Mrs. Grant went to check on Adam's work, Louisa was shocked that a boy of her brother's age could accomplish so much. The doctor's workrooms looked and smelled much cleaner.

"I mopped it twice," he said with pride in his voice. "Because I missed a few spots the first time. And I had to use all the rags. There was a lot of dirt on the outside of the windows. I stood on an old barrel to get to the top ones." He giggled a moment. "I almost fell off."

Louisa glanced at the windows, a rarity on the frontier. Most still had streaks but at least they were reasonably clean.

"I'm glad you didn't fall," Mrs. Grant told him, "or you might have become one of our patients. You did a fine job, Adam, thank you. I'm proud of you."

Adam's freckled face beamed.

Louisa was fairly sure her brother had never heard those words from their father. For certain, she never did.

"My husband insisted that his apothecary and clinic have windows. He believes sunshine and fresh air are better than any medicine. We had to order the windows from Nacogdoches," Mrs. Grant explained. "The glass has many waves and bubble pockets, but at least you can see through them and they're durable."

"What if someone shoots through them?" Adam asked.

"If there's trouble, we run to the Wyllie's cabin. Without windows, their cabin is more like a small fort," Melly said.

"Is that where we'll be sleeping?" Louisa asked, pointing to the two beds under the twin windows. She'd slept on one when she napped.

"Yes, dear. If my husband gets a patient who needs to stay overnight, we'll just have to put you two on a pallet in front of the hearth." Melly moved to the beds and began stripping off the linens. "Let's put clean linens on both beds." After she retrieved the linen and two softs quilts from a cabinet, she said, "Adam, watch how I make up the beds. After today, you'll be doing this whenever the linens need changing, usually every other week."

Louisa's eyes widened. So did Adam's. The beds they had always used were covered in only a rough, dirty blanket with one sheet that rarely saw washing.

"And you'll both be expected to make up your beds each morning," Melly continued. "Louisa, I have a screen we can move in here. You can use it to change behind. It will give you some privacy. And I'll have Baldy purchase a wash bowl, pitcher, and hairbrush for your use. It will take us a few days, but we'll make this room nice and cozy for both of you."

"We are terribly grateful, but will Dr. Grant be happy we're here?" Louisa asked. It seemed as though they were invading his workplace. And it surprised Louisa that Melly would hire both of them without getting her husband's approval first.

"I believe he will be delighted," Mrs. Grant said. "He enjoys teaching others about medicine. And he's been overworked lately. Ever since our arrival, we've had a steady stream of people coming here from the settlements. Some of them even bring their animals for him to heal. And he has a few creatures and wildlife that have to stay here while he treats them. I know he could use Adam's help caring for the animal patients. Adam can feed and water them and be sure they're all right."

"Where are they?" Adam asked.

"I'd like to help with the animals too," Louisa said. Her heart had always held a soft spot for anything with four legs.

"I'll show them to you shortly. For now, why don't you both take a break and help me make some shortbread?"

"Really?" Adam asked.

"Really!" Mrs. Grant said, tugging him along by the hand. "A day that includes cookies is a day sprinkled with happiness."

A large, stone hearth took up most of the left wall in the Grant's kitchen. In front of the hearth were a half dozen iron pans in various shapes and size, including two large iron pots with fireproof lids. Above the hearth, a mantel held an assortment of spices and herbs stored in jars. On the hearth's right side wall, various utensils hung from an iron bar along with cloths for picking up hot pans. Opposite the hearth was a window that provided light. Hung with hinges, it was opened to the outside to let out smoke, Louisa guessed. On the far wall, a cupboard held more pots and dishes on open shelves. Based on the mortars and pestles, used to grind spices, the counter below served as a work surface. In the center of the room, sat a large table with a butter churn and chair beside it.

"Do you have a smokehouse?" Louisa asked.

"Not yet. Game is so plentiful here there's been no need. But the men plan to build one this spring before the hog is slaughtered," Mrs. Grant explained. "Then we'll have some good smoked bacon. But for right now, we'll get a fire going and soon we'll have some splendid shortbread!"

Louisa had never made shortbread and she watched Melly work with interest.

Melly turned around to tell them, "The boys' love of shortbread came from their Scottish mother, Jane. Stephen's wife made it often and her daughter, Martha, taught me. The ratio you should use is four parts flour, two parts butter, and one part sugar."

Four, two, one, Louisa repeated to herself. Her first real recipe.

Mrs. Grant put the butter on to come to a boil and measured out and mixed the flour and sugar. Next, she made a hole in the mixture and poured the boiling butter in it. She worked the flour and butter together, formed it into a tight ball, and rolled it out into an oval. Then she cut the dough into short rectangular pieces and put a layer into the buttered Dutch oven.

Within minutes a delicious buttery aroma filled the kitchen and they were all devouring the shortbread with delight.

"That's the best thing I've ever tasted!" Adam declared with a mouthful of cookie.

After that, Mrs. Grant took them out to show them the animals that Dr. Grant was caring for. Inside a small shed, a row of cages and pens held the sick animals.

"We give all the animals a temporary name that's easy to remember. This is Rose the rabbit," Mrs. Grant said, pointing to a rabbit with a twitching nose. "She has a festering foot. This is Charlotte the chicken. She has a broken wing. A fox almost got ahold of her. And this is David the dog. He was bitten by a venomous snake. Poor thing almost died."

David raised his head and then resumed his nap.

"Will he live?" Adam asked her. "And can I pet him?"

"Yes, you can pet him. He's a sweet loving dog. He'll live, but he's still recovering. His body needs time to get rid of the poison and that terrible wound where he was bit needs to heal. Pet him as often as you like as long as you're gentle. Petting could even help him to recover quicker. But don't fall in love with him. He already belongs to a boy a little older than you. You know, that boy would make a good friend for you. He lives nearby."

Louisa couldn't recall Adam ever having a friend. Their father had moved them around so much. Even when they did land somewhere for a while their father kept Adam constantly busy with chores. Louisa's only friend had been her mother and later, and too briefly, Adam's mother. For the last six years, her only companions had been her brother and her now dead mare. She realized that part of the reason for her loneliness must be that her heart ached for friendship.

As if reading her thoughts, Melly smiled at her and hugged her shoulders. Just that simple contact spread a comforting warmth inside her.

Adam reached in and gave the dog a few gentle pats. "Get well soon, David."

Louisa loved rabbits. "What about Rose? Is her foot healing?"

"Yes, it's already much better. You can pet her if you'd like."

Louisa put a hand inside the cage and slowly stroked the back of the rabbit. "Don't be afraid. I'm your friend. I'll help you get better."

They gave the animals fresh water and then Melly showed

them where the two milk cows were kept, the chicken coop, and the garden.

"Adam, one of your jobs will be to chase deer out of the garden and to keep squirrels from devouring the growing crop," Melly said. "And chase out any rabbits you see too."

"I can do that," Adam said with a grin.

They spent the rest of the afternoon baking and cooking the evening meal which included a savory stew and fried cornbread. Louisa learned what spices made a stew flavorful and which of the vegetables they'd picked earlier should be used in the stew.

The remaining vegetables were stored in a small, one-room building, constructed over the nearby spring. The main purpose of the spring house, Louisa learned, was to keep their spring water clean by keeping out fallen leaves, animals, and dust. But it also functioned much like a root cellar, which she had seen before. The chilly water of the spring ran under the room's floor and kept a constant cool temperature inside the spring house throughout the year. Food that would otherwise spoil, such as meat or fruit could be stored there, safe from the havoc of animals as well.

By the time they finished preparing dinner, Adam's stomach was growling, and Louisa saw him sneak a piece of shortbread off the counter. Her eyes widened because she feared Adam would get in trouble.

Melly noticed the pilfering too and laughed out loud. "Adam, next time, just ask. If it's okay, I'll tell you. If it's not, I'll tell you why it's not." Adam nodded and she kindly gave him another piece of shortbread to tide him over.

Louisa's body ached from fatigue, but she couldn't remember when the two of them had a better day. She'd already learned a lot about cooking and household duties from Mrs. Grant. Simple things, really. But they were things no one had ever taught her or told her about.

After they carried all the food over to the Wyllie's cabin, they placed the pot and pans by the hearth to keep it warm, and Louisa added wood to the still glowing coals.

Then, Louisa even learned how to properly set a table. It was the first time she'd set a table. With Melly's help, they added wildflowers and some greenery to a pitcher, set it in the center, and put candles on either side of the bouquet. Normally, at home, they just filled a plate, grabbed a fork, and sat wherever they could. Somehow, setting a nice table made a meal more significant. More meaningful. Peaceful even.

About the time they finished setting the table, she heard the sound of horses riding up. She peered out and saw three large fellows dismounting near the horse shed.

Melly peered out too. "Those are Samuel's brothers. After they care for their horses, I'll introduce you and Adam."

"When will Samuel be back?" Adam asked.

"Soon, I hope," Melly said. "Along with Mr. Wyllie and my husband."

"I hope so too," Adam said.

Louisa could see the worry in the woman's kind eyes. Her husband and Mr. Wyllie had left that morning and had yet to return. The sun would be setting soon, and men didn't stay out in the darkness of the frontier any longer than they had to.

A few minutes later, the three young men all stormed in, laughing and jostling one another.

Louisa stared at them. Like Samuel, they were all enormous and well-armed. Clearly, working regularly in the open and Melly's cooking had made them healthy and strong. And their rugged appearance made her think they were all capable of defending themselves or their family. And like Samuel, they were all exceptionally handsome.

When they glanced her way, the three stopped in their tracks and stared.

"Where are your manners?" Melly asked. "Stop gaping and introduce yourselves properly. These two are Louisa and Adam Pate, neighbors from across the river. They are working for me now."

One by one the three stepped toward her, hand outstretched, and told her their names. Then they each shook Adam's small hand.

"Pleased to meet all of you," Louisa told them. "I hope you won't mind that my brother and I will be joining you for dinner."

"Oh no!" Steve blurted and then seemed embarrassed. Steve appeared to be the youngest of the four brothers. A swath of wavy dark hair hung on his high forehead. Like Samuel, his eyes were dark blue, but he seemed more reserved, almost somber. "You're welcome to join us."

"Of course, we welcome you, Miss Pate," Cornelius said. Cornelius, who seemed full of life, also had dark hair, but his eyes were a mischievous green and his smile playful.

"You too, Adam," Thomas said. His rugged features made Thomas appear older than the other two. His hair color, almost black, was the same as his father's and his eyes were the same light blue.

"Thanks," Adam said.

"Please, all of you, call me Louisa."

"We were sorry to hear from Samuel of your misfortune," Thomas said. "If any of us can help you, please, just ask."

Louisa nodded. "Thank you."

"Where are Father, Baldy, and Samuel?" Steve asked.

"Your father and Baldy still haven't returned from the settlement. Samuel went after them to see if they needed his help and now he hasn't returned either," Melly said. "Why don't we eat while the food is hot and if they aren't back by the time we finish, you boys can go see what's keeping them."

"I don't think that would be wise," Thomas said. "It's nearly dark. We could have another Indian raid. We'll need to stay and guard the horse shed and the bull." He winked at Adam. "You can help us guard the women, Adam."

"You bet I will," Adam said. "I know how to load weapons for Louisa."

Louisa could tell that Thomas possessed the same kindness of spirit that Samuel did. Most young men would ignore a boy, but Thomas took the time to speak to Adam twice.

The three removed all their weapons and washed their faces, forearms, and hands in a large bowl on a side table by the beds. After exchanging a few playful swats with their towels, they all took seats at the table on one of the two side benches.

"Why don't you two sit on the opposite side," Melly told Louisa and Adam.

Louisa took a seat on the end and Adam plopped down beside her.

After Melly took a seat, she said, "Adam, would you like to say the prayer?"

"It ain't Sunday," the boy said.

"We pray before all our meals," Melly told him. "To thank God for blessing us with food."

He frowned as he turned to glance up at Louisa. "Maybe that's why we never had much food—we never thanked God."

Embarrassed, Louisa frowned, but the Wyllie boys chuckled good-naturedly and Melly smiled.

"Ma'am, I ain't ever said a prayer before," Adam said, glancing back at Melly.

"We all had to start praying sometime," Cornelius said. "Tonight's your night! Just thank God for the food and anything else you might be grateful for."

"All right, I'll do it!" Adam said and inclined his head. "God, thanks for this food and make it good, 'cause I sure am hungry. And thanks for these nice people. And our new jobs. I hope we get to keep them. And thanks for sending Samuel to save us... And..."

"And bring my husband Baldy, Stephen, and Samuel safely back to us," Melly concluded, no doubt thinking that Adam might not be stopping any time soon.

They did have a lot to be thankful for.

"Amen!" the three Wyllie boys said in unison.

"Amen," Adam imitated.

CHAPTER 9

A S THEY RODE AWAY FROM Billy's place, Samuel, his father, and Baldy were all dirty, tired, and emotionally spent. Earlier, his father had dug down into Billy's grave a ways and then added Billy's scalp to the grave. It gave Samuel a small measure of comfort. What gave him more comfort, though, was the fact that the brave who'd displayed it was now dead. And the Indian would receive only what they called a sky burial—a burial by vultures.

Surrounded by the men at the settlement, Baldy had conducted a heart-rending service at the gravesite that left all those hardened men near tears.

Samuel tried to listen but spent most of the service agonizing over what had happened to his friend. He'd had to draw in slow, steady breaths to keep his anger at bay.

As soon as he could, he mounted his horse. He wanted to get away from this place. But as he rode, with his father and Baldy riding their mounts on both sides of Samson, anger continued to roll around inside of him like the dark clouds of a furious thunderstorm. Not wanting to talk, he mentally withdrew and remained quiet until they returned to the settlement.

Most of the men hurried to Mabbitt's and Wetmore's trading posts to stock up on weapons and ammunition. All except the two that were wounded who went with them to the tavern to have Baldy tend to their wounds.

As the group of them made their way inside, a lame man named Claude O'Neil, too fond of the bottle, snored in the corner. An old leather hat covered his face and his arms were crossed in front of him. Baldy once tried to determine if the man's lameness was the cause of his fondness for alcohol or if it was a physical or mental weakness, but Claude would have none of it saying he didn't trust doctors. Even so, he always seemed grateful when Baldy and Melly would sometimes bring him a plate of food or fresh warm clothing. When the fellow was awake and reasonably sober, he could saw on the fiddle though. Those who enjoyed his music would tip him a coin or two.

Over the long counter that served as the tavern's bar, the owner had hung a sign upon which he'd chalked in large letters, *'Pay to-day, trust to-morrow.'* And since ready money was in short supply in the settlement, a stack of skins stood behind the bar. For deerskins, coonskins, and beaver were as good a legal tender in the West as a New York shilling any day. And so the obtainability of a man's strong drink pretty often depended upon his keen eye and a good gun.

Baldy ordered and paid for a whiskey for both wounded men, one for himself, and one to sterilize the wounds. His service during the War of 1812 had given Baldy a great deal of experience treating battle wounds.

Meanwhile, his father ordered a whiskey and a double one for Samuel. Taking a table well away from where Baldy worked, the two of them took seats.

"I see more anger than grief on your face, Son," his father said.

Samuel stared into the amber-colored liquor in his glass. "I felt grief, lots of it, while I retrieved their bodies and dug their graves." He took a long sip. "But then, as I laid them in the graves and stared down at them in those cold holes in the ground, my grief turned to rage. Right now, I hate Indians. They murder and steal and make our lives here miserable. How can they expect us to live in peace with them?"

"I'm not sure they do. We think peace is always the goal. But it's not. They count coup anytime they even touch an enemy."

"Count coup?"

"A war honor. A blow struck against an enemy counts as a coup, but the most prestigious acts include just touching an enemy with the hand, bow, or coup stick and escaping. Also stealing an enemy's weapons or horses."

"They did a lot more than touch Billy," he swore.

His father nodded somberly. "I would hope that one day we can have peace, but I think that is likely to be many years off."

"You should have seen Billy!"

"I'm sorry you had to."

Samuel squeezed his eyes shut. "I can't get that image out of my head!" His voice broke with huskiness.

His father sighed. "It may take a long time for it to fade. But it will."

"When Louisa's father came to our place, he said some horrible things about Indians. He hates them and believes they should all be killed."

"Hardin said pretty much the same. He would have ridden into a likely trap just to satisfy his lust for Indian blood."

"I urged Pate to exercise restraint and caution, but now, I wonder if he might have been right," Samuel said. His mind reeled with confusion.

"You don't believe that. Not really. You're too good a man to believe that way."

He peered at his father. "I was. I'm not so sure anymore."

"A man can't live well or long on hate."

Mr. O'Neil woke and sat up. Blurry-eyed, he glanced around. When he noticed Baldy, he stood up on shaky legs and hobbled over to him. "Dr. Grant, can you buy me a whiskey? For medicinal purposes, I mean. I'll play you a tune."

Baldy placed a coin on the counter. "Whatever it is that's making you drink so much, Claude, you need to let me help you."

His leathery, despondent face twisted as he shook his head. "There's no help on earth for what ails me." He tossed back the whiskey and then hobbled over to his fiddle case.

Baldy shook his head and buckled up his medical saddlebag as O'Neill started playing and singing a forlorn tune.

"When she left me it broke my old heart.
I shed a tear for every mistake I ever made.
Don't worry about me, I'm just living under a dark cloud.
And these days, I can't tell the difference
Between the whiskey and the shade."

Samuel emptied his glass. He was in no mood for sad songs. "Baldy's finished. Let's go."

While they were on their way home, Samuel told his father and

Baldy about the rest of his encounter with Mr. Pate. "The man expressed concern for one thing only, the loss of his possessions. He didn't express thankfulness at all that his daughter and son lived through their ordeals. In fact, he heaped nothing but anger upon them."

"He probably panicked," Baldy said. "Losing your weapons, food, and household goods on the frontier can mean disaster."

"But that's no reason to treat your flesh and blood so poorly," Samuel protested. "He's a cruel man and my instinct tells me he'll mean trouble for Louisa. He intends to marry her for profit." The thought made Samuel's anger escalate even more.

"So what happened?" his father asked. "Did he take his children?"

Samuel hesitated a moment. "Well...no."

"No?" his father and Baldy both asked.

"When Louisa told him she would get a job to help pay for the supplies they would need to replenish, he ridiculed her and made her feel useless."

"What did Louisa say?" his father asked.

"She just looked hurt and defeated. It was Melly who took offense at what Pate had said. She especially didn't appreciate him ridiculing you, Baldy, because you're a preacher in a Catholic land and doing the devil's bidding. He said you weren't fit to sing a hymn to a dead horse."

"That's offensive in more ways than one," Stephen said.

"Offending my Melly is not something any man should dare do. If she didn't give him what for, I will," Baldy swore.

Samuel nodded. "I wanted to knock the man off his high horse and teach him better manners. But before I could, Melly heaped coals of kindness on Pate's head."

"How?" his father asked.

"She gave both Louisa and little Adam paying jobs," he told them. "She told Pate that she would give him their salary every Friday."

"Jobs?" Baldy asked.

"Yes. Louisa is going to help Melly with laundry and other chores. And Adam is supposed to help you, Baldy."

Baldy's dark eyes widened. "How is a little boy going to help me?"

"That's up to you," Samuel said. "But I suspect Melly has some ideas."

"That wife of mine…" Baldy said with a grin and shook his head.

"She was desperate to keep Mr. Pate from taking his children away," Samuel explained. "So was I. It was obvious to us that the man was a brute. There's no telling what he would have done to Louisa when he got her home."

"At least while they're with us, they'll eat properly," his father said. "The two look as though they've missed more than a few meals."

Samuel had a feeling they'd missed a lot more than just food. He suspected they'd known little happiness and even less love.

❧

Just as they were finishing eating, Louisa turned toward the front of the house at the sound of horses galloping up.

"Riders!" Steve said. "They're back."

"Thank God!" Melly said.

The three huge brothers leaped up and raced out the door.

Louisa guessed they were eager to hear what had happened at the settlement. She glanced at Melly. "Should we go out too?"

"No, let's let them have a few moments. They'll need to care for the horses before they do anything else. Adam, please shut the door. It helps to keep the flies and the dust out."

The light in the cabin abruptly grew dim as the sun fully set. Daylight was dying faster now in late September.

Melly lit a few candles and several oil lamps while Adam trailed behind her like a shadow.

A sense of calm filled Louisa for the first time in a long, long while. She gazed into the flickering candle on the table and let the moment's peace sink in. The candlelight soothed her all the way from where the soft rays touched her face to the deepest part of her. Was it possible that this moment was a new beginning? Possibilities meant hope.

How her life had changed in just one day. She'd experienced despair and desperation this morning and then kindness, and even joy, since coming here. But was this comfort merely temporary? Would her friendship with this family be short-lived? Would this small taste of happiness be ripped away? She feared it would be, and soon.

Her father still regarded her as a bargaining chip to gain a profitable alliance. He cared nothing for her happiness. He merely wanted to reap the benefits of having a daughter who men considered beautiful. And he would demand respect and obedience to his will. She swallowed her bitterness. She couldn't fathom being forced to marry a man she didn't love or even know. She also couldn't imagine defying her father.

But if her life could change this much in a day, perhaps her future would change too. Although she'd worked hard all her life around the numerous homes her father had moved them to, for the first time she had a paying job. Even though her father intended to take all their wages, at least here they would have a comfortable place to live and food. And here she could experience some measure of freedom and even a little happiness. She could also learn much from Melly and Adam could learn a great deal about medicine from Dr. Grant.

For Adam's sake, and for both their futures, she would do everything she could to make this opportunity work. For eighteen years she had survived living with her father's anger, resentment, and undeserved punishments. If she could withstand that, she could do what she must to earn a living and provide for herself and her brother. Despite her father's low opinion of her abilities, she believed she was strong and reasonably smart. She could learn. She could make something of herself.

As she watched Adam with Melly, she wanted so much to keep her brother this happy. But could she? Her father had left them here for now. But he would soon grow tired of taking care of himself and doing his own chores. The day would come when he would demand that they both return to him.

And they would have to.

She had never stood up to her father's wrath. Ever since she could remember, when he became angry, she would simply do as he wished and keep her mouth shut. She would swallow the words that she desperately wanted to fling at him. She'd learned early that even a pout or a cross glance at him would cause him to explode into an unpredictable rage. A rage he would take out on both her and Adam.

So, for Adam's sake, she carefully avoided doing anything that would cause his temper to flare.

She wanted her family to be peaceful, normal, happy. But it never would be. Her father didn't care about love, but he demanded respect. Not the kind of respect born of admiration or earned. The kind of respect born of fear.

And even though her fears often made her want to cry, she would never let him see her tears—not since that time when he'd hard-heartedly ridiculed her for crying. He'd heartlessly scoffed at her tears and made fun of her. Ever since, with a gritted jaw and a clenched heart, she kept her tears inside.

Now, there was nothing he could do to her to make her weep openly. But she soon learned that tears shed on the inside stung so much more. Perhaps because they held so much bitterness.

When the time came for her to marry whoever it was her father selected, she would do as he commanded. For Adam's sake.

Only for Adam's sake.

CHAPTER 10

AFTER SEVERAL SORROW-DAMPENED DAYS AND dark nights with little sleep, the tightness in Samuel's chest finally eased as he and Thomas rode together. They were on their way to the settlement to purchase supplies. The spectacular scenery along the trail that meandered alongside the Red River lifted his spirits. He inhaled the clean scent of pine wafting off the tall woods to the south and east and let the fresh air ease his grief.

In the distance, they saw two enormous black wolves jogging by, but they were at too great a distance to reach the predators with their rifles. And wild turkeys and deer repeatedly crossed their path, running as though they were in a great hurry to get somewhere.

From a bluff along the Red, they looked down upon a drove of about a hundred wild horses watering along the trickle that was left of the river. They stopped to admire the herd and watched as the horses ascended the opposite bank having been refreshed by the water.

They needed to buy coffee, flour, and some supplies for Baldy. Samuel also intended to buy Louisa at least one dress and some clothes for Adam. The boy was still wearing only Steve's shirt.

Both Louisa and Adam had settled in nicely and seemed to enjoy working for the Grants, although Louisa sometimes seemed troubled with her pinched brow and tense jaw.

During the last four days, while Thomas and Cornelius watched over the herd, Samuel and Steve built a split rail fence for a new large holding pen. The work was taxing, but he'd found the process of digging holes, planting posts, and laying the rails in an interlocking zig-zag fashion a welcome distraction from his thoughts of Billy. When Adam came by with a bucket of fresh water for them, he'd called it a snake fence because of its twisty pattern.

After evening meals, Samuel found himself looking forward to Louisa's company. They'd spent the last four evenings together talking on the porch for hours. The more he talked to her the more he understood how difficult her life was. He'd learned that although she was young and beautiful on the outside, inside she was old and worn. Her soul crushed by unhappiness. Her heart heavy with despair. Her mind troubled by fear. Especially her fear that her father would soon come for her and her brother. After having met Mr. Pate, Samuel could certainly understand that worry.

Despite her difficulties, Samuel sensed that within Louisa, welled untapped courage and strength. And if given half a chance, she could be a vibrant, happy woman. She was full of life, but that life was imprisoned. She needed to be freed.

It would take a great deal of strength to stand up to her father. Could Louisa rise above the rubble of her wretched life? Could what was beaten down inside her be brought back? Could he help her free herself? He certainly hoped so, for she seemed to be a fine person who cared deeply for her younger brother. The more he got to know her, the more he wanted to know and the more he wanted to help her. He'd sought out opportunities to see her as often as he could. He wanted to learn all about her—her thoughts, her dreams, her hopes.

Lately, when she was near, he found himself keenly aware of her female appeal. Whenever she smiled at him, a sudden heat would erupt within him and he would long to hold her in his arms. And whenever she left to go back to the Grant's cabin, an undeniable melancholy would grip him inside.

Up ahead, they saw two men riding toward them. Relieved that they were not Indians, Samuel waved a greeting. But his relief was short-lived because he saw that it was Pate and another man who appeared to be a military man based on his attire.

He and his brother drew their horses up when they met the two on the trail.

He noted that Louisa's father was wearing what appeared to

be a new suit of good quality. Had he used the silver Melly gave him to try to pass himself off as a man of means? A man of means with a young, beautiful daughter. A daughter of marriageable age in a land with exceedingly few unmarried women.

"Mr. Pate," Samuel said with little sociability in his voice. "This is my brother, Thomas."

Pate grunted and gave Thomas a slight glance but said nothing. Neither did Thomas.

The other man, who rode a quality thoroughbred spoke up. "I am Herman H. Long, a lawyer and plantation owner from Louisiana. I am also the commander of Texian forces at Camp Freeman at Nacogdoches." The impeccably attired man appeared to be around thirty and would be considered good-looking by women. His shirt of fine white cotton had a tall standing collar and his wide cravat was tied in a soft bow. Over the shirt, he wore a waist hugging coat with long tails in the back. Tightly fitted leather riding breeches reached almost to his boot tops. A red silk sash was wrapped at his waist and an expensive-looking sword hung at his side. His tall black boots of the finest leather gleamed in the sun.

If the man was trying to stand out on the frontier, he'd certainly succeeded. Or maybe he was trying to flaunt his obvious wealth.

"Texian forces?" Samuel asked. "Just why are you here at Pecan Point, Commander Long? Are there troubles nearby that we need to know about?"

The man seemed to assess both Samuel and Thomas with haughty green eyes before he answered. "I assume you are both loyal citizens of our United States?"

"Indeed," Samuel said. "We are. As are my father and two other brothers."

The arrogant man seemed satisfied with his answer. "I am here to encourage the settlers at Jonesboro and Pecan Point to become comrades in arms and to cooperate fully with the struggle to make Texas independent of Spain."

Samuel was not expecting that answer. "What struggle exactly? Are you operating under the directive of the U.S. government?"

"No. Washington politicians are slow to act and when they do it is not in our best interests. In fact, they are now writing the Adams–Onís Treaty to settle the Louisiana Texas border dispute. It will cede much of Texas to Spain. Prominent citizens of

Louisiana, including myself, are opposed to the treaty and are recruiting men who are like-minded. Because of my background in the law and the military, I have been placed in command and we have established a provisional government in Nacogdoches."

"So you're a filibuster," Thomas said, getting straight to the point.

Their father recently read a newspaper article aloud that explained that filibusters engaged in unofficial military expeditions into foreign countries or territories. Their purpose was often to ferment or support a revolution. The editor of the newspaper inferred that such illegal activities were developing in Texas and they'd all heard rumors of filibustering expeditions into the Province. But their father considered such activities ill-advised. Samuel agreed.

Long raised his long, straight nose a bit. "Some might call me a filibuster. Others call me a patriot. And some call me a trailblazer."

"And I'd call him a born leader," Pate said.

Seated atop his tall horse, Long reminded Samuel of a cocky, crowing rooster sitting on a fence. He suspected this puffed-up citizen-soldier had never been tested in battle, much less a war. "Forgive me, Sir, for my bluntness, but I'd call your intentions foolish. I agree it would be unfortunate to see any of Texas ceded to Spain in a treaty. However, you can't seriously expect the few hundred settlers in Texas, already preoccupied with fighting Indians and building their homesteads, to take on Spain's army."

"Many of my forces are courageous men from Louisiana who no longer want Spain as a neighbor to their lands," Long said. "The men here will feel the same."

"How many courageous men?" Thomas asked.

"Enough, for now," Long said evasively. "Soon, more will be joining us."

"Still not interested," Samuel said.

"I knew you were a coward," Pate hissed.

"Get down from your horse, Mr. Pate," Samuel ordered. "It's time someone taught you some manners."

"Let's not get embroiled in a dispute, gentlemen," Long said. "We are here to join forces, not fight each other."

"We will *not* be joining forces with you, Sir," Samuel said.

"Circumventing the U.S. government's policies and plans can only mean trouble. In fact, many would consider it treasonous."

Thomas nodded. "Although your goal may be worthy Commander, your odds are poor. You can't win. Spain has a mighty force in San Antonio. You cannot hope to win without a large, well-disciplined army, which you clearly do not have, or you wouldn't be here."

Long shook his head. "But I will win. And soon. Spanish power in Texas is unraveling due to events elsewhere in their empire. The Napoleonic Wars in Europe for one thing. Troubles in Mexico for another. It is only a matter of time before we will be in position to take control."

"They say timing is everything," Samuel said. "And in this case, the time is not yet here. I urge you to postpone this risky venture."

"That's where we disagree, Sir," Long said. "The time is right to gather our army. Texas has millions of unclaimed acres that I can promise to those willing to fight."

"Under whose authority will you give away Texas lands?" Samuel pressed.

Long's brows rose. "Under my authority. I intend to be the first president of Texas."

"We were just on our way to your place," Pate told Samuel, pretending civility and changing the subject. "I want Commander Long to meet my daughter."

"Why?" Samuel asked although he had a good idea. His protective instincts flared as his stare bored into Long.

"I am unmarried," Long said, "and I desire to set up a home, a second plantation, in Nacogdoches. While I am recruiting for our cause, I am also keeping an eye out for a potential bride. Mr. Pate tells me Louisa is a rare beauty of marriageable age and I would like to meet his daughter."

"I plan to join the Commander's cause and move to Nacogdoches," Pate said.

Long smiled with satisfaction. "If Louisa is as beautiful as Mr. Pate says she is, and I find her acceptable, he is agreeable to arranging a marriage."

Acceptable? Samuel's dislike for this high and mighty man increased tenfold. His jaw tightened as his mind filled with contempt. Long was so big-headed and tedious it was no wonder that he should get into politics.

He couldn't stop Pate from taking Long to meet Louisa, but he could be sure he was there to protect her.

"Come along, Thomas," Samuel told his brother as he turned his horse around. "Our supplies can wait."

As Samuel and Thomas rode up to their home followed by Pate and Commander Long, he found his father and Baldy working together between their homes chopping wood. The unique thunk, kerracking sound of axes striking wood was always a sure sign that the chill of winter was not far away. But today, his temper heated at the thought of another man here to see Louisa.

He had to come up with a way to stop this.

Samuel, Thomas, and the Commander dismounted but Pate remained on his mount.

Samuel curtly introduced Pate and Long to his father and Baldy and then told them briefly about Long's intention to raise an army against Spain.

"The Spaniard's are foreigners in what should be *our* country," Long said. "All we need is courage, confidence, and resolve."

"And about five-thousand well-armed soldiers," Samuel said, shaking his head at the man's naiveté.

"The Spanish are nothing but crows who seek to pick out our eyes," Pate said from still atop his horse. "We must shoo them off."

It was difficult to believe but Pate was even more naïve than Long.

"I assume you know that Governor Martinez has issued an order that all Americans exhibiting even the least suspicious conduct should be arrested?" his father asked Long.

"And perhaps you've forgotten what happened in San Antonio five years ago," Baldy added.

Samuel hadn't forgotten the Battle of Medina and what happened in 1813 to the last filibusters who challenged Spain. A large force of Spanish soldiers under the command of General Arredondo advanced on San Antonio. The disorganized filibusters met Arredondo's forces in what became the bloodiest battle yet in Texas. Refusing to allow the filibusters to surrender, the Spanish killed more than a thousand rebels and executed every resident of San Antonio de Bexar who had conducted business with the usurpers.

"Sir," his father said, addressing Long, "no group can hope to gain control of Texas without the assistance of a well-disciplined, fighting force of great number."

"That's what I told him," Thomas said.

Long continued to address their father. "I know that, Mr. Wyllie. That is why I am here now hoping to recruit some of you to our cause. And I would hope that you will encourage the other settlers to join us. We will muster our forces in Nacogdoches on October 1. I expect your full cooperation, or at least that of your sons, in our struggle to make Texas independent of Spain."

His father's jaw grew rigid and his piercing blue eyes stared into Long. "You may expect it, Sir, but you will not get it. The time is not yet right. I did not raise fools for sons. They will be the first to enlist in the defense of Texas when called upon by the United States government or a legitimate, lawful government of Texas. But your ill-conceived filibustering efforts will only get you and those that follow you killed."

"Why not wait until the United States buys the rest of Texas?" Thomas asked.

"I agree," Samuel said. "Furthermore, since this part of Texas is already part of the United States through the Louisiana Purchase, there's no reason for us to raise the ire of Spain's powerful army."

Pate gave Samuel a taunting look and then turned to Long. With a curl of his lip, he said, "I told you he was a bloody coward."

Samuel shot his long arms up and grasped Pate by his waistcoat. He yanked the man off his horse and hammered his legs into the ground. Samuel wanted to send his fist right down the man's throat, but he settled for slamming it against Pate's jaw. That sent the man's hat flying off. Then his left fist smashed Pate's face on the other side, drawing blood. Pate staggered backward, blood dripping from several spots on his face. Next, Samuel sent his clenched right fist upwards under Pate's chin which made the man ignominiously topple to the ground on his backside.

Samuel stood over Pate, fists still clenched. "That was the third time you called me a coward!" he spat. "I'd advise you not to let there be a fourth time." The man would die if there was.

"That's enough, Samuel," his father said. "You've hit him three times. One good blow for each insult. Let Baldy see if he needs any doctoring."

Samuel stepped back, breathing heavily, although his fists ached to deliver a few more blows. He wanted to beat the man senseless. Not for calling him a coward, but for his mistreatment of Louisa and Adam.

"Do I have to?" Baldy asked, with a half-smile. "Seems to me he got exactly what he deserved."

Rubbing his bloodied chin, Pate glowered first at Baldy and then at Samuel. He pointed a dirty finger at Samuel but spoke to Stephen, "Your son beat me up!"

"Keep a sharp eye out. He may beat you again," his father said.

Long turned to Pate. "I can see there's nothing to be gained here. These men can decide later if they want to join our noble cause. Let's get on with the other reason we've come. Where is your daughter, Mr. Pate? You said she works here?"

Samuel's fists clenched again.

CHAPTER II

SAMUEL FIXED A HARD, HEATED stare on Pate as he watched the man shift his attention to arranging Louisa's marriage. It was highly likely that this topic might warrant giving the man an even more robust beating. If Pate wasn't Adam and Louisa's father, he would have thoroughly trounced the infernal skunk instead of just giving him three thumps on the chin.

"Where is my daughter, Mr. Wyllie?" Pate asked Samuel's father as he wiped the blood from his busted lip with the back of his hand.

"She's working," was all his father said.

"Dr. Grant, where is she?" Pate asked Baldy.

"Doing something useful," Baldy told him. "Which is more than I can say for you, Sir."

"Louisa!" Pate yelled loud enough to be heard clear across the Red. "Louisa! Come out here. Now!"

Samuel longed to hit the despicable man again. He hoped Louisa would ignore her father and just stay inside.

Pate picked up his hat and dusted himself off. Then he mounted his horse and rode closer to Baldy's home and called again. "Louisa! Adam! I'm calling you!" he yelled.

Regrettably, Louisa stepped out of the Grants' home. So did her brother and Melly.

Samuel noted that Pate didn't greet his children and they didn't greet him.

Louisa just looked at her father warily.

Adam's head leaned against Melly's leg.

"Follow me, girl," her father ordered and turned his horse back toward where Long stood waiting.

Samuel watched Louisa's face as she bravely took steps toward them. Then he saw her grip her skirt with clenched fists. She was hiding her fear. Her eyes sought him out and when their gazes met, she seemed to gather her strength.

Samuel's mind raced. He had to stop this somehow. It was all happening too fast. He had thought he had more time. He'd been so distracted and grieved by Billy's death, he'd hardly given much thought to her father's plans for her.

He wished now that he'd made his tender feelings for her known. Was it too late? He was definitely mightily attracted to her. And she seemed to enjoy his company. In fact, he often caught her gazing at him during mealtimes. But their responsibilities and the presence of his three brothers and her little brother left little time for courting.

Louisa carried herself with dignity as she followed behind her father's mount and closed the remaining distance to Long.

Melly and Adam followed closely behind her.

"What's this all about?" Melly asked in a loud voice.

"I have asked Commander Long to meet my daughter," Pate told her. "This is none of your business, woman."

Melly harrumphed. "We'll see about that. And my name is Mrs. Grant."

Long stepped forward and extended his hand to Louisa. "I am Herman H. Long, commander of the army at Camp Freeman at Nacogdoches. I am organizing a Texian army to take the Province from Spain."

"Pleased to meet you, Commander Long," Louisa said.

Then Long nodded to Melly. "Pleased to make your acquaintance as well, Mrs. Grant. You're Dr. Grant's wife?"

"Yes, indeed I am." Melly eyed him and then Pate with a cold-eyed glare.

Baldy moved to stand next to his wife on the other side of Adam. He rested his big hand on Adam's little shoulder.

Pate turned toward Long. "I apologize for the state of my daughter's attire. She's obviously wearing borrowed clothes, too large for her petite frame. Her entire wardrobe was stolen by thieving Indians."

Entire wardrobe, indeed, Samuel thought. He doubted that she had more than two shabby dresses to her name before the Indian raid.

"You should see her with her hair all fixed up and shining like gold. Isn't she a beauty, just like I told you?" Pate asked Long. "She's got perfect teeth. She's slim, but she's strong and long-legged."

Samuel bristled. The man was talking about his own daughter as if she were a horse to be sold and bought.

"Indeed, she is a beauty," Long agreed, staring at Louisa. "An enchanting young woman who could utterly inspire a man to gentlemanly feelings."

Gentlemanly? Samuel could almost hear the man's lust in his flirtatious voice.

"All she needs is a fashionable, quality gown and she'd be the belle of any ball," Long added.

Louisa's cheeks flamed and she cast her eyes down.

"The bloody Indians stole my son's clothing as well. Oh, that's my son, Adam," Pate said as though it were an afterthought and pointed to the boy.

Adam wrapped his arms around Baldy's leg.

"What are you hiding from, boy? Step out here and meet Commander Long," Pate ordered Adam.

Adam took two tiny steps forward. "Morning, Sir."

Long glanced only briefly at Adam and then waved him away with a flick of his hand. "What about her schooling?"

Adam hurried back to Dr. Grant.

"She's a smart one," Pate said, avoiding the question. "I've always believed an ounce of horse sense is worth a pound of book learning any day."

"Might I have a word with your daughter, in private, Mr. Pate?" Long asked. "We will only stroll for a little ways. Perhaps to that bench by that lovely tree."

Seeming enormously pleased, Pate nodded. "Certainly, Sir."

"Certainly not," Samuel said. "You can bloody well talk to her right here."

Long ignored Samuel's protest and wrapped an elbow around Louisa's arm. "Discussing marriage requires privacy, doesn't it, dear?"

Louisa glanced over at her father.

The man dismounted, leaned his head slightly forward, and gave her a cold, hard stare. The implication was obvious to everyone.

Samuel saw the briefest glimpse of fear in Louisa's eyes. She remained absolutely motionless for a moment and then nodded toward Long.

Long stepped away with her, taking long strides toward the bench that sat under the shade of the nearby enormous oak tree.

For an instant, Samuel stood there staring after them, feeling helpless. But what could he do? He had no claim on Louisa. He had no right to interfere. And no plan to stop this. Or did he? He turned toward his father who cocked a brow and then gave him a slight nod. That was all the encouragement Samuel needed.

"Just a moment, Commander," Samuel called after them, his voice hardened.

Long and Louisa halted in their tracks and turned around to face him. The Commander appeared extremely displeased with the interruption.

Samuel straightened his back and stood taller. "Louisa hasn't given you permission to touch her person. And neither have I."

"Stay out of this, boy," Pate warned, his face full of loathing. "This is none of your affair. I have given my permission."

In Samuel's heart, there were no doubts. In his mind there were still questions, but not in his heart. "This *is* my affair. Very much so. For I have already asked Louisa to be *my* wife."

Louisa's eyes widened and her mouth fell open. Fortunately, neither her father nor Long noticed for their eyes were focused on him.

He stared at Long with possessive firmness. "Louisa will be *my* wife."

"What is the meaning of this?" Pate demanded. "Why didn't you say anything earlier, on the road, when I told you we were coming here for Commander Long to meet Louisa?"

"Because it wouldn't have made a difference to you. And I had not yet discussed the matter with my own father. But you've heard me now, Sir," Samuel said. "I intend to marry Louisa, with or without your permission. But I would prefer to have your blessing."

Pate didn't want to hear anything Samuel had to say. He whirled around and faced his daughter. "Is this true? You planned to marry

Samuel Wyllie? I won't have it! You'll pay for this disrespect!"

For a second, Louisa flinched at her father's words.

With a bewildered look in her eyes, she took a few steps toward them. What would she say?

Long followed too closely behind her.

When Louisa stopped, her eyes peered back and forth between her father and Samuel. He could see the struggle on her face as she grew more confused by the second. But he would have to let her internal battle play out. This was her life they were all talking about.

Samuel had no idea what she would say since he'd never discussed courting with her much less marriage. He hoped she would go along with his ruse to save her from Long. Was it a ruse? Surprising himself, he decided it wasn't. A trick maybe. Or a ploy to gain control of the situation, but not a ruse. He really did care for Louisa. She just didn't know it yet.

Any other woman might have dissolved into a blubbering puddle of tears or even fainted in a situation like this. But not Louisa. She seemed to be mustering her courage. She opened her mouth to speak, but Pate interrupted.

"Louisa, I forbid you to even consider marrying Samuel Wyllie! He's merely a poor squatter. Not a gentleman."

Commander Long agreed with Pate. "These men are here because they did not prosper in regular society."

The man's low opinion of frontiersmen was a common misconception and prejudice perpetuated by arrogant landowners like Long who never dirtied their hands.

The Commander continued, haughtily, "They are too shiftless to acquire either valuable property or a gentleman's profession. They have no skills other than to fell trees, build log cabins, and lay open the ground to cultivation. All things done by slaves back in Louisiana. This kind of man merely prepares the way for those who come after him. People like me. And your father, Louisa."

"That's right! That's why I'll decide who you will marry!" Pate nearly shouted at his daughter.

The real reason was clear to Samuel. He was counting on Louisa's marriage to gain him not only economic security but also favorable social standing.

Raw hurt glittered in Louisa's eyes. Maybe she did care for

Samuel. But she couldn't muster the strength to voice a choice that would defy her father.

"I assure you, Sirs," Samuel said bristling with anger. "I am neither poor nor shiftless. When I marry, I will have a thousand acres here at Pecan Point and will soon have that many cattle." Samuel's father had started paying him a man's wage when he was fourteen. Ever since, for six years, he'd saved nearly all of it. The sum now amounted to an impressive number. "And as far as being a gentleman, the men of my family and this settlement are the finest sort of gentlemen if being a gentleman requires a courageous heart and the enterprise to settle new lands for a growing country."

Long scoffed. "That merely requires a strong back and calloused hands."

Samuel ignored him. "I request your permission, Mr. Pate, to marry Louisa. I will provide her with a fine home and care for her the rest of my days." He knew his appeal was pointless but he had to try.

Pate merely scowled at Samuel. "Commander Long, are you interested in marrying my daughter?"

"Indeed, Sir. She is one of the loveliest women in the entire province. Of course, I would like to get to know her better before I make a final decision. Perhaps we can host a few parties in Nacogdoches before we have our formal engagement ball at my plantation in Louisiana."

Samuel suspected what Long likely meant by 'get to know her better.' Over his dead body.

Pate nodded excitedly. "Then it's decided. We will travel to Nacogdoches with you, Sir. That should give you both a chance to get to know one another."

"Splendid!" Long said and gave Louisa a brazen smile. "You've made a wise choice, Mr. Pate. My destiny is bright, and your beautiful daughter will shine alongside me."

Samuel glanced at Louisa for a sign of objection. But her obvious fear of her father kept her mute.

Long straightened his waistcoat and the red sash around his waist.

Samuel sneered. This self-proclaimed hero of Texas would likely wind up in a Spanish prison. Or dead. But that wouldn't be soon enough to save Louisa.

Pate glared at Samuel. "I warn you my word is final in this matter."

Teeth bared, Samuel glared at Pate. "Well, here's my word. You and the so-called Commander can get the hell off our place. Now!"

Pate addressed Melly. "Mrs. Grant, please pay my daughter and son what you owe them. We are leaving."

"As you may recall, Sir," Melly said in a voice that would intimidate a Comanche chief, "I paid you in advance. You took a week's wages from me already, and they still have three days left to work off that advance."

Pate's face grew even redder, and he started to speak, but Baldy stepped forward which stopped him.

"You heard her," Baldy said. Baldy still held the axe he'd been using earlier. "Don't you even try to argue with or even intimidate my wife, Sir. I am a surgeon and know where to cut a man to make him die quickly." Not only was he holding an axe, the doctor always carried several knives of different lengths on his belt.

Samuel glanced at Adam. He was now completely hidden behind Melly's skirt.

Long turned to Pate. "Gentlemen, there is no need for further disagreements. We will wait three days. I need to spend some time recruiting at the settlement and in Jonesboro anyway. Louisa, you are a lovely young lady. I very much look forward to getting to know you better. If our plans are successful in securing Texas as an independent country, soon you could well be married to the first president of our new republic."

"Like hell!" Samuel growled through gritted teeth. "Now you understand, *Commander,* if you come anywhere near Louisa, you'll never have the chance to be president of anything."

A sense of satisfaction filled Samuel when a glimmer of fear flashed in Long's green eyes.

He had to come up with a way to stop this, short of killing Long, although that idea greatly appealed to him at the moment. But by custom and by law women were under the control of their fathers until they married. A father could give his daughter away in marriage without her consent. If Long didn't marry Louisa,

Pate would just find some other wealthy man for her to marry. Legally, women were decidedly dependent, subservient, and unequal.

He was helpless to stop this sham of a marriage.

And from the expression on Pate's face, her father knew it.

Louisa kept all emotion from her voice as she said, "Come, Adam, we must get back to our work." Woodenly, she took her brother's hand and they walked away.

CHAPTER 12

IN A SHOCKED DAZE, LOUISA returned to the Grant's cabin. She had been too startled by the suggestion that she marry Commander Long and too fearful of her father to offer any objection. And she'd merely stood there, blank, amazed, and shaken by his words when Samuel said he planned to marry her. Now, away from all of them, objections exploded inside of her.

As she folded the clothes that Melly had washed since Louisa's hands were still sore, her mind whirled with a jumble of thoughts, fears, and pure dread. They say misfortunes never come alone and they, whoever 'they' are, are absolutely right. First Indians, then quicksand, and now Commander Long and a forced marriage. What was next?

Three days! She'd disliked that Commander Long instantly. His smiling, lecherous face had disturbed her. Even now, the memory of it unnerved her. And he possessed enough arrogance for ten men. But none of that mattered. Her father cared nothing about her feelings. And in three days, he and Long would come to claim her. They would not be asking. They would be telling her she had to go.

And she would have to. A father exercised complete control over the course of events in his daughter's life until she married. At that point, the husband took control.

She had a feeling Long would be a controlling husband. He seemed to be the type of man who thought his opinion was more valuable than anyone else's. She couldn't stand the thought of continuing to be completely powerless. Of living a life without any control over even the smallest of decisions. Her father decided everything. Where they would live, what they would eat, what they would do each day, even what she would wear. At the Arkansas Post, she'd found a pretty yellow dress that wasn't that expensive. But giving her a hard glare, her father had snatched it out of her hands and tossed it to the floor of the shop. "You'll wear your durable muslin and be glad you have it," he'd shouted.

She truly didn't want to leave the Grants and the Wyllies. And neither did Adam. They both loved it here. Melly and Dr. Grant treated them with extraordinary kindness, slowly healing their sadness, soothing the wrongs done to them. But just when they'd both begun to feel at home here, her father had shown up again bringing back all the same fears and hurts. Once again, she felt drained, lifeless, and hollow inside. Most of all she felt no control over her life.

Or Adam's. When his mother died, she'd sworn she would protect him. But how could she protect him from his own father? Somehow, she would have to find a way for him to remain here with Dr. Grant and Melly.

Melly had spent every spare minute with Louisa, encouraging her, teaching her, and even showing her affection. The warmth and grace with which Melly treated her made Louisa realize that was exactly how she wanted to treat her own children someday. She would make them feel appreciated, safe, and loved. And she would give them choices. She would advise them, not dictate to them. She would earn their respect, not demand it.

And, that was how she wanted Adam to be treated. Already, Adam had learned a great deal from the doctor. Last night, as they were getting ready for bed, he'd proudly named all the major bones in his body. For Adam, working alongside Dr. Grant was more like attending an excellent school. Melly had told her that her husband had earned three degrees—one from a university, one from a medical school, and one from a seminary—all from first-rate schools in Virginia. The man could pass that knowledge on to Adam. Her brother might even become a doctor under his tutorage.

If she married Long, that would mean Adam would be left to live with her father. Doomed to a miserable life. What kind of a man would Adam turn out to be if life continued to treat him so cruelly? What kind of example would their father set for him as he grew up? She knew the answer—a poor one.

And marrying Long could also mean they might all be killed as he sought glory in battles with Spain's military. Louisa's brows furrowed. Did the man know what he would be up against? Even with her limited knowledge of politics, she knew Spain had a powerful army.

On the other hand, if she refused to marry Long, her father would take his anger out on Adam. He would use her brother as a pawn to get her to do what he wanted. She couldn't allow that. She could tolerate him beating her, but not her brother. That was more than her heart could bear. Just remembering those beatings that left several scars on Adam's back made tears well in her eyes.

She refused to let those tears fall. She blinked rapidly and wiped them away with her knuckle before she turned back to her work.

Then, out of her despair and confusion, with jarring clarity, she suddenly knew what she had to do. She would marry Long on the condition that her father let Adam live out the rest of his childhood here with Dr. Grant and Melly. That would protect Adam, although it meant a life of misery for her. She quickly waved aside any hesitation. She took a deep breath. To keep her brother safe and happy, she would do what she had to.

Reaching for another garment, she recognized it as one of Samuel's shirts. The same one he was wearing the day he pulled her from the river. She ran her hand slowly across the shirt's shoulder wondering what it would be like to actually touch his bare wide shoulders. The startling thought made heat flush her face and unfamiliar, tingling ripples course through her body. The sensation made her gasp in surprise and her pulse race.

Her heart also warmed as she thought about how Samuel had defended her. He stood up to her father and to Long. He even lied for her. And as an honorable man, she knew that could not have been easy for him. She clutched the shirt against her chest. What a lie it was! Obviously, he didn't truly intend to marry her. He was just trying to keep Long from taking her away. But she could not stop herself from pondering the idea. A tiny part of her wondered if maybe, just maybe, he might have feelings for her. Would he ever consider marrying a poor, nearly homeless, daughter of a man as disagreeable as her father? Who would want to be yoked to a relative like him? Nobody.

It didn't matter now anyway. She was going to marry Long to protect Adam. It was the only way to get her father to agree to leave her brother here. To give Adam a future.

She held the large shirt up and stared, picturing Samuel's broad shoulders and strong arms filling it out. She knew that within his muscled chest, a kind heart beat. He was the most considerate man she'd ever known, but that didn't mean he had feelings for her. Feelings of love. It was a big leap from friendship to love. Over the last week, they'd spent a good many hours together and not once had he expressed any fond feelings toward her. She could never love a man who didn't love her.

No, marrying Samuel was too much to expect. She refused to think of her own needs. She had to think of Adam first. Biting her lip, she quickly folded the shirt and set it aside. She had come up with a plan, and she would stick to it no matter how much the idea dismayed and disgusted her.

"I need a plan," Samuel swore as he paced back and forth in their home after the Commander and Long left. "Three days and that weasel will take Louisa away. Three days!"

Cornelius and Steve had returned to the cabin from hunting just as Pate and Long were leaving. Their father had explained everything and they'd all gone inside to talk.

His father and brothers, Baldy, and Melly, all sat at the table with him, all but Baldy were drinking coffee. Baldy drank a whiskey. The doctor normally didn't drink whiskey this early in the day. Samuel guessed it was Pate who had inspired the need for a strong beverage.

All of them wore sympathetic expressions as they listened to Samuel rant. "Did you see the way Commander Long eyed Louisa?" he asked. "It was appalling. And, I swear he is by far the most arrogant man I have ever met."

His father nodded. "Indeed. If you offered to make him a god, he would likely say he desired to be something greater."

"Hmm, I wonder what the solution might be..." Cornelius said, a merry glint in his green eyes.

Baldy smiled knowingly at Cornelius. His smile softened his

face. A face sculpted by the hard life he'd led for a time prior to becoming a preacher.

What the heck was there for the two to smile about? He frowned at Cornelius and the doctor. "What is it? What's got into both of you? This is serious."

Baldy was still smiling. "Have you forgotten that I am an ordained preacher?"

"Of course not," Samuel said, although sometimes the unconventional preacher made it easy to forget. Then he abruptly realized why they were smiling. "Now wait just a minute. I only told them I'd asked her to marry me to keep Long from taking her. But my ruse didn't work because her obstinate father chose Long over me. And, he wouldn't even let her speak."

Thomas sighed and rolled his eyes. "Are you sure that's the only reason you said that? We've all seen the dreamy looks you give her when she's not looking."

"It's enough to make me blush," Cornelius said, with a chuckle and a pat to his cheek.

"Yup, you're sweet on her," Steve said. "We all know it and you know it. Might as well 'fess up."

"It's understandable," Baldy said, "she's a beautiful young woman. If I weren't already married…"

Melly rolled her eyes.

Samuel was ready to beat the stuffings out of all three of his brothers and Baldy too. He would trust each of them with his life. But his love life was off limits. He glared at them until his eyes widened with the realization that their teasing comments held nothing but the truth.

"Thomas, Cornelius, and Steve," Father said, "go finish chopping up those logs. I want it all done by dinner. Chopped *and* stacked."

"But…" Steve started.

Cornelius interrupted. "We're just trying to make him see what we can all see."

Their father held up a hand stopping him. "Your brother has important *private* decisions to make."

After the three trudged out the door and shut it, his father turned to Samuel. "Marriage to you would be a solution. But no one can make that choice but you. Marriage is an important and lasting step. There will be no going back. From my perspective, Louisa is a fine young woman, and you would have my blessing even if you don't have her father's."

Samuel was glad to hear that. His father's blessing was far more important to him anyway.

"But she deserves a husband who loves her," Melly said. "Not one who is merely trying to save her."

Samuel suspected he did love her. But was he ready to marry?

"Keep in mind if you marry her, you are marrying her father too," Baldy said, shaking his head. "That man would try God's patience."

"And you'd likely be accepting responsibility for her brother too," his father added.

"None of that bothers me," Samuel told them. "But I just met Louisa a few days ago. We've talked a lot, but we haven't actually courted yet. And with three days left before she has to leave, we'll hardly have any time together. What my brothers said is true though. I am strongly attracted to her. I think I even love her. But that doesn't mean I'm ready to marry her. I just don't want anyone else to."

His father rubbed his chin. "Seems to me you have two days to be certain you've fallen in love with her and you want her to be your wife. If you don't have strong feelings about marriage at the end of two days, you won't marry her on the third day."

"I have to agree," Baldy said. "The bloom of love opens pretty quickly. You'll know at the end of two days, if not sooner if your hearts are reaching out to each other enough to marry. Then on the third day, we can have a wedding. Alternatively, when Long comes, we can say our goodbyes to Louisa and her brother. Though I've grown used to having that smart little fellow underfoot." He glanced over at Melly. "He surprised me. He's actually been a good helper."

"We can't let little Adam go back to that beast of a man," Melly protested. "Or Louisa." She stood up and tossed her apron down on the table angrily.

"We can't prevent it," Baldy said. "They're his children, Melly."

Samuel agreed with Melly. He didn't like the idea of saying goodbye to them at all. Not one bit. But something else worried him. He placed his hands palms down on the table and leaned toward his father. "You need me. So do my brothers, Baldy, and Melly. There are threats all around us. Indians to the north and west. Spain to the south. Cattle rustlers and freebooters in between. If I marry Louisa, I'll mostly be protecting her and her brother, not you."

"Samuel, you're twenty-one. It's time to think about your own life. With Baldy and three other sons, I'll rarely if ever be alone. And I'm certainly not defenseless myself. I may be getting older, but my guns are still loaded, and I still shoot straight. If you decide that the time is right for you to marry, whether it's Louisa, or someone else, you can build a home close by. You won't be far away."

Samuel shook his head and started pacing. Something was making him hesitate. The image of Billy's wife came to mind. Remembering the sight of the arrow in her made the thought of marriage and children freeze in his chest. "After what happened to Billy and his wife, the thought of building a home and getting married seems rash. It is too unsettled here. I never want to face having my wife and child murdered by Indians."

"I have a feeling it will be many years before this part of Texas is truly settled," Father said. "You can't put life on hold because of danger. For danger is always with us. Before you were ever born, I lost a brother to an unexpected danger. Whether it's back in Kentucky or here or somewhere in between, danger is a part of life. But we are stronger than most because we have each other. Billy was alone. We are seven times stronger than Billy was." He glanced up at Melly. "Yes, I'm counting you too, Melly."

"Thank you," she said with a nod.

"We can all trust in each other for protection," his father said, "and trust in our weapons. That's as much as any man can expect when it comes to starting a family."

"And trust in God," Baldy added.

Samuel and his father both nodded, acknowledging the truth of that.

"As tough as life is here, it's rewarding when you make a home out of nothing and fill it with love," Melly said. "And you will be establishing a foundation for future generations so *they* will have a safer and better life."

His father nodded. "Love has no guarantees—it can last a day or a lifetime. Love promises only one thing. Every day *with* love is worth the risk of losing it any day."

Father had deeply loved Jane, Samuel's mother, and it was easy to tell that he loved her still. Since Steve was born, his father had struggled to live with her loss. But Samuel also knew his father treasured every day of their marriage.

Samuel wanted that kind of love too someday. Perhaps someday was now. He nodded his head decisively. "All right. I'll court Louisa for two days. But don't say anything to her about this. I want her to respond to me because she truly cares for me. Not because she's looking for a way to escape marrying Long or to avoid going back to her father."

Melly smiled broadly. "With love, all three of those things are possible."

"When will she be through with her work for today?" he asked her.

"She had some laundry to fold and then a chicken to pluck and cut up. That hen wasn't laying eggs so I decided she would make a good soup tonight. We can't tolerate freeloaders around here," Melly said with a grin. "Louisa should be about through folding the clothes. Why don't you go volunteer to help her dress the chicken? After that, she normally helps me to prepare dinner. But tonight, Baldy can help me. I think we need to prepare the doctor's specialty."

Baldy grinned at his wife. "Chicken soup. Good for colds, moles, and sore..."

Melly wagged a figure at him. "Don't say it!"

Samuel dashed out the door before anyone could say anything else. He didn't need any more advice. He just needed to learn if he truly loved Louisa and if she loved him. At the thought of her loving him, a thrill ran through him and with a sense of urgency he hurried toward her.

CHAPTER 13

LOUISA SAT AT THE OUTSIDE work table staring down at the gutted chicken Melly left for her. She felt as though her own guts were ripped out. Her scheme to strike a bargain with her father seemed the perfect solution when she'd thought of it, but now…

She needed to stay strong and stick to her plan, for Adam's sake. If her father would agree to leave Adam here in exchange for her cooperation, her brother would be assured of a happy life. When her father arrived at the end of the three days, she would take him aside and strike her bargain with him.

To convince Samuel that she intended to marry Long, she vowed to show nothing but indifference toward him over the next three days. She would prove to them both that she was immune to him. It would mean keeping her distance from him as much as possible. She prayed she would not betray her true feelings—that she loved him.

"Let me help you with that chicken," Samuel said, as he strode up to Louisa. Her hair, which she normally wore loose in long graceful waves down her back, was tied at the nape of her neck.

She held the headless hen by the feet and dipped it in an iron pot of scalding water hanging over their outdoor cook fire. Scalding allowed the long hard flight feathers to come off easily.

When she finished, Louisa stared up at him. "Don't you have more important work? Plucking and cutting up a chicken is one thing I do know how to do." She sounded unusually curt.

"Right now, I'm going to help you with that chicken."

She nodded indifferently. For some reason, she didn't seem too happy to have him there.

They sat down at the outdoor work table and he withdrew his knife from its sheath on his belt. "Louisa, I know you have a lot on your mind, but we need to talk," he said as he cut the feet off. "I must ask your forgiveness for telling your father and Commander Long a lie about asking you to marry me."

Louisa shook her head. "No need for forgiveness. I know why you did it. That was actually quite clever of you and I thank you for it. But this is my problem and I'll have to figure it out."

"We can figure it out together. If you'll allow me to help." He waved away a feather that floated between them.

She swallowed and tugged at a wing feather. "No, I don't need any help. Besides, there are no good solutions."

"Why do you say that?"

"Because if I refuse to marry Commander Long, my father will take his anger out not just on me but also on Adam. And if I agree to marry Long, then my father will also take my brother to Nacogdoches with us. Adam won't have a chance for a decent future. The kind of future he would have here learning from and helping Dr. Grant. So there's just one option…never mind."

Samuel wondered what she'd been about to say. "What option?"

"Samuel, I said *I* would have to figure this out."

"Does your father beat Adam?" he asked, trying to probe gently.

She sighed heavily. "Yes. Especially if I defy him. When Pa gets angry with me, Adam starts to cry and that makes my father furious."

"Why?"

"I don't know. He often ridicules and taunts us, even offering to pay us if we'll cry."

"Does he?" Samuel asked, incredulous.

"No, he's just mocking us. Besides, I stopped crying a long time ago. But Adam still cries."

An uncomfortable silence hung in the air between them while Samuel tackled cutting the chicken up with a vengeance.

Their situation was even worse than he had imagined. "Louisa, that man is a brute. He treats you like property and doesn't hesitate to punish you with violence. You both must stay away from him. If you don't, I'm afraid of what might happen to one of you."

She nodded gloomily. "I've been worried about that for a long time. I live in fear that someday he will hurt one of us seriously. His temper is so bad I honestly think he's capable of murder. Sometimes, the look in his eyes..." She swallowed. "It's like a stab to my heart." A terrible tenseness seemed to grip her.

"I promise, I will help you figure a way out."

She gazed up at him. "Don't promise what you can't offer."

"I don't know yet what I can offer. And neither do you."

"I know that my fate is set by a higher power, greater than both of us. A power that knows my future far better than I do. I must learn to live with the life I'm dealt and be grateful for the blessings I do have. Somehow, Adam and I will survive."

The woman's saint-like statement left him stunned. "Being grateful for blessings does not mean you can't fight back against injustice. Against the wrongs done to you. And all the obstacles you mentioned have to do with your brother. You have to think about your happiness too. How you want to live *your* life." He threw the last piece of meat into the pile of cut up pieces.

"I really must get back to work," she said.

He wasn't going to let her avoid talking about this. "Did you like Commander Long? Are you interested in marrying him?"

"No! I found him haughty, presumptuous, and a man who would likely use my father and me for his own ends."

It surprised him how relieved he was to hear her say that. "You're exactly right. He is all three of those things."

"I need to help Melly in the kitchen." She grabbed the tray with the cut-up chicken on it and headed toward the Grant's cabin. "Thank you for your help. Goodbye, Samuel."

Samuel hurried after her wondering if courting Louisa was always going to be this challenging. "Melly told me you have the afternoon off. Baldy is going to help her make one of his specialties."

Louisa frowned. "Baldy? I didn't know he knew how to do anything other than boil water."

"He's actually a good cook. When he was a circuit preacher traveling throughout Kentucky, he had to cook all his own meals.

What do you say we go for a ride? I'd like to show you our herd and tell you about my plans."

"I can't. I'm working," she said as they stepped inside. "I have things to do."

"I already spoke to Melly. She said you are off duty for the rest of the day."

Louisa didn't look pleased. "First, I have to put this chicken in the pot to simmer and then I need to check on Adam," she said.

They rinsed the chicken pieces and their hands in salted water. He added some wood and kindling to the embers in the hearth while she tossed the chicken along with some seasoning into the large iron pot Melly used to make soup.

"There, now all Melly and Baldy have to do is add the vegetables," she said.

"They should be here shortly," Samuel said.

They found Adam in the doctor's apothecary where Baldy kept his potions, tinctures, and medicines. Baldy was extremely knowledgeable in the use of plants and herbs to make medicines.

He also kept a good supply of medical supplies such as Dr. John Sappington's fever pills for malaria. Baldy said malaria pills contained quinine, dogwood bark, licorice, whiskey, and a couple of other ingredients Samuel couldn't remember. In the summer, settlers around the settlement, especially those who lived closest to the river, often suffered attacks of malaria's chills and fever. It was of an unknown cause and a danger against which no rifle could protect.

Adam stood on a stool in front of a work table and seemed to be concentrating on his work.

"What are you doing?" Louisa asked him.

"Dr. Grant wants me to crush these mustard seeds with this mortar. Then I'm to shave these sassafras roots. When I finish that I'm supposed to grind up this chicory root a little at a time with this other mortar."

"Are you sure you know how to do all that?" Louisa asked her brother.

"Sure! Dr. Grant showed me. It's not hard. It just takes time."

"Looks like you're doing a fine job, Adam," Samuel told him. The boy certainly was a quick learner and seemed particularly bright for his age.

"Thank you, Sir. I'm also learnin' what he treats with all these. Mustard seeds are for making a poultice for chest colds. Tea made from Sassafras settles stomachs. And chicory helps people go."

"Go?" Louisa asked, looking confused.

Adam grinned. "You know…down there." The boy pointed to his rear end. "Dr. Grant says people sometimes have problems with that."

Samuel and Louisa laughed while Adam snickered. Samuel knew from his own brothers that all boys seemed to find matters of digestion terribly funny. In any case, he was grateful that Adam had managed to make his sister chuckle. She laughed far too infrequently.

When Louisa had recovered herself, she told Samuel, "I'm too tired for a ride. Perhaps another day." She turned to leave.

Samuel's chest flooded with disappointment. "Please, Louisa. I have important things I want to discuss with you."

She sighed heavily and then nodded. "All right. Just a short ride. Adam, I'll be back soon. Will you be okay by yourself?"

"Sure I will. After Dr. Grant showed me what to do, he told me he would be back soon to see how I was doing."

"Keep up the good work, Adam," Samuel told him as they left. "But be sure not to eat or drink any of this stuff."

"I won't. Dr. Grant warned me about that too. He said if I put the wrong thing in my mouth it could make my tongue fall out. And if my tongue fell out, then I wouldn't be able to jabber like I always do. He said the only thing I was allowed to put in my mouth around here was milk, fresh spring water, and Mrs. Grant's good cookin'."

"That's good advice," Samuel said. "Because I like hearing your chatter."

"I like to talk to you too," Adam said.

As soon as they were outside and walking toward the horse shed, Samuel took hold of Louisa's hand. The mere touch of her hand sent a shiver racing up his arm and down his back. Thanks to Baldy's miraculous ointment, her hands were nearly healed now, but the soft flesh of her hand was marred by hard callouses. Her work-hardened hands were much like her life. She'd had to be thick-skinned to stay sane and protect her brother.

He frowned when she pulled her hand out of his and crossed her arms in front of her. When had her feelings toward him become so cold? His own head swirled with doubts.

"Your horse shed is bigger and cleaner than most people's houses," Louisa said.

"Father won't have it any other way. He's extremely particular when it comes to horses."

Samson was still stalled in the shed. He'd planned to go to the settlement for the supplies they didn't get. But, again, the supplies would have to wait.

"What's up the stairs?"

"It's a private room," he said but didn't explain further.

Samuel saddled Samson and then an older but dependable bay mare that Melly sometimes rode.

Within a few minutes, they rode past the house and pulled up next to his brothers. Two of them were still chopping wood while the other one stacked. They waved and smiled knowingly.

Samuel shot them an annoyed look. "Tell Father we're going out to check the cattle."

Riding away, they passed between two stands of pines and then into the openness of the immense pasture. The sunny meadow always seemed welcoming to him and he inhaled the clean scent of grass seasoned with pine. Here, plentiful fall grasses rose up from the earth, still lush and springy and full of nourishment for his cattle.

Louisa appeared comfortable on a horse and rode well. He loved how her long hair spread out in the wind as they rode. He remembered her brother saying that the Indians had killed her mare. Undoubtedly, that was yet another heartache for her to bear. He resolved to buy her another horse even if his courtship didn't go well. And if he could find one, he'd get Adam another dog.

"Did you know that herds of wild cattle and horses roam the Great Plains?" Samuel told her as they rode at a leisurely pace. "In Louisiana, there's a large market for these animals."

"Is that what you and your father intend to do? Sell stock in Louisiana?"

"No, there's already a lot of competition for that market. With my brothers' help, I intend to round up or buy as many cattle as we can and then sell them to the government for use at their forts.

That's what we did in Kentucky and it was quite profitable. Next month, I'm buying five hundred head for $6 each with the calves thrown in for good measure."

"Really! That seems like a lot of cattle. And a lot of money."

"I've been saving for a long time."

"Who is selling you the cattle?"

"I'm planning to buy from Martín De León, he herds feral cattle from south and central Texas. Normally he sells in Louisiana, but his men are driving a herd north to Nacogdoches next month and selling them there. We have been corresponding and he promised to put aside five-hundred head for me."

"How do you know the government will buy them from you?"

"We moved here bearing letters of recommendations from the commanders of Kentucky forts. Because of those letters, I've been designated as a government stock raiser. The appointment carries a contract of $20 a head. Since beef sells for far higher than that in the East, they think that's a fair price."

"That's a $14 profit per head," Louisa said, impressing him with how quickly she did the math in her head.

"Exactly right. And there are a dozen forts within a reasonable distance from here. The first one we are selling to is Arkansas Post, about two-hundred and fifty miles to the east. My brothers and I will be driving the cattle to the fort next month or in early November. And next spring, we are making our first trip to Fort Smith."

"We came through Arkansas Post on the way here. We stayed about a month," Louisa said. "The people there will be glad to see your cattle coming. Beef is a real luxury there. People mostly have to eat deer and buffalo."

"Tell me what you remember," Samuel said.

"Well, the Post contains about thirty houses inside its walls in rows along two streets. The inhabitants are mostly French. American settlers live in a separate village north of the post, but Americans are now building within the fort too. A large, prosperous trading post on the north end is operated by a man named Mr. Bright. There's talk of the Post becoming the first capital of the Arkansas Territory."

"Will there be water for my cattle?"

"Oh yes, the Arkansas River feeds several bayous surrounding the Post."

"And Indians?" Samuel asked.

"I read that last year the Cherokees signed a treaty with the United States that establishes a large reservation between the Arkansas and White rivers. They're mostly farmers."

Astonished at how informed and knowledgeable she was, he gazed at her with admiration. "Your father said you can barely write. How is it that you can do math and know so much?"

"It's true, I'm not yet good at writing, but my mother and step-mother taught me math and we read our Bible together. I can read well. I mostly read newspapers. I read the *Arkansas Gazette* every day while we were there at the Post. The printer's apprentice gave me free copies. I think he might have been smitten with me."

That didn't surprise Samuel at all. "You're so pretty, I'm sure he was besotted."

She blushed prettily and looked away.

"The settlement's trading posts sell Louisiana newspapers," he said, "but they are always at least a month old."

"Mostly, I've learned to just keep my eyes and ears open. I love learning new things. You never know when knowledge will come in handy."

Stretched out before them the herd grazed on waving grass that tickled their undersides. The sight always brought joy to Samuel's heart. He had no interest in farming and no intention of ever leaving the back of his horse to stand behind a plow. Like his father, he wanted to be a cattleman. To travel the prairies rounding up or buying cattle. And then to travel to other places to sell them. And Red River country, with its wide open spaces, was the place to do it. A cattle operation needed enough land that during times of drought the cattle could still find grass to forage. And during winter, there would be enough freeze-dried grass to still provide some nourishment.

"Your herd is impressive," Louisa said. "How many cows is that?"

"About three-hundred, not counting the bulls and calves."

"So with the five-hundred you'll be buying you'll have more than eight-hundred head."

"And our herd will grow fast because we'll be keeping all the heifer calves. In a couple of years, they'll all be calving too.

They'll be the beginning of our Red River Cattle Company. As his oldest son, and the one with the most interest in raising cattle, my father has turned over the management of our cattle operation to me. I'm the majority owner and my brothers each have a third of the other half of our cattle company. Besides my brothers, I plan to hire about five more men to help us drive the cattle to various markets."

For their first cattle drive, Billy had agreed to be the first man Samuel ever hired. He swallowed his disappointment.

Samuel rode closer to the cows. Many of them glanced up but then quickly resumed grazing while stocky little calves frolicked together in the grass between their mothers. He loved how the calves always played together like children. As he always did, Rusty grazed off by himself a little distance away. The bull's long, smooth horns glowed in the sun like a crown.

"If our cattle operation grows as I think it will, we'll be able to provide seasonal jobs for most of the men at the settlement."

"What made you want to be a cattleman?"

"Well, my family has always raised cattle. So I guess it's in my blood. What I like about it is that I am able to support and improve my cattle business from the raw materials nature provides like water and grass. That's all cattle really need. That and a few hands to watch over them to be sure they don't roam off too far. And I don't have to worry about a freeze or a flood or a drought destroying my crop. Most of all, I like not being confined to a few acres standing behind a plow and an ornery mule all day. I can roam the open pastures and travel even further when I buy and sell."

Louisa gazed out over the herd. "It sounds as though you have a lot of plans for the future," she said with a wistful note in her voice.

"Forgive me for talking so much about my plans and my future. What about you? What do you want?"

"I wish I could plan my own future. I wish I even had a future to look forward to. I wish I had something to hope for." She pressed a closed fist to her lips and shook her head. "As the Scottish proverb says, 'If wishes were horses then beggars would ride.'"

This strong and beautiful woman—a woman he'd been attracted to since he first saw her in the riverbed—was admitting things to him that made him want to make the world right for her. A place where she would have a future. A world where she could be happy and feel loved.

Loved by him.

The thought gripped his heart with astounding force.

"Maybe you do have a future," he said. "Maybe you *can* control your future."

She didn't look like she believed him. In fact, she looked aghast. "How? Just how would I do that? You don't understand anything about me. A woman has no rights to her own future. I'm just as much a slave as any slave. I have to do what I'm told. Live where I'm told. And give myself to a man just because my father picked him! If I don't, I'll be beaten. Maybe not with a whip. But the cruel words and punishments my father lashes out..." she paused searching for the right words. "They rip at my heart."

"Louisa, I..."

Louisa turned to him with burning eyes. "I've tried to please my father my whole life, but it is never enough. I'm sick to death of it. I want to live. Marry for love! But I can't! I have to..."

Her voice rose with each sentence and Samuel could see the hurt on her reddened face.

"Have to do what?" he asked.

Bristling with anger, she said, "Don't follow me. I don't want *any* man near me!" She whirled the mare around and took off at a gallop.

"Louisa!"

CHAPTER 14

LOUISA'S HEART ACHED AS SHE rode. She shouldn't have raised her voice at Samuel. He'd been nothing but kind to her. But her pent-up emotions got the best of her. Unable to repress them any longer, she'd let all her frustration and resentment out on him because he didn't seem to understand that she had no control over her future. No control over anything. No options. No hope. Samuel just didn't understand what it was like to have someone control her every decision.

And the more she'd listened to Samuel and heard the pride in his voice as he told her of his wonderful plans, the more she wanted to be with him. Not Commander Long! She'd been so furious at her situation she couldn't speak. She could only run away at a gallop. With each powerful stride of the horse, another question assailed her. Where should she go? What should she do? She felt like just riding and riding. Letting the mare and the wind fly her somewhere where she could lead her own life. Be her own person. Make her own decisions.

But she couldn't. She had Adam to think of. She shuddered at the thought of going through with her plan. Nevertheless, she had to. And she would!

For now though, for a few reckless moments, she could experience freedom. She would taste what it felt like to be free. And then she would remember the feeling in the months and years to come whenever she felt trapped in her loveless marriage.

She let her body follow the horse's rocking motion, forward and back, forward and back. The sensation was a breathtaking combination of speed, energy, and blessed freedom.

She turned the mare into the woods and riding dangerously fast between and around trees she wove her way deeper and deeper into the ancient forest. Soon the underbrush was so thick she was forced to slow. She gave the mare her head, letting the horse find the best path. She glanced behind her several times, trying to keep track of where she was and the direction she was going.

The solitude here was glorious. The breeze whispered to her through the tall pines, and their thick boughs softened the sun's light giving the forest an ethereal quality. Here and there berries or flowering understory trees sprinkled the forest with spots of cheerful color. She inhaled deeply and let the soothing, woodsy fragrance fill her lungs.

As she took another deep breath, the breeze kicked up and carried another scent. From behind her, the air bore the rancid smell of bear grease. She'd gotten a whiff of the unique odor once before at the Arkansas Post when some Osage braves came there to trade. They'd passed by her and Adam on the street and their chilling appearance and strange odor frightened both her and Adam. When Adam wrinkled his nose, a woman nearby told them that Osage braves used bear grease to make their hair stand on end and to keep their bodies warm.

She knew what that scent meant now.

Indians.

Her heart beat hard in her chest at the realization. She chanced a quick glance backward. The sight froze the breath in her chest. Three Osage braves. Their eyelids, cheeks, and upper body painted bright orange made her gasp with terror. And the red crest of hair on their heads, stuck with feathers at the back, made them look like vicious predators.

She gasped and fear grabbed her. She booted into the mare's sides and took the horse to a full run despite the heavy woods. She wished now that she was riding Stephen's big black stallion. She would be lucky if she could stay ahead of the Indians on this little mare.

The three Indians let out shrill yelps that echoed threateningly into the forest as they followed closely behind her, no doubt waiting for her horse to tire and slow.

She shivered as panic began to claim her. Why had she ridden away from Samuel? What a fool she was! She would be violated by these braves, taken away, and then she would truly be made a slave. She would never see Adam again.

Or Samuel.

Her throat tightened at the thought. *Oh, God, please let me see them both again.*

As she tore through the woods, limbs and branches slashed at her, snagging her gown and ripping the skirt. One branch snapped back on her face and the sting brought hot tears to her eyes. She blinked them away. She needed to stay strong. Somehow, she would survive this.

Up ahead in a small clearing she saw the wispy smoke of a campfire and her heart leaped with hope. "Help! Help! Indians!" she yelled repeatedly as she sped forward. She leaned down and urged the mare to run even faster. She had to reach the campfire and get help.

As she charged toward him, a man sprang up and grabbed his rifle. He appeared to be a leather-stocking. Trappers were often called leather stockings because their dress was generally deerskin, unlike the more conventionally attired settlers.

He raised his longrifle and at once she heard the braves' horses slow.

As she reached the trapper, she spun the mare around and faced her pursuers.

The Indians jerked up on their horses and skidded to a stop about fifteen yards away. Fortunately, none of them held rifles or pistols. The one in front clutched a knife in his hand. The other two held tomahawks. All three narrowed their eyes as they assessed the leather-stocking menacingly.

The trapper yelled something to the braves in what she assumed was their language. His stern voice and fearful countenance left no doubt that the words he spoke were meant to stop them. He kept the rifle held high, aiming at first one and then another, constantly moving the barrel back and forth between them.

One of the braves held up a hand and nodded. The same brave said something back.

The trapper spoke again. "Gud'baz fiendz." This time his words seemed to bid them a friendly farewell.

To her astonishment, the three Osage nudged their horses and left, calmly walking past the man's camp and disappearing into the deep woods beyond.

As they passed, Louisa again caught their scent. It was one she would never forget. She stared after them. Beneath her, the mare's sides were heaving at the same rapid pace as her own racing heart.

"Thank you," she said, still breathless.

The man nodded and rested his rifle against the log next to the fire.

"What did you say to them?" she asked.

"I told them you were my wife."

"What?" she asked, shocked, and still very shaken.

"The Osage respect those who learn their language. And I've also studied their tribal customs. They have well-defined rules regarding marriage. They believe in the concept of commitment to one person in marriage. Telling them you were already claimed by me was the only way to keep them from taking you short of killing them."

The man looked to Louisa as if he were perfectly capable of killing all three. He appeared to be a skilled fighter. An ornate sword rested near his fire. She'd seen one like it on a Spanish officer at the Arkansas Post. How had this man come by it? Leaning on his saddle, which rested on the ground, was a painted Indian case containing a bow and arrows. And the claws of a mountain lion or bear hung on rawhide from his neck. The most intimidating part of this man's appearance, though, was the cougar head and skin that sat atop his gray-haired head. Although the cougar was eyeless, the animal's features glowered fiercely. He also wore a hunting coat made of buckskin, and his leather leggings were gathered under his knees by beaded Indian garters. His wide belt held a large hunting knife with an antler grip. A bone powder horn dangled to his right and a leather ball pouch hung to his left.

Despite his menacing appearance, Louisa sensed that she could trust this man. There was something in his eyes that conveyed honesty.

She dismounted and nearly stumbled because her knees were still shaking so badly. She tied the mare on a pine bough and patted the horse's sweaty neck. "Thank you for running so fast."

Blowing hard, the horse snorted and took a deep breath.

The trapper's gelding and pack horse whinnied and nickered a greeting to the mare.

Louisa also took a deep, calming breath before she addressed the man who had saved her life. "My name is Miss Louisa Pate."

"I'm William Williams. My friends call me Old Bill because my hair grayed at an early age. Even if we ain't really married, I figure we're at least friends now, so call me Old Bill."

"How is it that you speak the Osage language, Old Bill?"

"I served as a scout and translator with the Mississippi Mounted Rangers during the War of 1812. As I encountered local tribes, I learned their languages and studied their customs."

"What brought you all the way to the Province of Texas?"

"Beaver, mostly. Along the bayous of the Sabine and the Red Rivers. I also wanted to learn the languages of the Osage, the Caddo, and Spanish. I've about got all three mastered."

"That was indeed fortunate for me."

"Please sit," he said, indicating a log by his fire.

She tried to sit down gracefully but nearly crumpled to the ground.

"You look like you could use some coffee," he said.

She nodded and he poured her a pewter cupful. After handing the coffee to her, he sat down by the fire. "If I may ask, Miss Pate, what are you doing out here in the woods all by yourself?"

"I was wondering the same thing," she said. She was so disappointed in herself. Maybe her father was right. Maybe she was just a foolish girl.

After blowing on the hot brew, she took a few restoring sips. "I was riding with my friend Samuel Wyllie. For some foolhardy reason, I decided to go off on my own."

"I'm guessing you thought you had a good reason at the time."

"In fact, Sir, it was a terribly rash and foolish thing to do. He gave me no reason to run off. But freedom called to me."

"Freedom does that. If there is anything in life worth living for, it is freedom. I guess that's why I became a trapper. I'm free to go where I want when I want."

"What does it feel like to be truly free?"

He studied her for a moment. "Out of my distress I called on the Lord; the Lord answered me and set me free. Psalm 118."

"That's lovely," she said.

"If your heart and mind are free, your spirit is free. But if one or the other becomes trapped in sin or life's troubles, then your spirit cannot know freedom."

Could she free her heart and mind of all that troubled her? She'd been praying a lot lately, but God had yet to set her free.

They both looked up and stood at the sound of a rider coming fast.

Samuel. Thank God. He must have tracked her. "That's my friend, Samuel," she told the man as she stood and gazed into the forest.

The trapper turned back to face her. "From the look in your eyes, I'd say he's more than a friend."

Samuel raced toward her, both worry and consternation on his handsome face.

Louisa was surprised at how much joy the sight of Samuel brought her. When the Indians were chasing her, her first thought had been escaping. Then she wondered if she would ever see Samuel again and the thought of losing him deeply saddened her. How much more sadness would she feel when she married Long?

When Samuel reached them, he leaped off Samson and dashed to her. He hauled her up and into his arms and hugged her fiercely. Old Bill must be right. Samuel was indeed more than a friend.

Despite her resolve to keep her feelings for Samuel secret, Louisa let herself hug him back. A profound feeling surged through her—a feeling that Samuel cared for her and she cared for him. The sensation was joyous. In that instant, their hearts joined. But that was all that could ever be joined. Soon she would strike her bargain with her father and marry Long.

When he finally released her, Samuel's words rushed out on his nearly breaking voice. "I thought those three had gotten you!"

"They were Osage, Samuel," she cried. "They were about to overtake me when I spotted Mr. William's camp."

"Thank God you did," he said and kissed the top of her head.

"I'm so sorry. I should never have gone off on my own."

He nodded and took hold of her hands. "I wanted to leave you alone, as you asked, and decided to watch you from a distance. When I saw you head into the woods, I followed your tracks. The trees were so thick I couldn't see you. I had to take it slow so I wouldn't lose your trail. I knew I could find you as long as I could detect your path. Then I saw the tracks of three horses join yours. The deep ruts told me they were racing after you. When I heard their yelps in the distance, I knew you were being chased by Indians. I feared I would be too late."

He wasn't too late. But, sadly, it was too late for them.

One of his hands slipped down her back, and he brought her close to him again. He cupped her face with his right hand and gazed intently into her eyes. "I don't want to lose you—not to Indians, not to Commander Long, not to your father—ever!"

Regret surged through her veins. "Samuel...I..."

Samuel finally noticed the trapper watching them and he released her. He extended his hand and introduced himself to Old Bill. "I am greatly indebted to you, Sir. Thank you for saving Louisa."

"I only saved her from three Osage. I have a feeling you will save her from a great deal more."

CHAPTER 15

§●

SAMUEL INVITED OLD BILL TO dinner. It was the least he could do after the man saved Louisa's life. He still couldn't believe she'd come so close to death or a fate worse than death. And it had been his fault. If he'd just told her how he felt about her, and given her some hope, she wouldn't have reacted the way she did. And he should have stopped her. But he wanted to give her a taste of the freedom he knew she craved.

The only good thing to come of Louisa's ordeal was that it forced him to the realization that he genuinely loved her. He likely would have come to that conclusion soon anyway, but when he'd thought he'd lost her, it made him intensely aware of how deeply he cared for Louisa. He'd never felt worry and fear so deeply. Only love could make a man hurt like that.

On the way back, Louisa explained to Old Bill the situation with her father and Commander Long. Perhaps she wanted her rescuer to understand why she'd felt the need to run off into the forest alone.

"My father wants to marry me off to a man named Commander Long, a plantation owner from Louisiana," Louisa said. "Long intends to raise an army to rise up against Spain and take the Province of Texas from them. The Commander appears to be a man who is promoting his own interests and he needs a wife purely to gratify his ambition."

"But why pick Louisa?" Old Bill asked Samuel.

"I've wondered the same thing. Aside from her obvious beauty, I think he wants to be able to say to his supporters that his wife is a Texan."

"Long isn't so much picking me," Louisa said. "My father is picking *him*. And Long is flattered enough to go along with it as long as I meet his needs. He needs me merely to decorate his arm as he proceeds with recruiting his army."

"In any case, he's a big-headed, brash filibuster," Samuel said with disdain. "He'll have to do his filibustering without you, Louisa."

She glanced over at him but she didn't smile.

He couldn't wait to get her alone. He wanted to share that he loved her. He'd meant what he told her earlier when he let his tongue say what his heart thought. No one was going to take her away from him. Ever.

The trapper asked few questions and listened intently. "That's why you were asking about freedom," he told Louisa.

"Yes," she said. "I've lost all control over my life. I'll be commanded to marry against my will and forced to live with someone I don't love for the rest of my life—that's…"

"Not going to happen," Samuel finished for her. "I won't let it."

"Sometimes in life, we don't have choices. We just do what we have to do," she said, and rode on ahead.

He stared after her, baffled by her comment.

When the three of them reached the cabins, his brothers were still chopping and stacking wood. They glanced up at them and then concern showed on all their faces as they took in Louisa's disheveled and scruffy appearance.

"What happened?" Steve asked.

"I'll tell all of you at once. Where is Father?" Samuel asked.

"He's in the barn grooming George," Cornelius said.

"Baldy, Melly, and Adam are all in the clinic. A patient of his just left," Thomas added. "I'll go get them." He took off at a sprint.

"Tell Baldy to bring salve for Louisa's face," Samuel called after him.

Having heard them arrive, his father emerged from the horse shed.

"You can feed and water your horses over here, stranger," his father called.

The three of them rode up to the horse shed and dismounted. His father glanced at Louisa with concern but didn't ask any questions. Samuel knew he could also tell the mare and Samson had both been ridden hard.

Samuel introduced Old Bill to his father.

"We'll explain everything when we're all together," Samuel said.

"Go on inside then. There's coffee already made. I'll take care of these horses and join you shortly," his father said.

They dismounted and strode toward the house.

"Nice setup," Old Bill said, glancing around.

"We've only been here six months, but the seven of us managed to accomplish a great deal in that time," Samuel told him. "Louisa and her little brother recently started working here too."

They entered their home, poured coffee, and Old Bill and Samuel took seats at the table as they waited for everyone else. Louisa washed her face and hands, put an apron on, and then started to bustle around making preparations for dinner. Samuel kept an eye on her in case she needed any help as he discussed the trapper's recent beaver hunts with the man.

"Where are you going from here?" Samuel asked.

"Further south. Toward Nacogdoches," Old Bill said.

"Why leave the area?" Samuel asked. "There are plenty of beaver along Pecan Bayou. My father won't mind your trapping on our place. The beavers' dams jam up the waterways and cause flooding. Their dams force water out of the natural stream channel and spread it across our pastures, which can turn them into marshes. And that takes grass away from our cattle and in turn, food away from people."

Before Old Bill could answer everyone else filed into the house.

Samuel and Old Bill stood. He introduced the trapper to everyone.

"Old Bill saved my life," Louisa said as Melly, Baldy, and Adam put all the food on the table. Then she told them all about her hair-breath escape from the Osage.

"Let me see that welt on your face," Baldy said. He took a close look and told her, "It's only reddened. It'll disappear in a day or so. Put some of this on it tonight when you go to bed." He handed her a small jar of salve and she stuck it in her apron.

While the women finished preparing dinner, Adam told the trapper, "Samuel saved Louisa and me. We got ourselves stuck in quicksand in the Red. We were gonna die. But Samuel pulled us out with a rope."

"Don't feel bad about getting bogged down, sonny," Old Bill said. "That river is so quicky in places it might even bog down a butterfly."

Adam laughed at that.

In a few minutes, Melly and Louisa had spread out a bountiful meal of chicken and vegetable soup, fresh bread, butter, and two pecan pies for dessert. Melly had said pecans trees were plentiful in the area, hence the settlement's name Pecan Point, and their nuts had just ripened. Tomorrow, they would gather more nuts to replenish their supply.

After Baldy said the blessing, they all ate, asking Old Bill a number of questions about all the country and happenings between Mississippi and the Texas Province. Besides the occasional newspaper, travelers were about the only source of news in the settlement.

"One important thing," Old Bill said, "in April, Congress adopted the flag of the United States as having thirteen red and white stripes and twenty stars, one star for each state. Stars will be added whenever a new state is added to the Union."

"What will be the next state?" Adam asked.

"It looks like it will be Illinois," Old Bill said.

"Once the Illinois star is added, we'll order a flag," his father said.

"Have you ever killed an alligator, Old Bill?" Steve asked.

"Why yes, I have," Old Bill said. "On the Sabine, I came across a woman with three little children in her wagon. Hysterical, she could only scream and point to the river where the water was churning furiously. When I realized what was happening, I raced my mount some distance into the water, jumped off, and plunged into the water."

"What was happening?" Thomas asked.

"The poor man had waded out into the river to see if it was safe to ford with his wagon. He was seized by an alligator and drug under. By the time I got there and planted my knife in the creature's skull, the man had lost his left hand."

"Good heavens!" Louisa said. "Are there alligators in the Red River?"

"Indeed," Old Bill told her. "It's best to view the Red from afar."

Both Louisa's and Adam's eyes widened as they glanced at each other.

"I'll be glad when they finish building that ferry," Melly said.

"It's only useful when the water is high enough to float it," Stephen said.

"What happened to the man?" Baldy asked. "How did you stop the bleeding?"

"I made his wife press cloth to it while I made a fire real quick. While the fire heated, the man emptied my whiskey bottle, with just a wee bit of help from me. Then I heated my knife and charred that stump."

"Well done! You saved that man's life twice," Baldy said. "If you hadn't done that, he would have bled to death or the wound would have festered."

"Please, let's have no more talk of such things at the table," Melly said.

"Where's the prettiest spot you've been too?" Steve asked him.

"Why it's here, young Sir. I've never seen taller trees. The grass is as thick as lamb's wool. And even though the Red is a trickle right now at the end of summer, I can tell she's a beauty when she's running strong."

"The Red River, whether a torrent or a trickle, is always treacherous," Stephen told Louisa. "It is navigable only seven to eight months of the year and nearly dry the rest of the year. That's when quicksand makes it treacherous for uninformed travelers."

The trapper was pleasant company during the rest of their dinner, and they all talked of politics, nature, and bear hunting. Steve and Adam continued to pepper the man with questions, which Old Bill patiently answered. Sometimes his answer was a long, fantastical story and sometimes it was a short quip.

Samuel didn't want to be rude and leave, but he was getting anxious to speak privately with Louisa. However, she seemed to be as enthralled by the trapper's stories as everyone else was.

"How is it you've survived this long in the wilderness and among Indians?" Steve asked, gazing at the trapper with open admiration in his eyes.

Old Bill grinned. "Sleeping or waking, I've made it my habit to have one eye open and the other not more than half closed."

Their father laughed aloud. "You sound a lot like my oldest brother, Sam. He always said the West required keeping an eye out for threats in four different directions at the same time."

"When Captain Sam said that," Baldy told them, "the western edge of the frontier was Kentucky."

"True," Father agreed, looking thoughtful. "Twenty years later, the West is now about seven-hundred miles further west."

"Both places require a person to stay vigilant and be ready to act," Samuel said.

"Indeed," Old Bill said. "The West is no place for amateurs. As for Indians, I've found that if you can talk to them, especially in their language, and you're not planning on staying too long, most tribes are quite tolerant."

"I presume you're just traveling through then," Thomas said.

"Presume anything you please," Old Bill said, with a half-smile. Then Old Bill's expression became serious and he turned toward Samuel and Louisa. "What about Commander Long? I sense the man's spirit is here disturbing both of you."

Old Bill's observation was true. "Louisa and I are about to go discuss that," Samuel answered. "But if you have any suggestions, they're welcome."

"Only one. Live boldly while you have the chance, and when the time comes, die bravely."

"When will you return, mister?" Steve asked.

"About the time I come back," Old Bill said with a wink.

It was time to live boldly. The second they were alone in the woods, Samuel reached for Louisa and kissed her. Their lips melted together like butter on hot bread and the kiss grew even more delicious with every second. When she opened her mouth for him, and he deepened the kiss, he felt his soul touch hers. And the touch seared his heart, branding him as hers. And branding her as his.

It was then that he knew for an absolute certainty that he was meant to marry Louisa. He intended to shield her from further hurt. He wanted to make her hopes and dreams come true. And he needed her to make his own hopes and dreams come true.

But when he held her tighter, she stiffened in his arms. He sensed that she was holding back. Baffled he released Louisa and gazed down at her. He marveled again at her natural beauty and her alluring body. Perhaps she just needed to be reassured of his feelings. "You're as lovely tonight as wildflowers blooming on the prairie in the spring."

"Some of those wildflowers have barbs," Louisa said and stepped away. "You have to be careful which ones you pick."

Her life was a thorny mess. But he would do whatever he had to to make Louisa his wife. He moved around in front of her and gazed into her face. "I'm a careful man, Louisa. That's why I'm twenty-one and still unmarried. But I know I want to pick you for my wife. You're one of the purest and most beautiful of all God's creatures. But I want more than your beautiful body. I want your heart. If you'll have me, I'd like for us to be married."

Her eyes widened a moment and her cheeks flushed, but she didn't say anything. Instead, confusion paraded across her beautiful face.

"I have been as bothered as a fly in a tar pot about how to get you out of this mess," he said. "The surest way is for us to get married."

She stood there thoughtfully. Then, with a sad look on her face, she shook her head. "I can't."

That was not the reaction he was expecting.

She turned away from him. "I can't marry you. I must marry Commander Long." Her voice was firm, final.

Samuel grabbed her elbow and turned her around again. "What? You can't seriously intend to marry that pompous ass."

"I do intend to. I have to. To save Adam," she cried. "I'm going to agree to marry Commander Long but only if my father agrees to let Adam stay here and live with Baldy and Melly. I have to think of Adam first."

Now he understood why she'd been trying to push him away. "Adam wouldn't want you to make that bargain. And neither to do I."

"I'll do anything to protect him. His life will be so much better with Baldy and Melly. It's a bargain I'm willing to make for my brother's sake."

"Louisa that is an exceedingly bad idea. You can't trust your father to keep that bargain. Once you're married, he could easily renege and come and get his son. Legally and rightfully, the boy is his."

Her brow pinched and her lips tightened as she struggled with that truth. "I hadn't thought of that." Clearly confused, she sighed heavily and took a few steps away again.

"You know it's true, Louisa. He considers Adam his property. Just as he does you. He won't give him up."

"But I'll get him to swear to me…"

"You know you can't trust him. He may pretend to agree just to get you to commit to this marriage, but he'll soon come for him. And by then it will be too late for you. You'll already be married to that mad man."

They stared at one another across a sudden thunderous silence.

The shock of defeat held her still. He could almost see wretchedness fill her as her shoulders slumped. With a groan of distress, she stepped away again.

"I can protect Adam," he said. "But not without you. If you're gone, we would have no right to claim Adam. But as his adult sister, his blood relative, you could. Marry me and I'll get you out of this mess."

She raised her chin and turned to face him. "I'm not getting married to get out of a mess."

"Yet you were willing to marry Long?"

"Not for me. For Adam!"

"If you go off with Commander Long to Nacogdoches or he sends you to some Louisiana Plantation, Adam will be miserable," Samuel told her. "You think you're doing what's best for him, but you're not."

"It's the only way to save my brother," she insisted.

"No, it's not. Marrying me is the only way."

"If I marry you, I won't be able to protect him. My father will make Adam's life a nightmare."

"Louisa, it's you who needs to wake up."

She gasped. "How dare you."

"I didn't mean…" Samuel suspected it would be hard for a man to remain coherent while discussing marriage under normal circumstances, but this situation was downright befuddling. "I'm not good at this."

"Just for the moment, let's put Adam's future aside," she said. "Why do you want to marry me? Tell me what you're thinking. Just say what's on your heart. I need to know how you really feel before I can give you an answer."

Samuel decided to just say what he was thinking. He took a deep breath and began pacing. "All right. It's true we face more than minor obstacles. The first problem being your father. He's been blinded by greed and the prospect of power. The second being Commander Long. He's blinded by your beauty and his vainglorious belief that you would want to marry him because he may become a powerful man in this province. Neither one is going to give you up easily."

"Respectfully, Samuel, I know that's what they want. And I know my own feelings. But I can't understand yours until you tell me. What is it that you're after? What is it you feel?"

"You're right. I should have told you this before now. If I had, you wouldn't have run off into the woods." He paused to gather his thoughts. This was important and he had to get it right. "Louisa, love is our best defense. Because love is an unbreakable bond. Together, we are twice as strong as we are separately. They can never take you away if we are married. But that isn't why I want to marry you. I want us to marry because I love you and I dare to hope that you love me. I realized how much I love you when you were in so much danger. I understood then that I wanted you to be a part of my life."

Her face softened. "I do love you, Samuel. And not because I want you to get me out of a mess. I would never use you that way. I love you because you are an honest, decent man, who has shown my brother and me nothing but kindness. I love you because you made me realize the world is not quite as dismal and unkind as I thought. The world is a beautiful and caring place because of people like you. My brother and I were alone in the wilderness, but you came and saved us. Not with your rope, but with your heart."

He nodded, too full of emotion to speak.

"I've known loneliness most of my life. A loneliness so complete I even felt that God had deserted us. Then, He sent you to save us. But not just from the quicksand. You saved us from a desperate, miserable existence. Now, I don't feel alone anymore.

You stood up to my father and no one has ever done that. And just now, you helped me to see the truth. You kept me from making a terrible mistake. You are my sword and my shield. You are my hero. You always will be."

Samuel's eyes widened. A hero? His heart swelled at the thought of being her hero. He would gladly serve as her hero, and he silently pledged to forever be her sword and shield.

"My Red River hero," she whispered, as she came close.

Her words were so beautiful he had to glance above them as he blinked away tears. He wouldn't have been surprised to see the tall trees around them bend their tops to listen in. Or the clouds that passed overhead laughing out joyfully. Even the wildflowers of autumn around them glowed as if they had just turned into beautiful gems.

"Bless your sweet lips," he said as he turned his gaze back to her.

She grasped both of his arms as her eyes filled with promises and tenderness. "I love you so much. I would love to marry you, Samuel."

An intense pleasure filled him as pure joy surged through his heart, mind, and soul.

"But I have one condition," she said, her voice determined. "My brother must stay with me. Whatever it takes, we can't let my father take him. Ever."

"I agree. Of course. I swear he will stay with us no matter what your father says or does."

"But you said, legally and rightfully, Adam is his. How will we prevent him from taking my brother?"

"We may have to fight to keep him. But I doubt your father would dare challenge all the men in my family. If he does, though, are you willing to let me do whatever is necessary to win?"

Louisa hesitated for only a second. "Yes. I never want to let him near Adam. Never again."

"Till this is over, one of us will watch over Adam at all times until there's no longer any threat of your father coming for him. I promise to protect Adam as if he were one of my own brothers."

She exhaled a long sigh of relief. "Thank you."

"Do you have any other worries?" He wanted no more distressing worries, no crippling fear, and no agonizing confusion to come between them and getting married.

"Only that we've only known each other such a short time."

"True, but my attraction to you was immediate," he said. "And my feelings for you were there from the very beginning. From the start, I wanted to protect you—from your father, from Long, from the whole world. Soon, I wanted you in my life. Not just for a while, but always. What I feel for you is unaffected by time. It is unchanging and enduring. It's the one thing in our lives that will never change."

She gave him a tender smile. "For as long as I live, I will give you my heart."

He cherished her words in his own heart for a moment before he asked, "What else concerns you?"

"Truthfully, I'm a bit uneasy about us living in a place as dangerous as this. But I think I understand now why people want to live here. It's the lure of land and the promise of a fresh start. But most of all it's the desire for freedom. I've come to realize how important freedom is. When you don't have it, it's the most precious thing in the world."

Samuel agreed. Life here with him would entail a certain amount of risk. She was right to be concerned. She and Adam might be safer in one of the eastern states. The West was no place for the faint-hearted. "Yes, Texas offers all of those things and more. But there's one thing we must all realize. The connection between freedom and war is as real and powerful as exploding black powder. Freedom isn't guaranteed here on the edge of the West. We'll have to fight for it. Whether it's fighting Indians, Spaniards, or Mexicans, in between times of peace we can expect conflicts. Our rifles will remain an important part of our survival. Are you willing to live with that?"

"I am. Freedom is worth fighting for. So is being able to live here with you. You may have to teach me to be a better shot, but I'm willing to learn what I need to. Especially if I'm fighting to defend my family. And I want Adam to learn to be a strong man, just like you."

"He's already strong. He just needs to learn a few more survival skills. But he'll have four brothers to teach him."

"And Father Wyllie and Baldy."

"Louisa, I promise I will strive to make you happy here," he said. "No one will cause any more heartache in your life. And no one, including me, will control you."

"Promise?" she asked with the cutest grin he'd ever seen.

"I promise that we will be equals and respect each other's wisdom and feelings."

Tears of happiness welled in her eyes. "Can we marry tomorrow? Before my father comes back?"

"Yes!" He tugged her to him and sealed his promises with a kiss.

A kiss that must have made even God smile down on them.

CHAPTER 16

THE NEXT MORNING, LOUISA WAS still smiling as she gazed out the apothecary windows at the colorful sunrise. Glowing pink and purple clouds dangled against a turquoise blue sky. She would marry Samuel later that afternoon. She could hardly believe her good fortune. She already felt herself growing stronger, blossoming because of Samuel's love. His kisses caused her to feel sensations she didn't know were even possible. And his embrace wrapped her in a warmth that she could no longer live without. She sighed, wanting to feel his arms wrapped around her once more.

Until the ceremony, she was trying to stay busy helping Adam in the apothecary. A man soon arrived seeking Dr. Grant's care. She showed him in, and he introduced himself as Caleb Robbins. He wore no weapons and judging by the soil on his clothing he looked to be a farmer.

"Dr. Grant will be right with you. Please have a seat," Louisa told him. After sending Adam to fetch the doctor, who was still drinking coffee with Melly, she resumed her work.

While Dr. Grant examined the man who complained of a persistent sore wrist, the two men spoke about what Commander Long had been up to at the settlement.

Adam stood by watching the doctor and ready to help if necessary.

Louisa listened to the men talk with interest as she folded the bandages she'd washed and boiled for the doctor.

"In order to rise in men's estimation, he's drinking and treating freely, nearly emptying the settlement of every drop of strong spirits," Robbins said. "And he promises them everything."

"That's because promises cost nothing," Dr. Grant told him. "Politicians like him are all things to all men."

Robbins nodded. "He's making long-winded speeches, composed mostly of wind, in front of the tavern, talking of his unselfish devotion to the Province of Texas, railing against Spain, and saying he'll be the backbone of American citizens in Texas. As though he believes we have no backbone of our own!"

"That man is featherbrained, reckless, and pompous," Baldy said. "I have no doubt that the time when Texas will be received into the glorious Union is in the not too distant future, but for now, she must grow stronger with more American blood and muscle."

"Well, Commander Long is encouraging anyone he can find to tell him of their grievances against Spain."

"If he keeps it up, he'll have a one-sided war on his hands and drag the settlements into it with him," Baldy said.

"Other than a surly fellow named John Pate, he hasn't found any men to follow him yet, but I think there's a couple sitting on the fence. Both of them young men."

Baldy let out a disgusted humph. "Unfortunately, men like him, draw idealistic young men and naïve civilians into wars. Poor planning and being unprepared will cause untold hardship, suffering, and anguish. I know because I tended the wounded in two wars."

"Ouch!" Robbins yelped when Baldy's probing fingers found the exact sore spot.

"Americans have proven twice already that they are not afraid to fight when necessary," Baldy declared. "But it seems to me, the time isn't right."

"Nope, the time ain't right just yet to fight," Robbins agreed. "We have enough trouble with Indians to keep us busy."

Commander Long was nearly a stranger to her and yet, like the doctor, she'd found the man intolerable from the start. Nevertheless, she'd been willing to marry him for Adam's sake even though her instincts had told her that a future with the man held only heartache and trouble. Now, thankfully, she no longer had to worry about marrying Long to protect her brother. Later today, her future would be made safe. And so would Adam's. At 4:00

o'clock she would marry Samuel. And he'd sworn to her that he would keep Adam safe, even fight for him if needed.

Until the wedding, she would have to stay busy or her excitement might make her swoon. Samuel had gone to the settlement for supplies that he said could not wait. And the rest of the family were busy getting everything ready for the wedding. Old Bill had been asked to stay for the ceremony, and he had volunteered to go hunt a fat turkey for the wedding feast.

Melly told her to do nothing except help Baldy in the apothecary, if he needed it, or just rest.

"You have a sprain," Baldy told Robbins. "Give me a minute to mix up a batch of healing herbs for your wrist."

While Baldy went to the high pine table where he mixed medicines, Robbins stood and started wandering around the treatment room and apothecary. He snatched up a Bible that rested on Baldy's desk. "What's this? A *holey* Bible?" he asked and chuckled.

Louisa wondered how on earth the man had never seen a Bible before.

Robbins pointed into a hole in the Bible's hard leather cover. "Lord Almighty, this Bible has a lead ball stuck in its pages!"

"That Bible saved my life soon after we left Kentucky," Baldy told him. He patted his waistcoat pocket. "When I'm out and about, I make it a habit to carry the Good Book right here."

The man shook his head. "I've never seen anythin' like it."

"I'm not the first sinner that book has saved," Baldy said and gave the man a grin as he made something for Mr. Robbin's wrist. "If you haven't, you'd do well to read it for yourself."

Robbins nodded. "I confess I've neglected that lately. Too concerned with trying to keep my family alive and fed."

"That book is food," Baldy said. "Food for the soul."

"I heard that you're a preacher as well as a doctor," Robbin's said.

"A man often needs healing in several ways," Baldy told him.

Adam cocked his head and glanced up at Baldy. "Who is God? Has anyone ever seen him? If we haven't seen him, how do we know he's real?"

Louisa wondered if all eight-year-olds asked so many questions.

"And what does he look like?" Adam added.

Dr. Grant smiled down at Adam. "Well, the answers to those excellent questions could fill a dozen books. But the simple answer is that God is the maker of everything including our souls. And love is how we know He is real. Humans didn't just imagine love. God gave it to us. As to what God looks like, the Bible says that He made man in His own image, so I guess he looks like a perfect version of us."

Adam whistled. "He must be really handsome!"

Louisa, Baldy, and Mr. Robbins all laughed.

"What is our soul? And what is love?" Adam asked the doctor.

Louisa pitied Baldy. She'd learned that answering one of Adam's questions always led to another question. But she listened carefully, anxious to hear Baldy's answer.

"Our soul is the innermost part of us that isn't made up of flesh and blood. Our bodies have a heart, bones, organs, and lots of other messy things inside. But those parts are just organic matter. They don't contain our soul. Our soul is made of a spirit that only God could put in us. That's why God's word says we are born once of a woman and once of the spirit."

"Is that where love is? In our spirit?"

"Love is a feeling that is guarded by our spirit. There are many forms of love, but they are all the best thing we humans can ever feel."

Adam nodded, satisfied for the time being. "I love my sister."

"And I love you, brother," Louisa told him.

Her brother watched Baldy closely as the doctor worked.

"I'm using rosemary, marjoram, camphor, and menthol," Baldy told Adam. "I'll mix those with some oil."

"What will it make?" Adam asked the doctor.

"A liniment good for sprains and sore muscles."

Baldy poured the mixture into a jar and walked over to Robbins. Then he rubbed some of the liniment on the man's wrist and wrapped it with one of the bandages Louisa had just folded. "Rub this liniment onto your wrist three times a day. And a wrap like that will help support it until your wrist has a chance to heal."

"For how many days?" Robbins asked.

"Until it feels normal and one day past that," Baldy told him.

Robbins paid Baldy and they bid the man goodbye. On his heels came another man complaining of a severe bite, but he couldn't remember being bitten.

"That looks like an Asp Caterpillar injury," Baldy said. "Did you pick any caterpillars off your trees?"

"Why yes, I did. But it was just a caterpillar," the man said.

"Asp caterpillars are covered in what appears to be a deceivingly soft coating, but it contains stinging venomous spines," Baldy explained. "Exposure results in immediate skin irritation in that grid-like pattern." He pointed to the man's finger. "I know it's a severe, radiating pain. But it will only last for several hours."

"Can't you do anything for it?" the man asked, his forehead wrinkling with his discomfort.

"Chew some tobacco and put the wad on it. It will help draw out the poison. Next time, use a stick to remove caterpillars. Sorry I can't be of more help, but some problems just take time to heal," he said with a grin at Louisa. "No charge today since I couldn't do a thing for you."

"Thanks just the same, doctor. I'll try the tobacco juice," the man said and left.

"Adam, thank you for your help," Baldy said after the man left. "Next time we have a patient with a sprain, I'll let you mix up the liniment while I watch. But today, you are relieved of further duties. Please go check on my animal patients, and be sure they all still have water and their shed is clean. After that, I want you to spend the afternoon playing."

Complete surprise filled Adam's face. "Playing? Playing what?"

Louisa grimaced as she realized Adam had spent so little time playing in his life that he didn't even know how to go about it. Truth be told, their chores prevented both of them from finding time to play. They understood work, but not play.

Baldy rubbed his chin. "Well, just use your imagination. You can pretend to be a knight, a soldier, a doctor, or even an Indian. The point of play is to have fun and be whatever you want. Do whatever you want. Run, jump, explore, see what nature has to teach you."

Adam appeared thoughtful. "I'll try." He went to Louisa and took her hand. "I'm glad you're goin' to marry Samuel. I like him a whole lot!"

"Me too!" Louisa said.

"I don't like him as much as you, of course." He hugged her and ran out the door.

After Adam left, Louisa picked up the Bible and examined the hole the lead ball left in it for herself. "Truly remarkable."

"Have you ever read the Bible, Louisa?" Baldy asked.

"I used to. We have one. Our mothers wrote our birthdates in it. It's the only thing the Indians left behind. Samuel said he'd go fetch it for me sometime."

"When he brings it back, read the gospel of John. It's my favorite. I believe you will find it thought-provoking."

Louisa liked how he simply left it up to her to draw her own conclusions after reading the gospel.

Baldy moved back to his worktable to put away all the ingredients he used for the liniment. "How did your mothers die?"

"I've always wondered about that. They both seemed fine just before they died. My mother died unexpectedly when I was about Adam's age. Soon after, Pa married Adam's mother and we moved away. Then, suddenly, about three years later when Adam was about one, she died too. I was around eleven. I'd grown especially fond of her." That was the last time she'd felt wanted and loved. Since then, her mind-numbing loneliness had grown every day.

"So that was about six or seven years ago. And you never learned the cause of their deaths?"

"I was so young I barely knew what death was, much less what caused it. In both cases, one day they were there taking care of us and the next they were buried in the ground."

Baldy frowned and appeared thoughtful. "That must have been terribly hard for both of you."

"It was."

Compassion filled Baldy's face. "Well, let's not dwell on the past any longer. This is your wedding day and you have your entire future ahead of you. I realize you haven't known Samuel long, but I'm certain it was long enough for you to realize what a special man Samuel is."

A smile that came all the way from her heart broke out on her face. "I knew that the first time I met him. I said 'yes' when he asked me to marry him because he's already my hero. Not just because he saved our lives, but because he makes me happy—

truly happy."

"Samuel is a proud and spirited son who comes from a truly heroic family. His father and all four of his uncles are valiant, principled men. And their sons are as well. And both of Stephen's daughters are equally brave and honorable. Even though my past was spotted, they welcomed me and then Melly into their family with grace and love."

"Just as they have done for Adam and me."

Baldy nodded. "Indeed. You are a part of our family now."

His words made Louisa's eyes water. "I truly appreciate how you are teaching Adam medicine. He's a smart boy. Perhaps he can even follow in your footsteps and become a doctor someday."

"I would be delighted if he did," he said with a kind smile. "I'm going to go see if I can help get things ready. They might need an extra pair of hands. Let me know if any more patients show up, but you're under orders to stay here and rest."

Louisa wasn't sure how much she could rest, but she laid down on her bed anyway, just to think. She thought about Samuel's last kiss last night, which felt equally sensual and heavenly bliss. The feel of it would likely stay with her for days, yet she longed for another kiss, and more. She wanted to be held against his strong body. She wouldn't have to wait long. The thought sent tingles racing down her spine.

Abruptly, a thought interrupted her musings and she sat upright with widened eyes. Where would they go after they were married? They couldn't sleep here, of course. And Samuel slept with his brothers. The settlement had no inns. And it was too dangerous to set up camp in the wild.

Oh dear! Had Samuel given this any thought? she wondered.

She laid her head back down. Were she and Samuel doing the right thing? Had they really thought this through? Had they known each other long enough? Perhaps they were rushing things too much. Should they build a home before they married? But if she didn't marry today, her father would demand that she and Adam go to Nacogdoches with him. She rubbed her forehead, beginning to ache with the worry of it all.

None of that matters, she told herself. Only one thing mattered now—they loved each other.

She closed her eyes and let Samuel's smiling face fill her mind.

A wonderful, contented peace flowed through her once again.
  Moments later, she was sound asleep.
  Minutes later, she wanted to scream.

CHAPTER 17

BEFORE SHE COULD SCREAM, HER father gagged her while she was still in the bed. With the Commander's help, her father tied her hands despite her desperate struggles to keep him from doing so. Then Long tied her feet while her father held down her legs. With disbelieving eyes, she glared at her father as he stood there while Long threw her over his shoulder. They were abducting her! They were going to keep her from marrying Samuel!

Ignoring her glares, her father straightened the bed to make everything look normal before they snuck out the cabin's back door. Long went first and her father followed. As she tried to glower up at him, she noted that her father's face bore bruises and swelling from Samuel's blows. The sight actually pleased her. Normally, it was her or Adam with banged up faces or bodies.

Three horses were tied nearby. She tried to scream through the gag, but Long tossed her over the saddle of one of the horses and knocked the breath out of her.

"What about my son?" her father whispered as they swiftly tied her on the horse.

"Never mind him. We can come back for the boy when I have more men to back me up," Long said in a hushed voice.

"After you're married, I'll come back for him myself," her father said.

Her heart hammering, alarm swelled through her.

A moment later, they trotted into the forest with Long pulling the horse she was on.

Long turned his head toward her. "Louisa, I wouldn't be doing this, but Samuel threatened to kill me if I came near you. Still, I wish we could have just talked and not gagged you. But we couldn't risk alerting them to my presence. No telling what that ruffian, Samuel, and his brothers might do to me."

"That's true, look what he did to me," her father said. "And we didn't have time for an argument. If our plan was to work, we needed to act quickly and get in and get out without delay. You saw them as we watched from the woods. They are clearly getting ready for a celebration. Samuel intends to marry Louisa right away. We had to act first."

Long turned his head back toward her. "Louisa, I'll take that gag out and untie you just as soon as we are well away from the Wyllie's place. Then we'll make plans for our own wedding."

Louisa's stomach churned and she forced bile down. She could choke if she retched while gagged. It wasn't the bouncing horse making her nauseous, it was the thought of being forced to marry Long. She tried to think. But only questions raced through her mind. How long would it be before Samuel or someone else discovered she was missing? How far away would she be? Where were they taking her? Would Long try to kill Samuel if he came after her? Would Samuel kill Long?

Then Long spoke. "I've changed my mind, Mr. Pate."

Louisa's eyes widened with hope. Had he given up on this foolish plan? Was there an ounce of decency in the man after all?

"What do you mean?" her father asked.

"I don't think we should take Louisa south to Nacogdoches. It's about a hundred and fifty miles away. And the Arkansas Post is an even further distance north of here. I've decided I don't want to wait that long to marry your daughter. We can't risk Samuel coming for her."

"What do you want to do then?" her father asked.

Long remained quiet for a few moments before he said, "I need Louisa. Having a beautiful wife like her by my side will aid in my recruitment of men to our cause. She'll draw them like bees to nectar. They'll see I am a family man fighting for freedom!"

What about my freedom? Louisa thought. What about the freedom of the slaves on his plantation? What about their mangled and shackled hearts? How can a man fight for freedom and deny it to those he controls? The irony of the situation would be laughable if it weren't so sad.

"But how will you wed? The only preacher around here is that ungodly Baldy Grant. Men say he plays cards and drinks whiskey and who knows what else. He claims it's so he can reach sinners. But if you ask me…"

Long interrupted him. "We'll do a handfasting with a *spousal de futuro*, a marriage contract to be made official at a future date. It's binding, especially if it's consummated, as long as you give your approval as her father."

"It would be my honor, Commander," her father said. "That's a brilliant solution."

Louisa's panic increased ten-fold. She could easily believe her father was doing this. He'd always put his own interests before hers or Adam's. However, she couldn't believe Commander Long would force her into marriage. She didn't know what the word consummate meant, but she suspected it meant she would be forced to lay with him.

They continued riding through the woods, staying well away from roads and trails, likely because people might question why they had a woman tied on a horse.

The rumble of distant thunder rolled toward them and it suddenly grew darker. Louisa turned her head and glanced up trying to see through her long hair hanging in her face. Gray, churning clouds filled the sky. A thunderstorm would soon be upon them.

"We need to find a shelter," Long said. "We can't take her to your place. It's the first place they'd look."

"You're right we can't go to my place. Hm."

"Well?" Long demanded. "Think man, think."

"A young couple was killed by Indians a few days ago. Their cabin would be empty. You two could use it tonight. I can just go back to my place. If they show up, I'll just say I don't know where Louisa is."

"Do you know where that cabin is?" Long asked.

"Never been there, but I heard men talking about where the attack happened. It was west of here, a little more than a mile from the settlement. I think I could find it and we're in luck, we've been traveling in that direction anyway."

"Lead the way then," Long said. "And hurry. Those clouds are getting darker by the minute."

Samuel crossed one thing off his mental list of things to do before the wedding. He'd found a puppy for Adam. The fluffy yellow dog with one white paw, a male, was spread across the saddle in front of him. Based on the size of his paws and huge tummy, the pup would soon grow into a large dog that would provide protection and companionship for Adam. The dog's company would be especially important after his sister wed.

The puppy licked his hand as he rode toward a place owned by a man known for selling excellent horse stock. From the looks of the herd of quality horses grazing nearby his home, the man's reputation was well warranted.

"I'm looking for a small, already trained mare for my future bride, Mr. Jackson," Samuel told the man when he arrived.

"Got just the horse for ye. We bred her ourselves. She's a cute, well-mannered, four-year-old filly on the smallish side. She may be a wee horse, but she's got some real strength in her."

Sounded a lot like Louisa, Samuel thought.

They strode over to a horse paddock and the man pointed. "There she is over there, the chestnut close to where my three sons are training those geldings."

Samuel took a long look, admiring the mare's conformation and color. "She is a pretty thing. Would you please saddle her up and let me ride her?"

"Sure thing."

Jackson led the mare to his horse shed and saddled her while Samuel petted the back of the pup. Missing his mother and litter mates, the puppy whined pitifully. "I know a little boy named Adam who is going to love you a whole lot," he cooed against the puppy's downy ear. The whining stopped and the puppy resumed licking Samuel's hand.

Samuel observed the calm mare as Jackson saddled her. Her ears were relaxed and so was one of her back legs. She showed no hesitation accepting the saddle and bit, and she kept her head down as Jackson slipped the headstall on her. He liked what he saw so far.

"She's ready for you, Sir," Jackson said as he buckled the last strap and then held out the reins.

"Thank you, Mr. Jackson. If you wouldn't mind, could you hold this little fellow for me?"

"Happy to. Nothing better than hugging on young pups and young babies."

With a smile, Samuel handed the pup over and mounted. "What's the mare's name?"

"Don't have one yet. Never name the ones I intend to sell."

Samuel put her through left and right turns, turning in a circle, backing up, and then took her to a gallop before stopping her abruptly. The horse responded well to all the tests he put her through. The only thing left to do was to determine a fair price.

"How much?" he asked.

Jackson cocked a brow at him. "You said she's for your bride-to-be?"

"Yes, we're to be married this afternoon. Her name's Louisa Pate."

"I always was a romantic," Jackson said and then named a more than fair price.

"Sold." Samuel counted out the appropriate gold and silver coins. "If you'll remove your saddle and tack, I'll be on my way."

"I heard you're the owner of Red River Cattle Company," Jackson said and handed the pup back to Samuel.

"That's right."

Samuel put the pup down and let him walk around a bit so he could relieve himself before their trip back into the settlement. When the deed was done, the little fellow romped around playfully. Adam was going to love that little guy.

"I tell you what. If you give me your company's horse business and send your friends who need horses my way, I'll throw in that saddle and tack."

Now that Billy and his horses were gone, Samuel had no reason not to take his offer. The man and his sons were obviously excellent horse trainers. "My thanks, Sir."

After Jackson tied the mare onto Samucl's saddle, he mounted and placed the pup on the saddle in front of him. "Before I go, my compliments to you and your sons on this mare's excellent training."

"Thanks. It's what we love to do. The trick is keeping the Indians from sneaking in and stealing them. My sons have lost a lot of sleep protecting our herd."

"I know what you mean. They tried that at our place recently, but my brother and I were on guard. We had to kill three braves just yards from our horse shed."

"I heard about that. We're posting a well-armed guard every night now. Hope your gal enjoys her horse. I can tell she's going to be a lucky bride marrying a fine young man like you."

"I'm the lucky one, Sir."

"Greetings to your father and brothers."

Samuel nodded. "Good day to you, Sir."

With the two hardest tasks out of the way, the only thing left to do was to visit the trading posts for dresses for Louisa and clothes for Adam, since the arrival of Commander Long had interrupted his previous trip into town for supplies. He also wanted to purchase a ring, but he doubted either of the traders did any business selling jewelry. A ring would have to wait until his trip to the Arkansas Post.

Ten minutes later, he rode up to Wetmore's trading post and tied both horses on the rail in front. He nodded to a cluster of men he knew well standing nearby. They were all dressed in buckskins, and the straps for shot pouches and powder horns crisscrossed their chests. They wore their hair long and loose under worn tricornes or shapeless floppy hats.

"Howdy, Samuel," Elijah Anderson said. "That mare is a bit on the small side for ye, ain't she?"

"Your feet will be dragging the ground, sonny," Elijah's brother Bailey said and laughed.

"When she gets tired of carrying a man of your size, you'll have to let her ride you a while," Mr. Johnson said.

Samuel chuckled at their good-natured ribbing. "She's for my bride to be," he said unable to stop the wide grin that split his face.

With a glance up at the heavy, ash-colored clouds, he decided he needed to make haste. He placed the pup on his shoulder and hurried in. On their journey from Kentucky, they'd visited numerous general stores and trading posts along the way. They all held the same pleasant scent. He could only describe the aroma as friendly.

The well-stocked store, which also served as the post office, held a good supply of guns, ammunition, blankets, kettles, and pans made of copper and iron, tin cups and plates, tobacco, bolts of cloth, sacks of grain, and jugs of strong-spirits. Stacked in a corner were several sizes of finished rope made from hemp. They also had staples such as coffee, flour, cornmeal, spices, and other essentials. Household supplies included baskets, pails, torches, paper, and wicks and wax for candles. And an assortment of jars holding glass beads, used for trading with Indians, added a rainbow of color to one shelf. Behind the store, the owner kept basic blacksmithing equipment and pitch and tar for waterproofing.

Samuel hoped they sold ready-made clothes too. Taking a deep breath, he savored the blend of fragrances unique to a trading post. "Mr. Wetmore," he called.

The man emerged from the backroom and smiled. "Samuel! What are you needing today? I just got two freight wagons loaded with goods and provisions in so I'm well-stocked."

"Good day to you, Sir."

"That's a cute pup you got there."

Samuel petted Adam's puppy, already growing attached to it himself. "Do you have any readymade gowns for ladies?"

"I do, nothing fancy though. Just got a new shipment in and it included some in small, medium, and large in two styles."

"I'll need two dresses in the small size. And I'll take one of each style." With a storm brewing, he wouldn't take the time to look at them now. "Do you have any clothes for boys?"

"Well now, that's harder because most mothers sew their children's garments. But I do have something he might could use. A woman brought some clothes in because her own boys outgrew them. I traded her some flour and sugar for the garments." He went to the back and brought out a good-sized stack of used clothing.

Samuel sorted through the stack and found two pants and three shirts he thought would fit Adam. "I'll take these, and I'll need to order him a pair of boots."

"Who are they for?"

"Adam Pate, an eight-year-old. His father lives across the river. I'm marrying his sister, Louisa."

"Congratulations, Samuel. Just measure Adam's foot and bring the measurement to me. For youngsters, I always order a couple of sizes up because by the time we order and receive them, which could take at least a month, he'll have grown into them or soon will."

"Good thinking, Sir. At least he'll have them before it gets really cold."

"Will that be all?"

"Well…I don't suppose you have any wedding rings?"

"No, sorry, don't have any."

Disappointed, Samuel sighed.

"But I do have a necklace you could give her instead." He pulled out a case kept under his counter and opened it. "A simple pearl with a gold chain, but it's lovely."

Samuel nodded. "I'll take it. And add two jugs of whiskey and three bottles of wine to my bill." It wasn't every day a man got married.

Four more things were now crossed off his list. It was time to go home and get married. Excitement raced through him. While Wetmore totaled up his bill, Samuel's thoughts turned to his upcoming marriage. He just hoped he could be a good husband and make Louisa happy. She deserved that. Her life had not been an easy one. He truly wanted to be her hero.

Wetmore glanced up at Samuel. "You know, you can't just hope for a happy marriage, you have to create one."

"How does a man go about that, Sir?" Samuel asked, wondering if the man had read his mind.

"Well, here's my take on it. True love means you stand by that person. And in hard times, you stand even closer. And here on the frontier, hard times are just about guaranteed."

They both glanced toward the window as a flash of lightning filled the trading post with a sinister light.

CHAPTER 18

HERMAN LONG BROUGHT HIS MOUNT to an abrupt stop. "Mr. Pate, hold up a minute. I'm going to untie Louisa. I don't want her to get sick on our wedding night."

"I'm not sure that's wise," her father said.

Long dismounted and handed the reins of his mount to her father. Then he untied her from the horse she was on and untied her feet. After he set her upon the ground, he left her hands tied and yanked the soaked gag from her mouth.

Louisa swallowed and sputtered. "You're doing this for nothing. I'll never marry you!"

Her father glowered at her. "Louisa, be respectful to your betrothed."

"We are not betrothed!" she shouted, boldly meeting her father's intimidating eyes. For once in her life, she was going to stand up to her father. Was it Samuel's love that gave her the strength to do so? Or did she have the strength within her all along? She wasn't sure. But something had been unleashed within her, and she vowed to defy both of these men.

Her father's eyes widened in shock and intense astonishment filled his angry face. He wasn't used to Louisa challenging him. "You are promised to the Commander because I said so," he hissed.

Every muscle in her body tensed in defiance. "I never agreed to marry Commander Long."

Stunned, her father's jaw and fists clenched. He started to say something but froze when lightning exploded nearby.

Startled by the ear-piercing clap splitting the air, Louisa's body tensed even further, but she turned to face Long. "We are not betrothed!"

Long smiled at her. "Oh, but we are betrothed, my love. Your father and I reached an agreement." His voice sounded like a tone that would be used on a sulky child. "Don't you remember?"

She did remember. She shot her father an angry glare.

"Louisa, listen to me," he warned with a stern face. "Those Wyllie people wanted to work you like a servant. And that woman wouldn't let you leave. Well, now we've rescued you, and you are free to follow your heart."

She suspected it before, but now she was certain. Her father was a raving lunatic.

Commander Long eyed her as though she were now a misbehaving small child. "If you promise to behave yourself, my love, I'll untie your hands."

Louisa raised her chin. "If you behave, I'll tell Samuel to let you live."

Long chuckled. "You won't have any more contact with Samuel."

Louisa's panic rose a notch but not as high as her anger. "Untie my hands and take me back. Now!"

"There's no need to play hard to get or act coy," Long soothed, "although it is somewhat endearing. But we are soon to be married, my dear. You just need to get to know me better. After all, we've had so little time together. But it was long enough for me to know how appealing you are." He stood closer and touched her cheek with his index finger. "Long enough to know how exceptionally charming and fetching you are. I have been enthralled with you since I first saw you. And today I'm learning how feisty you can be as well. I consider that an asset. A spirited woman is so much more...exciting." He ran his finger and his eyes slowly downward, from her neck to the cleft of her bosom.

If her hands had been free, she would have slapped him. Instead, she shot him a disgusted glance. "I *am* about to be married. To Samuel Wyllie! And yes, I'll be hard to get—impossible, in fact—for I love another and could never marry you."

Long's lips tightened and he shook his head. "No, Louisa, you're not going to marry him. You are too exquisite for a man like him. Your beauty would be wasted in this primitive settlement. You deserve to shine in society among the genteel, the upper sort."

"I have no desire to join society," she said. "I'm happy with Samuel and his family."

Long gave her a patronizing look. "That boy is nothing but a poor cow man living in a crowded cabin. I'm a well-respected, successful lawyer and the Commander of Texian forces. I have a large, prosperous plantation in Louisiana and can provide the kind of life you deserve. You'll have servants and slaves, fine silk gowns, and live a life of luxury beyond your wildest dreams."

Her father muttered his agreement. "Listen to the man. He's right."

Louisa cast her eyes between the two men. She saw a devil lurking in the covetous look Long gave her. And her wicked father was surely one of the devil's minions.

"Pa, untie me!" she pleaded. "Please, help me."

"I can't do that. You are going to marry the Commander whether you like it or not. As your father, I know what's best for you."

"You've never known or cared about what's best for me. Or Adam. You've only wanted what is best for you."

Her father drew back his meaty hand and slapped her. "Enough of this back talk! What's best for me is best for you," he yelled. "Someday he will be the leader of all of Texas. And you'll be by his side. So will I. Commander Long has promised to make me one of his highest ranking officers. While his army takes control of this land and we make our fortunes, you will live in Louisiana at his plantation. You'll thank me someday."

"No, I won't. And I loathe you today," she spat, her cheek still burning. Her father's thinking was as warped as Long's.

A chilly gust a wind blew against her face and tossed her hair about. Above her the sky relentlessly grumbled, as unhappy as her heart. A major storm was brewing.

Long moved to stand between her and her father. "Let's quarrel no more. Mr. Pate, please refrain from laying a hand on my future bride. Louisa, please don't aggravate your father. He only wants what's best for you. So please try to be civil. The three of us have much to look forward to."

"If you want me to be civil, untie my hands. I'll show you just how gracious I can be." She looked forward to graciously planting her boot between his legs.

"Regrettably, I will have to leave your hands tied, for now," Long said. "But we will untie them shortly. When you learn how wonderful I can make you feel, I'm sure you will want to return my affections. You'll see when we consummate our marriage."

If he did that...Louisa knew she would be ruined. No man would have her. Probably not even Samuel, because she could be carrying another man's child. The thought of Long being the one to take her virginity made her scream, "No!"

A new and unexpected resolve surged through her as Long took hold of her, preparing to lift her onto the spare horse. This was her life, and no one was going to ruin it for her. And no one was here to save her from that ruin except herself. She had to save herself. She pulled away from him. "I said, no!"

As if they had a mind of their own, Louisa's legs took off running. She'd always been a fast runner, but now she ran as if her life depended on it. Because it did. She bolted in the direction they'd come from. Each long stride took her closer to Samuel. Closer to freedom. Closer to being able to decide for herself what kind of life she would lead.

"Stop!" Long commanded. "You won't get far."

That made Louisa run even faster. She glanced over her shoulder.

Encumbered by his long sword and heavy, knee-high boots, Long trailed behind her a short distance. Beside him, her father's eyes shot daggers at her and his clenched fists promised punishment.

She leaped over a fallen log, darted between trees, running like a scared rabbit being chased by a hungry fox. No! She was no scared rabbit. She was smart. And swift. And determined. By God, she would escape or die trying. Keeping her breathing steady, she pushed harder and went faster.

As she ran, the sharp wind out of the north bit at her face and stung her eyes. The clouds above grew almost black. Beneath the canopy of the forest, the filtered light was so dim she had a difficult time seeing. The wind blew her hair onto her face and she repeatedly swiped at it with her tied hands. She zigged and zagged among the large trees, running with the wind, hoping to lose them. She glanced behind, only Long followed now.

Lord, help me!

Lightning cracked and the sky seemed to drop. Icy cold rain stabbed her skin but still, she kept running. As the rain poured down, she tried to remain hidden amongst the trees, running behind first one large tree trunk and then another. Her heart throbbed as she fled further and further into the cold, wet woods.

The dark sky was mostly hidden above the canopy of the forest. Then she heard the sudden crack of a lightning bolt as it shot across the sky and then downward. The flash lit the woods in an eerie glow and shook her heart. The rolling, growling roar of the thunder that followed nearly instantly vibrated within her causing every nerve in her body to quiver.

Her path across the forest floor grew slippery and her boot nearly slipped from beneath her. Soon the weight of her soaked clothes made running even more difficult. The trees provided no shelter. Droplets the size of pecans crashed through the foliage above. Shadows shifted to menacing gloom, and the rain kept pouring.

Suddenly she entered a sizable clearing, and the unobstructed rain there fell on her as if she were standing in a waterfall. She glanced behind her but could see little. The world was just a wet blur. At least she didn't see Long on her heels.

Her chest heaving, her breaths came in short, rapid gasps. She stopped, taking a moment to catch her breath. Even the air felt wet as she sucked in deep mouthfuls of air. Water ran freely from her long, wind-tangled hair and flowed in a sheet down her back. Her borrowed shirt and skirt stuck to her like a cold second skin. A flash stream ran over the tops of her muddy leather boots, and water seeped into the stitching making her feet even colder. Her bound hands trembled.

Her mind raced, still frantic with thoughts of escaping. As she glanced around and tried to get her bearings, the tall pines around the clearing bowed to the gale. A forked bolt shot across the unbroken clouds that blanketed the sky. The lightning illuminated the open field in an unnatural, blue-gray light. The thunderous boom that followed the lightning roared a warning too late.

Eyes widened, breaths ragged, and shaking from the cold, she stared, disbelieving.

She jammed her fist into her mouth to stifle a scream.

A single Indian, riding a horse and holding a long lance, watched her from across the large clearing.

Her legs were frozen in place with sudden terror and fatigue, so she crouched down and crawled and dragged herself toward the edge of the woods. Maybe he hadn't seen her. Her heart thumped madly as she clawed at the earth trying to pull herself back into the cover of the forest.

She glanced back, her eyes narrowed to keep out the relentless curtain of rain.

The brave was coming, his horse's steps slow, threatening.

There was no point in trying to get away now. There was no place to hide. And if she ran, the horseback Indian would be on her in seconds, perhaps driving that long lance into her back. A shudder ran down her spine.

She wondered where Commander Long was. Had he gone back to get his horse and her father? She was sure they were still coming for her. Would they wait until the storm ended? The thought of seeing either one again turned her stomach.

She would never forgive her father for his betrayal. He had stabbed her in the back just as surely as if he'd used the spear this Indian held. His treachery had pierced her heart like a sharp, ragged blade.

But, still, she wouldn't let him make her cry.

She wasn't sure which would be worse—to be a prisoner in a loveless, arranged marriage or to be made a slave in an Indian village. Either way, her life would be covered with a blanket of doom. A life of continued unhappiness. And she would never be with Samuel.

Perhaps neither fate awaited her. This Indian might kill her. Her long blonde hair would likely be a prized scalp. The horror of the thought made cold terror creep through her.

Still crouching in cold water and mud, she turned her head around.

The Indian continued his slow march toward her. His hawkish gaze drilled into her.

Panting with panic, she clutched her bound hands against her chest. Despair and hopelessness assailed her, crushing her heart. *Oh, Samuel, if only we'd had a chance together. A chance for happiness. A chance for love.*

But that life was a fading dream now.
She most likely wasn't going to make it out of this alive.

CHAPTER 19

L OUISA REFUSED TO DIE WITH the Indian's lance in her back.

If this brave was going to kill her, he would have to do it to her face. Her legs were still trembling with cold and fear, but she pushed herself up, wiped her mud covered hands on her skirt, and straightened her back. For Adam's sake, she couldn't give up. Not yet. She was still alive. And as long as she was alive, there was hope. Even if it was only a raindrop's worth, it was enough hope to let a storm of courage flow into her heart.

She pushed her wet hair out of her eyes, lifted her chin, and waited as the storm let up.

The Indian rode closer, his proud, bronze face and dark eyes studying her with piercing scrutiny as he approached. Large earrings adorned his ears and his head was shaved except for a scalplock, one long lock of hair on top of his head. He wore no shirt, but a cloth jacket covered his broad shoulders. Leather leggings protected his long, sinewy legs. A powerful, young brave. She guessed he was of the Caddo tribe because Old Bill said he'd encountered a number of Caddo hunters in these woods.

The brave's white stallion was also young and powerful. Eagle feathers hung in the horse's mane and from his reins. And the horse's chest and shoulders bore strange, crimson-painted shapes. Louisa wondered at the meaning of one design in particular. It was a circle with a smaller circle in the center that had four logs in the shape of a cross pointing outward from the central circle. One log pointed north, one east, one south, and one west. Smeared by the rain, the designs made his horse appear as menacing as the brave.

"Kua'a," he said when he reached her and held up a hand. It sounded like an almost friendly greeting.

Trying to keep her voice from shaking, she said, "Hello."

"Hello," he repeated.

"You speak English?" she asked.

"Some." He gestured around them and to the sky. "Today, the storm God rides." His words were rough and guttural, but she understood them.

"Yes," she said, nodding. And her father and Long were probably riding toward her too. She glanced behind her, still worried that they might ride up at any moment. Caught between them and this Indian, she had nowhere to run. She turned back to face the Indian and tried to hide her fear.

The brave glanced at her bound hands and his eyes searched the forest beyond her. His brow furrowed. "Man follow you?"

She nodded. "Yes. Bad man. He carries a long sword." She gestured to her side.

The brave nodded once, indicating his understanding. He gracefully slipped off his horse and stuck his spear in the ground. He withdrew his knife and strode toward her.

The sight of the blade and the frown on his face made a wave of terror sweep through her far colder than the north wind that blew up her skirt. Was this brave going to scalp her? She backed away and nearly stumbled when her boot stuck in the mud.

He stopped, pointed to her wrist, and then made a sawing motion with his knife.

Her relief was so profound she felt light-headed.

His sharp blade swiftly cut through the rope and he tossed the fragments aside.

Her wrists freed, she tried to rub the soreness out of them, but it hurt too much. The wet rope had tightened painfully and made her skin raw.

"Where home?" he asked

She thought for a moment about what to tell him. Were the Wyllies his enemy or were they his friends? "Wyllie," she said, making her voice firm. "The place on the Red River where there are many cows." It *was* her home now. For the first time in her life, she felt she belonged somewhere.

The brave's eyes narrowed, and her heart skipped a beat.

"Brave warriors," he said.

"Yes, they are brave. And good men." Somehow, she knew this Indian was a good man too. She sensed a bizarre connection to him, as though he had purposefully come here to help her.

"You go now," he said and took a step back. "Run from bad man."

Louisa exhaled her relief. He was going to let her live.

When she didn't move, he gestured with a sweep of his arm that she should go.

"I am lost." She gestured trying to indicate her confusion. She pointed in each of the four directions, shrugged her shoulders, and opened her palms. Since it was so cloudy, she couldn't tell north from south, east from west. "I don't know where to go."

The brave actually chuckled. Then he vaulted upon his horse, reached down, and pulled her up behind him as though she weighed nothing at all.

Surprised, she stared wide-eyed at his broad back. After the heavy rain, the man's scent wasn't bad, it was just distinct, almost like the musky fragrance of freshly toiled earth.

A soft mist still falling, they rode toward a stand of towering pines. The warmth of the brave and his horse beneath her legs made her trembling ease and her numb feet began to thaw. Her nerves also settled down and she heaved a sigh of relief. Ironic that she should she feel far more comfortable and safe with this brave than she had with her father and Commander Long.

All too soon, though, she heard riders coming from behind them. At once, her heart clenched into a tight knot.

They had found her.

Louisa hung on to his coat as the brave whirled his mount around.

It was Long and her father some distance behind them, both coming at a fast gallop. The sight made her breath solidify in her chest.

"Bad men?" he asked her.

What should she tell him? Yes, they were both bad men. Nevertheless, she didn't want them killed. She couldn't speak. An unintentional whimper escaped her though.

That was all the Indian needed to hear apparently because he lowered her off his horse and trotted off to the side. The muscles of his body tightened as he readied himself for battle. He held his deadly spear up, but made no moves toward the approaching riders.

Astounded, Louisa stood there aghast as she realized this Indian stranger was going to fight to protect her. Her own father would not protect her from Long, yet this young brave was willing to.

Long galloped toward the Indian with rage on his face. She saw him withdraw his pistol as his horse came within firing range. Why hadn't he waited to see if the Indian was friendly? Why hadn't Long given her a chance to tell them that the brave was only helping her?

The brave bent over his horse and took off at an angle, riding at an incredible speed.

The boom of the black powder weapon echoed through her and then reverberated through the forest.

Long's shot had missed. He sheathed the pistol and withdrew his long sword.

"Stop!" she yelled.

Holding his rifle, her father caught up to Long, his face and eyes lit with the hatred he held for all Indians. He tried to aim the rifle, but he couldn't hold his horse steady enough to take a shot.

"No! Don't shoot him, Pa!"

Riding in a wide arc, the Indian swiftly circled behind both men. She'd never seen a man ride with such skill. He seemed to be one with his magnificent white horse, remaining well-balanced even without a saddle. And both the horse and the brave exuded a surreal strength, the aura of their courageous spirits radiating from within them. A force unseen, but one she could sense nonetheless.

Her father jerked viciously on his reins as he tried to turn his horse around. The gelding balked at the rough handling and let out a high-pitched neigh that left no doubt he was unhappy with his harsh treatment. Her father had never treated his horses well.

Or his children.

Swearing at his horse, her father quickly dismounted, held his rifle to his shoulder, and tried to aim at the brave.

The Indian sneered with disgust and galloped toward her father, his lance raised. The brave's fearless eyes made known his intent—death.

"Pa!" she cried.

Her father's shoulder jerked back as he shot at the brave.

At the same instant, the white horse cut sharply to the right at an almost impossible angle. The shot missed.

The brave managed to stay atop his horse and then angled back again. This time, heading directly for her father.

A second later the brave's lance pierced her father's chest.

Louisa stared in horror, her eyes disbelieving.

As her father fell, she ran toward him. She collapsed to her knees next to him. His head rested in a pool of muddy water. She slipped her hand behind his neck and raised his head. With her other hand on his cheek, she gazed into his eyes, hoping to see love and perhaps regret.

"I loved you and your brother…in my own way." Then, an all too familiar anger filled his eyes as he took his last breaths.

The brave rode up, reached down, and jerked out the spear.

She watched her father's blood drip in a surreal slow motion off the spear point, each drop flooding her with drowning disbelief.

She looked away from the lance, disoriented, too stunned to react or to cry. She wondered if she would ever cry for her father. Would the rain that fell from her lashes be the only tears she would ever shed? Could she mourn someone who had never comforted her? Someone who had only intimidated and terrified her? She had always been afraid of him. She couldn't remember a time when she wasn't. The scars she bore on her heart were proof that her fear of him was real and deep.

Now, she would never have to fear him. But she still did, she realized in a dazed exasperation. And that made her angry. Pent up resentment spilled from her and she beat a fist against his bloody chest. It wasn't grief that provoked her rage. It wasn't his death. It was that her father took with him all her hope that one day he would become a good father. He would never tell her he was sorry. He would never give her a father's love. It would never be right between them.

She glanced up and shuddered when Long let out an unearthly howl from a considerable distance away.

The Commander charged toward them. Long held his sword high and glowered at the brave. Would the Commander meet the same fate at the end of the Indian's deadly lance?

Or would this brave Indian die defending her?

She didn't want either one to die. "No!" she yelled toward Long. "Please stop!"

The brave, still mounted and beside her, raised the bloodied lance and prepared to take aim. His lance was far more lethal than Long's sword because the Indian could throw it from a distance.

Long must have suddenly grasped the same deadly truth. When he saw the Indian take aim, he yanked his horse's reins, jarringly turned the mount away, and took off at a gallop. His spurred boots beat against the sides of his mount as he sped away, retreating at an even more rapid gait than when he approached.

Her father's horse took off, running hard to catch up to Long's mount.

The brave glanced down at Louisa. Was he trying to decide whether to stay with her or go after the fleeing man?

For an instant, she thought about waving him on. Long had intended to dishonor her and force her into a loveless sham of a marriage. A marriage created by some obscure law—not by God. Now, Long was leaving her in the hands of an Indian brave to face, as far as he knew, an unknown fate. He was a disloyal and a dishonorable scoundrel. The coward deserved to die. But there had already been enough bloodshed. She would not be the one to decide Long's fate.

"No." She shook her head and stood.

The brave stared after Long's retreating form with an intense fierceness. Finally, he said, "Not his time to die."

Not yet, Louisa thought.

She squeezed her eyes shut and took a moment to calm herself and to collect her thoughts. She had to get back to Adam. He would be so worried about her. And she had to find Samuel. This was supposed to be her wedding day. She hoped the brave would still help her find the Wyllie homeplace.

They would have to come back later to bury her father. She made a mental note to try to remember where this place was so she could find her way back.

"What is your name?" she asked the brave as he rode closer to her.

"Kuukuh. Means water."

"Thank you, Kuukuh, for helping me," she said. "I am Louisa."

"What does name mean?"

She had no idea. She thought for a moment. "A new life."

He nodded and a corner of his mouth pulled into a slight smile.

"Are you a Caddo?" she asked.

"Yes. Still, my spirit is free."

He brought his horse up next to Louisa, reached down, and pulled her up behind him.

Again she gripped his coat to keep from falling off. They rode a while in silence, Louisa lost in her turbulent thoughts.

"Who was man I killed?" Kuukuh finally asked.

She considered the question a long moment before she answered. "A bad man. An awfully bad man."

CHAPTER 20

"WHAT DO YOU MEAN SHE'S missing?" Samuel demanded of his father as he dismounted by the horse shed.

He'd waited out the worst of the storm at the settlement. As soon as it let up, he'd left. When he arrived home, he'd found his father, Baldy, Thomas, and Cornelius, all saddling their horses preparing to launch a search party.

His father appeared worried. "When we saw the storm coming, we stopped all the wedding preparations and pulled everything inside. After the storm let up, I sent Thomas to the Grant's cabin to go check on Louisa and Adam. But they weren't there, so he searched the entire cabin. When he still didn't find them, he ran back."

"Then we all started looking for them and calling their names," Melly said. "They were nowhere to be found."

"Adam was playing the last time I saw him," Baldy said. "But that's been some time ago. He must be with Louisa."

Samuel tried to remain calm. Something was terribly wrong. Louisa would not have left on her own. She was getting married today.

"Hopefully, they just went for a walk and got caught in the storm and are on their way back now," his father said, but he didn't sound convinced.

"Cornelius, take this pup and hide him somewhere in the horse shed. I want it to be a surprise for Adam."

Cornelius took the tired pup into his arms. "Cute little guy."

"That's a smart looking little mare," his father said. "For Louisa?"

"Yes. A wedding present," Samuel told him hurriedly. "Steve, wipe her down and then brush her. I'm going to look for Louisa."

"Sure," Steve said, taking the mare's reins.

"I'm going with you," his father said.

"I'll come too," Baldy said. "If they're hurt, they might need me."

"I'm coming too," Thomas said.

"Cornelius and Steve, stay here and guard Melly," their father ordered. "If Louisa and her brother come back, fire one shot into the air."

His father, Thomas, and Baldy were already well-armed and their horses saddled, so the four of them mounted up.

"Let's circle around the Grant's cabin and clinic to see if we can spot anything," Samuel suggested.

"The storm would have washed away any tracks," Baldy said.

Samuel headed in that direction anyway and the other three followed.

They rode around to the back of the cabin and Samuel studied the ground as did his father. They were both excellent trackers and if there was something to be found, they would find it. He spotted something and rode over to it. Two piles of soaked horse droppings.

Baldy frowned. "Why would there be horse droppings behind my cabin? None of us ride back here."

His father leaned down to study the ground and the nearby bushes. "Someone had three horses tied here, but not for long."

"I can guess who," Samuel said, anger welling up inside him. "Those two ratbags, Pate and Long, stole her away! And they took Adam too!"

"That's the most likely explanation," his father said. "I knew those two were not to be trusted."

"Any hope of following their tracks was washed away in the storm," Thomas said.

"Where do you think they might have gone?" his father asked Samuel.

"Long mentioned Nacogdoches. But I doubt they would attempt a trip that far in this weather." He glanced up. The sky still appeared unfriendly and the north wind still held a serious chill.

"They wouldn't take them home. They'd figure we'd look there first," Samuel said.

"Agreed," Baldy said. "I suspect they'll be looking for a preacher to perform a quick wedding. What about Jonesboro? There's a lay preacher there."

"We have to hurry," Samuel said, already turning his gelding toward the front of the cabin. "We can't let Long marry her. If he does, I'll have to kill him." He fought to control his anger. At the very least, Long was on the eve of an almighty thrashing.

"We'll stop him," his father said. "One way or another."

As they came around the corner of the cabin, Old Bill jogged up. His back was bent with the weight of a fat turkey. "Hold up," the trapper said, raising a hand and breathing hard. "I spotted a Caddo brave with Louisa riding behind him on a white horse. Since I was on foot, I didn't want to risk him taking off with her, so I stayed hidden and ran all the way here."

"Is Adam with them?" Samuel asked.

"No, it was just Louisa," Old Bill said.

"Is she okay?" Samuel asked. Real panic took hold of him. He'd been so sure that that Long had abducted Louisa and Pate had taken Adam. But being taken hostage by an Indian could be even worse. "If that Indian has…"

"She appeared calm," Old Bill interrupted. "So I doubt he touched her. From the direction they were traveling, I believe they are actually on their way here."

Samuel prayed that was true. "Perhaps a friendly Indian is trying to help her. Maybe she and Adam got lost and the brave found her. But where is Adam?"

"I sure hope the boy isn't hurt," Baldy said. "Let's go."

"Show us where they are," Samuel told Old Bill.

"They're not far," the trapper said.

"Drop that turkey and climb up," his father told Old Bill. "My stallion can carry us both."

Old Bill grabbed the back of George's saddle and hopped up with surprising ease.

The five of them rode nearly a mile at a gallop before they spotted the brave with Louisa riding behind him.

At the sight of her, Samuel's heart bumped. "Thank God."

The brave caught sight of them and halted. He turned his head toward Louisa and spoke to her.

Samuel urged his horse to an even faster run but he did not pull out any weapons. "Don't shoot," he called back to the others. He didn't think his father would, but Thomas might.

Louisa slipped off the back of the Indian's horse as Samuel reached them.

He quickly dismounted and she ran into his arms as the rest of the men rode up behind him. She was soaking wet, disheveled, and filthy, but the feel of her in his arms was the cleanest, purest heaven. "Are you all right?"

"Yes, thanks to this brave. Oh, Samuel, I was...I was...afraid we would never be able to marry." She was trembling.

He hugged her tightly to his chest. "*No one* will ever stop you from becoming my wife."

"They almost did. This is Kuukuh," she said, glancing up at the brave. "He speaks some English. He saved me from the Commander and my father. They stole me away and were going to force me to marry Long, even without a preacher, using some legal term about a future bride. I knew I had to save myself. So I escaped and ran and ran. They chased me, but Kuukuh found me before they caught up to me."

"We suspected they took you," Samuel said heatedly when he noticed her raw wrists. "And Adam? Do they still have him? Is he all right?"

"No, they only took me." Alarm filled her eyes. "Where's my brother?"

"We're not sure. We thought he was with you. I promise we'll find him. You know how little boys are—always running off to play." He'd said that to ease her worry, but where was Adam? At least Pate didn't have the boy.

"Dr. Grant told him to go play," she said.

"He's probably back by now," his father said. "He must have waited out the storm under a tree. We'll have to let him know how unsafe that is."

Samuel strode over to the brave. "Thank you, Kuukuh."

The brave nodded and held up his lance. "Killed one bad man. One ran like rabbit."

Samuel turned his head back to face Louisa. "Which one did

he kill?"

"Father."

Everyone stood still in stunned silence. Even Kuukuh seemed astounded. He must not have known that he'd killed Louisa's father.

"He was only my father in name. Not in my heart," she said.

"And Long?" his father asked.

"When Kuukuh threatened him with his lance, he turned his mount around and fled," Louisa said. "Like the coward he is."

Samuel's jaw tightened. "You mean he left you with an Indian brave, not knowing what might happen to you? No offense, Kuukuh."

"Some braves hold no honor in here," Kuukuh said, thumping his fist on his chest. "Some would have hurt Louisa."

"And other braves have much honor," Old Bill said. "Like you." He repeated what he said in what Samuel assumed was the language of the Caddo.

Kuukuh nodded his thanks to Old Bill.

"Yes, Commander Long raced away and left me with Kuukuh," Louisa said. "Fortunately, this brave *is* a man of great honor. His name means water and he said the storm god sent him to help me."

They all glanced up as the sky reverberated with thunder.

"I'm grateful for Kuukuh's help. But if I ever see Long again," Samuel swore, "he'll be sweating blood instead of water before I finish with him."

He noticed that Louisa was shivering. He removed his jacket and placed it on her shoulders.

"Kuukuh, I am Stephen Wyllie, father of Samuel and Thomas." He pointed to each of them. "And these are our friends, Baldy Grant, and Old Bill Williams. We would be pleased if you would join us tomorrow for the wedding of Louisa and Samuel."

The brave gave them a slight smile. "Kuukuh thanks you, Wyllie. But the storm god sends me to someone else now. I must go to them."

Samuel had no doubt that God, the God of all men and all places, had sent this man to help Louisa. He would be forever grateful.

Baldy dismounted and went to Louisa. He took hold of her

hands and touched her face and forehead. "We must get Louisa somewhere warm. And the sooner the better. She's half frozen. I don't want her to grow ill on the eve of her wedding."

"I am cold to my bones. And I could certainly use a hot bath," she said. Her voice sounded weak and tired. "I've got an acre's worth of mud on me. But I have to show you where my father's body is first."

"I show them," Kuukuh told her. "You go. Sit by fire."

"But I thought you had to go help someone," Louisa said.

Kuukuh nodded. "Soon."

"Thank you," she said. "I would like to get back and check on my brother."

He smiled at Louisa and then turned his magnificent mount around.

"I'll take Louisa back," Thomas volunteered.

"And I'll go back with Old Bill," his father said. "We have to find Adam and then we have a fat turkey to pluck for your wedding feast tomorrow. I'm sorry we have to delay the wedding a day, Louisa, but this time tomorrow, you will be Mrs. Samuel Wyllie."

Louisa gave Samuel a broad smile and relief filled him as he tugged her shoulders to his side and hugged her. He hated to admit how terribly frightened he had been when he learned of her disappearance. It had felt as if someone had thrown water on the fire inside him, leaving nothing but dampened ash.

Baldy placed a comforting hand on Louisa's shoulder. "If you have no objection since foul weather threatens and it's getting late, Samuel and I will just bury your father where he is stretched out on the earth. I will say a few words and ask God to not punish him too harshly for the ill-treatment he doled out on you and Adam."

Louisa stared at Baldy a moment. Would she want her father punished? If she did, Samuel wouldn't blame her one bit. For whatever a man sows, this he should also reap. And Pate had sown nothing but grief in Louisa's and Adam's lives.

Finally, she said, "Yes, bury him there. It's a beautiful spot in the forest. Thank you."

"Samuel, I have a folding shovel in my saddlebag you can use," Thomas said.

"I have one too," Samuel said. "Baldy can use yours."

While Baldy and Louisa talked, Samuel got the shovel from Thomas and then withdrew the clothing he'd bought at the trading post from his saddlebag. He handed the package, wrapped in brown paper and tied with twine, to Thomas. "I bought these for Louisa and Adam. Give it to Melly and tell her to open it while Louisa bathes. She'll know what to do with it."

"Sure will."

Samuel shoved his second package, containing the whiskey and wine, into the other side of Thomas' saddlebag. "And make sure this wine is saved for the wedding feast."

Thomas grinned widely. "Glad I'm old enough to drink now."

"Can you put one bottle—unopened mind you—and a couple of Melly's special occasion glasses up in the shed's upstairs room?" He didn't think Louisa was going to be a jittery bride, but if she was, the wine would help her to relax. Truthfully, it would help them both to relax.

"You bet," Thomas said with a knowing smile and a wink. "Getting married can make a man thirsty." Thomas removed his sturdy leather coat and handed it to Samuel. "Since you put your coat on Louisa, you may need this."

Samuel donned the coat and stepped back over to Louisa. Even though she was clearly exhausted and freezing, her face held a stalwart strength and her eyes reflected a new sereneness.

"Is there anything else you'd like me to say before we commit your father's body to God?" Baldy was asking Louisa.

"No. But please say a prayer for my mother and Adam's mother. They suffered at my father's hand too, and maybe even died."

"I believe they may have," Baldy agreed as though she'd already discussed the deaths of the two mothers with him.

Samuel exhaled. If Pate had murdered them, it was one more example of the man's capacity for cruelty. Perhaps now, with her father gone, Louisa could find the happiness she deserved. He wanted no more sorrow to plague her life.

He prayed Adam would be there by the time she got back.

CHAPTER 21

AFTER LOUISA LEFT FOR THE cabins with Thomas, Old Bill, and his father, Samuel finally focused on Kuukuh. He owed the man so much and he regarded the brave with a mixture of gratitude and awe.

The Indian's appearance astonished him. Kuukuh was the most magnificent Indian he'd ever seen. Drops of moisture beaded on the brave's proud face and the bronze skin of his exposed chest. His body conveyed power and youthful strength. Yet his strong, striking features and dark eyes expressed wisdom beyond his years.

As soon as Samuel and Baldy mounted up, Kuukuh turned his stallion. With Baldy riding beside him, Samuel rode behind Kuukuh as the three of them left to find the body of Louisa's father. The brave kept his mount at a reasonable trot as they splashed through standing water and trudged through the mud. The unique earthy scent of a forest after a hard rain filled the air while moisture dripped from every tree and bush and little rivulets trickled along the ground.

He couldn't believe Pate was dead. He was ashamed to admit how relieved he was. Now the man couldn't force Louisa to marry against her will. Without having to defy her father, she was free to marry Samuel. And, the man couldn't hurt Adam or Louisa ever again. That pleased him just as much if not more. He was certain Pate was now facing the wrath of God for the Good Book is clear—fathers should not provoke their children to anger.

After about an hour, they arrived at the spot. Mr. Pate's long body was stretched out in the dead center of a clearing in a puddle of brown rainwater. Pain carved the merciless lines of the man's face. A large splotch of blood covered his chest. How had Louisa reacted to the grizzly sight?

He glanced around wondering where Pate's mount was. The horse was nowhere to be seen. "Pate's horse must have chased after Long's horse."

Kuukuh nodded his agreement.

High in the sky, a few buzzards began circling overhead. It wouldn't be long before other predators smelled death.

Kuukuh turned around and regarded Samuel, his face wholly serious. He pointed to Pate. "He was not good man. You be good man for Louisa." It was a command, not a request.

Samuel nodded and placed a hand over his heart. "I promise I will be."

"And I will be a good friend to her," Baldy said.

Kuukuh sat there and studied their faces with a stare that spoke clearly. Then he nodded, turned his beautiful horse, and rode away.

When Samuel had buried his friend, Billy, he'd also buried his youthful, idealistic opinion of the nobility of Indians. The harsh reality of the West and hatred made anger toward all Indians burn in his chest. Until today. Now, Kuukuh made him remember, once again, that there are good and bad in every tribe. He silently thanked Kuukuh for reminding him.

He glanced over at Baldy whose eyes were widened.

"They say God works in mysterious ways. I think something extraordinary happened here with Kuukuh."

"I'd have to agree," Samuel said, as he watched the brave ride away for a few moments. He removed his hat and stored it in his saddle bag. "I know Louisa and Adam will be better off without their father in their lives. If Kuukuh hadn't shown up when he did, Louisa would have been compromised by Long and forced into marrying him later. I would have…"

"Killed Long," Baldy finished.

The thought made him angry and Samuel shoved the spade into the wet earth.

"You dig for a while and then I'll dig," Baldy said.

"I can do it all. We've had so much rain, the digging should be easy enough," Samuel said. "While I dig, you can figure out what you're going to say about Pate. Good luck with that, by the way."

Baldy raised his brows and nodded. "As Voltaire said, 'To the dead, we owe only the truth.'" He retrieved his Bible and began studying it.

Samuel suspected it wouldn't be easy to conduct a funeral service for a man they both considered despicable. A man whose honor had faded to gray. A man whose heart was riddled with the black of pure meanness.

A cool mist fell from the leaden sky as he dug. Fearing another storm, Samuel hurried and soon, the grave was deep enough to keep predators from digging it up. "I guess we should search him?"

"Yes. He may have something on him that Louisa would want."

He searched Pate's pockets and found only a few coins that he would return to Louisa. He also kept the man's pistol.

"Ready?" Baldy asked.

"More than ready," Samuel said.

They each bent to take hold of the body but froze with Pate's head and legs just off the ground.

From the tree line, they heard a low, deep growl. A moment later, a nerve-wracking shriek that sounded like a woman screaming for her life ripped through the air.

Samson's head lifted and his ears pinned back.

"Whoa, boy, whoa," Samuel said, quickly dropping Pate and grasping the horse's reins. He snatched his rifle from his saddle, tied Samson's reins in a knot, and then gave the horse a smart slap on the hip to send him to safety. He knew Samson wouldn't go far.

Baldy's rifle was on his grazing horse, who had already moved some distance away, so the doctor withdrew his pistol.

"There it is!" Samuel said and pointed.

Narrow, yellow eyes scrutinized them from the darkness of the woods. After a few seconds, a cougar took a cautious step forward. Then another step. It was coming for them.

When the cougar decided to attack, he and Baldy could both be in serious danger. A cougar's strength and powerful jaws allow it to take down prey far larger than itself. And this monster appeared to be a huge male, based on the length of his body. His broad white chest stood out against the tawny color of his fur.

The animal's smoldering eyes fixed only on Samuel, perhaps because he was the first one to make eye contact with the cougar. Or perhaps because he was the larger of the two men. With an unnerving, burning gaze, the big cat stared directly at him with a look of pure contempt.

Despite his racing heart, Samuel glared back with a lethal fierceness. Cougar attacks on people were rare but usually deadly. He wouldn't let this be one of those times. When his aggressive glower didn't work, he yelled loudly, and waved his rifle and arms, hoping to scare the animal off.

Baldy did the same.

Unimpressed with their antics, the cougar snarled angrily. Obviously unhappy that they were disturbing his supper, the beast opened his jaws wide and growled.

Samuel knew he was about to fight for his life. Without flinching, he stood his ground. The muscles of his arms and back hardened. He would have to fight—man against the pure, savage wildness of the frontier.

"Save your shot in case I miss," he told Baldy.

With a sudden explosive burst of speed, the cougar ran toward them, a powerful and beautiful embodiment of nature's strength.

Samuel tucked his rifle butt into his shoulder, lined up his sights, and fired at the charging monster. The lead ball grazed the cougar's head and seemed to affect him no more than if a bee had bitten him.

In the next instant, the mountain lion bounded a dozen feet, and knocked him to the ground.

The impact and the animal's wild scent took Samuel's breath away, but he'd managed to hold on to his longrifle. Gripping the length of the rifle with both hands, he used the weapon to protect his face and head from the cougar's massive paws. After his hands took several bad scratches, he hit the beast violently with the butt of his rifle. Then he tried to repeatedly shove the rifle's end into the animal's neck.

The cougar soon had enough of that and the brute swatted the rifle out of Samuel's sweaty hands.

Out of the corner of his eye, he could see Baldy nearby trying to get a clear shot. But Samuel and the cougar were wrestling violently as he tried his best to strangle the animal. Samuel knew

Baldy wouldn't take the shot for fear of hitting him instead of the creature.

Rays of burning light darted from the cougar's bloodcurdling eyes as the beast growled and clawed at him, ripping Thomas' coat to shreds.

The cougar's neck was just too big, and Samuel gave up on trying to strangle it. He used his arms to protect his face, rolled to the side, and kicked at the animal with his boots. The second he had a chance, Samuel drew his big knife, the only weapon useful in fighting something at close quarters.

The cougar's mouth fastened onto his left forearm. Fortunately, he held the knife with his right hand. He felt the fangs begin to pierce his skin and plunged the knife at the cougar's right side. It felt like he hit bone. The fiend let go of his arm and Samuel withdrew his blade from the animal.

The cougar took a step back. The wound only made the beast limp a little.

He had to get to his feet. On his back, his neck was too vulnerable. He tried to stand but lost his footing on the slippery mud-covered earth.

The cougar's angry growls escalated as he wheeled about. Lunging from his powerful legs, the wild brute came at him again.

This time, Samuel aimed his blade for the fiend's eyes but hit his nose instead which only caused the animal to roar a cougar curse into Samuel's face.

The cougar stood over him a moment, gnashing his teeth, and rubbing his foreleg over his bloodied nose. Hissing with anger, the big cat's big head came up and he looked over at Baldy. The beast's eyes narrowed and his lips lifted, exposing vicious looking fangs. Now it wasn't just a huge beast. It was an angry huge beast.

It took a step toward Baldy.

When the cougar did, Samuel managed to scramble up and took a few steps back. He thought about sheathing the knife and drawing his pistol, but with only one shot, if he missed or just wounded the animal, he would be defenseless.

Baldy took aim. Only a shot between the eyes would stop an animal this powerful.

"You don't want him. He's old and tough." Samuel waved the

blade of his knife, brandishing it through the air to get the giant's attention.

The cougar changed direction and bounded toward him again.

"Watch out," Baldy cried.

Instinctively, Samuel shrank back. He took another step backward, tripped on Pate's body, and found himself toppling into the grave. As he hit the earth, he wondered if Pate's ghost had tripped him. He wouldn't put it past the foul man.

Instantly, the lion leapt upon him. The force knocked the breath out of him again. Samuel felt a claw rip into his ear and then hot blood run down the side of his neck.

The snarling cougar was a blur of violent motion, twisting and writhing above him. It was no wonder Baldy couldn't take a safe shot.

Growling, the animal seized Samuel's right thigh between his jaw. Fortunately, he'd worn his buckskin breeches, far tougher than cloth. But the cougar's razor-sharp teeth would soon penetrate the leather.

Samuel raised his upper body and with a desperate plunge, sunk the knife in the cougar's shoulder. This time the blade entered up to the hilt.

The cougar flinched and squealed in pain, but still the creature wouldn't let go of its hold on him.

Samuel heard buckskin rip. His leg was about to be lacerated.

Baldy leaned down and positioned his pistol close to the cougar's head and away from Samuel. The deafening report of the pistol, fired at close range, rang out.

The cougar's jaw released Samuel's thigh and the enormous creature collapsed on top of him. It was bad enough being in a grave, but the hundred and fifty pounds of a monstrous cougar on top of him felt crushing. Samuel summoned all his strength and pushed the cougar off of him while Baldy heaved it out by the tail.

Breathing hard, he sat up and rested his arms on the sides of the grave. "Good God."

"Sorry I took so long to shoot," Baldy said. "Only a head shot would kill him and I had to wait till you were clear of that beast. Didn't want the lead to pass through him and into you. And I thought you'd killed him with your knife. Twice!"

"The bloody brute wouldn't die!"

"When he got ahold of your thigh, I couldn't wait any longer. There are major veins in the leg and severing one can be lethal. Are you all right?" He offered Samuel a hand. "Let me look at you."

Gasping for breath, Samuel gripped Baldy's hand, stood on shaky legs, and stepped out of the grave. "I'm fine, but I never want to do that again." He brushed most of the muddy earth off, took a few steps, and collapsed to the ground again while he recovered his breath.

Baldy took one quick look at him and then tugged a folded white handkerchief from his waistcoat. "Here, hold this against your ear. Apply as much pressure as you can tolerate."

Samuel took the cloth, wiped some of the blood from his neck, and then winced as he pressed it to his ear. Abrasions covered his arms and his legs bled from several scratches. Otherwise, he felt all right, although he was still shaken.

"That cougar must have been drawn to the scent of Pate's blood. He'd claimed the body as his and went for a nap in the woods. When he saw us with it, he returned to defend his prize," Baldy said.

Samuel gazed over at the cougar. "Indeed. He fought well. I hated to kill such a magnificent animal, but it couldn't be helped."

Baldy nodded. "We had no choice. It was him or us. Since I only had one pistol shot, I had to wait until I had a shot that would kill him. Let me have a good look at you."

"That scream he let out at first was something," Samuel said. "Like a woman shrieking."

Baldy nodded. "Once heard it is never forgotten."

As he sat there, Baldy examined him from head to boot. "The top of your ear is sliced apart and will need quite a few stitches and you have a couple of deep scratches and gashes. The rest are just superficial. I'll doctor all of them after we get you washed up at home. Considering the viciousness of that attack, you more than held your own."

"I've had many a fight with a man, but they were all child's play compared to that."

Baldy whistled. "Best fight I ever saw."

"My clothes are ripped to shreds, and I'll owe Thomas a new

coat, but at least I'll get a nice furry rug out of this," Samuel said. "It can warm the floor of our room above the horse shed."

"While you were gone to the settlement, with Melly's supervision, we managed to make the barn loft a right comfy room for you and Louisa," Baldy said. "Melly even put a few candles up there."

Samuel smiled at the thought of having Louisa all to himself in candlelight. "It'll do until we get our house built."

Baldy nodded and then grinned. "With all of us helping, we'll have a new home built for you and Louisa before winter sets in real hard."

His breath recovered, Samuel stood up. "Well, we still have a man to bury. Can you say a few words over him?"

Baldy glanced down at the body. "He's like a thorn that still rankles, isn't he?"

"I think even God is finding him aggravating."

"Let me get my Bible," Baldy said. "I dropped it when that creature came at you."

"Reload first. You never know what else might come out of those woods."

Samuel hoped it wasn't Commander Long. He suspected, however, that the man was now racing back to Nacogdoches or even Louisiana.

CHAPTER 22

L OUISA WAS BESIDE HERSELF.
Icy fear gripped her heart. She'd returned to the main cabin cold to the bone, wet, and weary only to find her brother still missing. Adam was out there somewhere amid predators of all kinds, with another storm and night approaching. He was only eight-years-old for God's sake. She couldn't let anything happen to him. She'd promised herself that she would keep him safe.

"He must have run away!" Melly cried. "I've searched every-where!"

"So did Steve and I," Cornelius said.

"How long has he been gone?" she demanded.

"I don't know," Melly said.

"I fear he may be looking for me," Louisa said, pacing in front of the stone hearth.

"Where would he look?" Steve asked. "Your home?"

"No, I don't think so. We both almost died crossing that river. He's too smart to try that again on his own." She turned to Father Wyllie trying to keep panic from consuming her. "What are we going to do?"

"We're going to find him," he answered. His confident voice gave Louisa her first hint of hope.

"Please, you've just got to find him," she said. "He means so much to me."

"We will," Old Bill said. "I'll track him."

"Hurry!" Melly said. "Please hurry."

Thomas placed a reassuring hand on her shoulder. "I'll search too."

"We can search too," Cornelius said with a glance at Steve.

Steve nodded. "Of course."

"Let's leave now!" Louisa said, accepting a cup of hot coffee from Melly. Her hands shook so badly she had to hold the cup with both hands. "I'll just take one sip of this."

Father Wyllie shook his head. "No. Baldy said he feared you would take a chill. And from the way your hands are shaking, you may be. You must stay here and warm up. Take care of her, Melly. Get her warm and cleaned up. Cornelius and Steve, I want you to stay on guard outside on the porch. Keep your eyes open for any sign of the boy. If he returns, fire one rifle shot into the air."

"Yes, Sir," they said in unison and stepped outside.

With that, Father Wyllie, Thomas, and Old Bill turned toward the door.

Thomas reached for a package he'd set by the door and then handed it to Melly. "Samuel said to give this to you. But I think it's for Louisa."

"Melly peered inside. It's clean clothes for you, Louisa."

Samuel's thoughtfulness didn't surprise Louisa, but she was too worried right now to feel grateful.

Father Wyllie turned back to her as he donned his hat. "Louisa, has Adam ever run off or hidden himself before?"

She nodded. "Yes, several times when he feared our father's wrath. Sometimes he would hide for hours."

Father Wyllie's forehead creased. "Do you think he thought your father had come to take you away?"

"Since that's exactly what happened, it's likely," she answered. "He may have even seen Father and Commander Long. Baldy had sent him off to just play. He must have been outside playing when he saw them riding up!"

"And he would have feared that your father would take him too," Thomas said.

Louisa was on the verge of tears. "Oh dear God, he's out there hiding somewhere. Hiding from my father!"

Stephen, Old Bill, and Thomas ran toward the Grant's cabin.

Stephen couldn't imagine the fear that must have taken hold of the little boy at the sight of his father coming to take his sister away and maybe him too. The boy's first instinct must have been to run and hide.

After raising four sons and two daughters, Stephen could make himself think like a child when he had to. But his children had never lived in fear of a parent. A violent, mean-spirited parent who didn't know how to love. Since he'd been here, both Baldy and Melly had shown Adam nothing but love and kindness. No wonder Adam would hide to keep from being taken away.

"Does the cabin have two entrances and exits?" Old Bill asked.

"Yes," Stephen told him. "With all the people searching the cabin though, Adam's tracks are probably destroyed."

"But they all likely came and left out the front door. Let's see if there are any tracks leading away from the back door," Old Bill said. "He might have left from there to go play."

They raced through the cabin and out the back door to examine the ground. Standing beside each other, Old Bill and Stephen stepped carefully outside, and Thomas followed. Although the rain had washed most of the signs away, Stephen showed them where they'd found the tracks of the three horses earlier.

"Does the boy have shoes?" Old Bill asked.

"Not yet. Samuel has ordered some boots," Thomas said.

"There," Old Bill said and pointed. "A little bare footprint holding water. If it hadn't rained, we would never have seen it."

Stephen studied the ground for a few yards, pointing at two more little indentions in the mud. "Thomas, did any of you search the spring house?"

"I didn't. I don't know if Melly did."

They hurried toward the spring house until the tracks veered away and turned toward the shed that held Baldy's animal patients.

"The animal shed," Stephen said and ran toward it.

Stephen opened the Dutch door. Normally, the top door was left open, but both doors were closed. He gave his eyes a moment to adjust to the darkness while Old Bill and Thomas followed him in. They had built the small shed from scrap wood left over when they built their cabins and there was barely enough room for the three of them. All three of them had to bend over a bit to keep from hitting their heads on the low ceiling. The room held the scent of animals.

The light was dim, and he had to look twice before he spotted the boy, curled up with David the recuperating dog. They were both nestled deep in straw under an old blanket. Baldy or Melly must have given it to the dog to use while he recovered from the bad snake bite.

Adam was sound asleep with his little arm wrapped over the dog's back.

With his leg still healing, David didn't get up, but he flapped his long, hairy tail on the straw, no doubt hoping for a bone or other scrap. The dog was probably also enjoying the boy's company.

"Adam," Stephen said gently touching the child's small shoulder.

Startled, Adam jerked. "No! No! I won't go!" He squeezed his eyes shut and kicked at Stephen.

"Adam, it's me, Stephen. Thomas and Old Bill are here too."

Clearly still terrified, Adam sat up and started bawling. "I don't want to leave. I love Dr. Grant. Melly too. You too, Father Wyllie. Don't let my Pa take me away! I want to stay!" Deep sobs shook the boy's insides and he rocked back and forth in the hay.

Stephen sat down beside Adam and wrapped his arm around the boy's shoulders. "I promise, he will never take you away. You won't *ever* have to go," he told him. He would leave it to Louisa to break the news that their father was dead, but he could at least make that promise.

Adam's tear-filled eyes peered up into Stephen's face. "When you woke me, I thought you were my Pa." He seemed almost embarrassed.

"I know," Stephen said.

"I ran in here when I saw him and that Commander fellow ride up. I thought David would protect me like my old dog Buddy used to do."

Stephen nodded. "That was a right smart thing to do. Dogs are protective of those they love. And I can see that David has already grown to love you."

"We've been looking all over for you," Thomas said.

"What about Louisa? Is she gone? Did he get her?" Adam's lower lip quivered. "Did my father take her away? If he did, will you and Samuel go look for her and bring her back?"

"She's here, Adam. She's in the cabin. Come along now. She's worried about you," Stephen said.

Clearly relieved, Adam exhaled. "How'd you find me?" He patted the dog and then wiped at his tears and runny nose.

"Old Bill here and my father tracked you," Thomas said.

"Will you teach me to track?" Adam asked Old Bill.

"Sure will, if you promise to teach me something."

"What do you want me to teach you?" Adam asked as he stood up and cocked his head at Old Bill.

"Oh, it doesn't matter," Old Bill said. "Whatever it is you want to teach me."

CHAPTER 23

✒

"AND DO YOU, LOUISA PATE, take Samuel Wyllie, to be your lawfully wedded husband?" Baldy asked her, having already asked the same of Samuel.

She and Samuel stood facing Baldy in front of the candlelit mantel of the hearth in the main cabin. In his strong hands, the preacher held the Bible that had belonged to first her mother and then Adam's mother. Samuel had retrieved it early that morning from their old cabin so it could be used for the ceremony. Louisa knew her mother would be proud that she was marrying a man as fine and courageous as Samuel. And somehow, the Bible made it feel as though a part of her mother's spirit was there with them.

"To live together in holy marriage?" Baldy continued. "Will you love him, comfort him, honor, and keep him in sickness and in health, and forsaking all others, be faithful to him as long as you both shall live?"

Louisa nodded and said, with all the certainty she felt, "I do, happily and proudly." Samuel's love had already begun to heal all the raw places inside of her. He'd broken through all the hurt and obstacles and replaced them with happiness and hope.

"Then," he nodded at Louisa, "happily and proudly, in the name of God, I pronounce Samuel and Louisa to be husband and wife."

Samuel bent his head and kissed her, and the room erupted in cheers. Samuel's brothers clapped and stomped their boots too. Each of the brothers hugged her and called her sister as they congratulated them.

"Welcome to our family," Mr. Wyllie said with a hug. "That goes for you too, Adam."

"Thank you, Sir," Adam said.

"Adam, you'll have a home here with us for as long as you want," Baldy said.

"And Louisa too?"

Baldy chuckled. "Yes. And Louisa too. Although she'll likely want to live with her new husband when they get their cabin built."

"We may live in separate cabins," Father Wyllie said, "but our homeplace is home for all of us."

"Father Wyllie, you have always made us feel welcome," Louisa said. She couldn't ask for a better man to be her father-in-law and the grandfather of the children she and Samuel would have. She admired the man Stephen was, the father he was, and the friend he was to her and Adam.

She glanced down at her brother who stood next to her with his sleepy pup cuddled in his arms. Although he was still barefoot, Adam wore his new coat, shirt, and pants. He'd already gained some much-needed weight, and his cheeks were no longer sallow.

Early that morning, Samuel surprised Adam with the dog and her brother and the puppy became instant chums. Adam named him Caddo, after the Indian that had saved her. Although her brother never met the brave, the story of the Indian's help against Commander Long left him awe-struck.

They never told Adam that the brave had also killed their father. And her brother never asked how their father died.

She would always remember the Caddo brave, and she would be certain her children and grandchildren knew how much the Indian had helped her. She would only tell them that two bad men had captured her and not who they were. The important part of the story was that we never know whom God will send to help us, but with faith, help will always come.

Melly came over and hugged her tightly. "You are a beautiful bride, Louisa."

"Thank you, Melly," she said.

For the first time, Louisa felt beautiful and feminine. She'd worn the prettier of the two dresses Samuel kindly bought along with a lace shawl Melly loaned her. The high-waisted gown was yellow and trimmed with simple white lace around the scooped neck. The quality fabric draped loosely and would wash easily. Beneath the gown, she wore a chemise, borrowed from Melly until they could sew her one. And a delicate pearl drop necklace that Samuel put around her neck just before the ceremony hung from her neck. It was the first piece of jewelry she had ever owned, and she knew she would always treasure it.

Melly wanted to arrange her hair in what she said was the latest fashion in Louisiana, parted in the center with tight ringlets hanging over her ears and neck. But Louisa decided to just wear it long with her blonde tresses draping down her back in waves.

"Don't forget what I told you about your wedding night," Melly whispered. "There's nothing to be anxious about. You'll find being with your husband a great marvel."

She nodded and glanced over at—her husband—she couldn't believe she actually had a husband. He was a little worse for wear. But despite his stitched ear and numerous scratches, he was still the most handsome man she'd ever known. He wore what must be his Sunday best clothes. A dark brown, nicely-cut jacket covered a white hunting shirt, open at the neck, and he wore black trousers and black boots.

It frightened her even now to think she'd come so close to losing him. When they'd described the cougar attack, it horrified her. Even with Baldy there, if the beast's claw had sliced Samuel's neck instead of his ear, he could have bled to death.

With her father's death, instead of grief, relief filled her. It made her feel guilty that she should feel that way, but she couldn't deny it. A sense of independence and strength also came to her. And the despair that shadowed her life for so long abruptly vanished. She was free now. Free of the heartaches. Free to decide her own future. Samuel would be her partner in life, not her ruler.

What she noticed most of all was that she was free of pretending happiness. She was actually and truly happy. She no longer had to walk on eggshells and worry that she would do something to ignite her father's temper. Now, she could let that tense wall of self-preservation crumble. Louisa sensed though that a small part of her wasn't ready to let it totally fall away. Nevertheless, she trusted that Samuel's love would eventually heal her completely.

In him, there was no greed. No evil. No bitterness. Just love. Love was all she received from the man. She could probe deep within him, search every corner of his soul, and still, she would only find love. It was there from the very beginning, the first time he'd carried her from the river. It was there when he'd stood up to her father trying to protect her. It was there when he vowed to stop Long. It had been there in every kind gesture he'd made toward her and Adam.

Since it was so muddy and still overcast, they had decided to hold the celebration indoors. Old Bill started playing a harmonica and Cornelius opened a violin case, lifted out the instrument, and joined the trapper's melody. Both were quite good players and the cabin was soon filled with merry music. Earlier, they'd moved the beds against the walls to make room to dance. And when the musicians played the popular song, 'Hail Smiling Morn,' Samuel led her in a dance while Cornelius sang out the words. Old Bill and some of the others joined in on the chorus.

Hail smiling morn, smiling morn,
That tips the hills with gold, that tips the hills with gold,
Whose rosy fingers open the gates of day,
Open the gates, the gates of day,
Hail! Hail! Hail! Hail!

Who the gay face of nature doth unfold,
Who the gay face of nature doth unfold,
At whose bright presence darkness flies away, flies away,
Darkness flies away, darkness flies away,
At whose bright presence darkness flies away, flies away,
Hail! Hail! Hail! Hail!
Hail! Hail! Hail! Hail!

It was the perfect first dance for them. For the words, 'darkness flies away,' exactly described how she felt. The darkness in her life had flown away. And only the smiling light of happiness remained.

Melly soon started loading the long, beautifully set, candlelit table with all the dishes she had been working on all day. Father Wyllie and Old Bill carried in a large platter that held the turkey they'd cooked over a spit outdoors. Baldy opened a jug of whiskey and a bottle of wine and started pouring drinks for everyone.

Samuel grabbed hold of her hand and took her aside. "Happy?" he asked. He gave her a warm affectionate smile that made him even more handsome.

"You know I am. Not just for me, but for Adam too." She glanced over at her brother who sat on the floor, in front of the cheery hearth fire, playing with the pup. "Adam has never known happiness and comfort like this. For the first time I can remember, neither one of us is hungry or worried about our next meal. We're wearing clean clothes, thanks to you, and we're warm, and surrounded by our new family and friends. I feel incredibly blessed."

"Me too. I never expected to marry, much less marry a woman as fine as you, Louisa. Every time I gaze into your eyes, I am overcome by your goodness. By your inner strength. And by your beauty. I promise I'll move heaven and earth for you, just tell me where you want it."

She giggled and said, "Samuel, you make me so happy."

"I want to dress you in happiness and wrap you in a cloak of love. I'll spend the rest of my days striving to make you even happier than you are now."

"I am looking forward to each and every one of those days."

He smiled with joy and hugged her to him.

The feel of his strong arms wrapped around her and his fresh, clean scent reminded her of something she wanted to ask. "Samuel, I've been a bit worried about something. Is Adam going to spend the night here, in your bunk? I assume you'll be joining me in my bed at the apothecary." The thought sent shivers rippling down her back and a flush racing up her neck and onto her face, but she forced herself to continue. "We obviously can't have Adam there too. And it's an awfully little bed, but I suppose we could sleep on our sides. However, it's not terribly private since its part of Baldy's clinic."

"No and no," he chuckled, "although the idea of curling up next to you in a small bed actually holds a good deal of appeal. We will have a room all to ourselves."

"Where?"

"Above the horse shed. Remember the door at the top of the stairs? It leads to a rather large room. Melly and the others have prepared it for us. We're going to live there until we get our home built."

Louisa exhaled with relief. "Thank goodness!" She wasn't

exactly sure what went on in the marriage bed, but she had a good idea, and she knew it required privacy. A strange heat surged through her as she thought about loving Samuel up there. In fact, just standing close to him was making her pulse quicken and her lashes flap against her still flushed cheeks.

"I want to start building our home this week. Just as soon as my brothers and I can get the timber cut and hauled here. In the morning we can discuss the design and sketch it out. Tomorrow afternoon, I'll go to the trading post and order windows and boards for the floor to be shipped from Natchitoches. You can go with me and order whatever furniture you want and anything else you'll need. The owners of the trading posts accumulate orders for traveling furniture salesmen. It might take many months to get it here, but it will all arrive eventually."

She'd just learned something about her new husband. He certainly wasn't a procrastinator.

"Do you have the funds for all that?" she asked. "Windows and floorboards must be expensive. And I can't even imagine the cost of a cabin full of furniture."

"Yes, I have the funds. Remember, I've been saving for a long time. And once I deliver the cattle to the Arkansas Post, I'll have even more."

"I remember. I believe it was $14.00 a head profit."

"That's right." He frowned for a moment. "I was looking forward to that cattle drive, but not anymore. I'll hate being away from you."

"You'll be so busy the time will pass quickly. And while you're there at the Post, you can buy us pots, linens, other necessities, and…"

Samuel chuckled. "I can see I'll have to hire an extra hand just to drive our supply wagon."

She could hardly contain her excitement at the prospect of having a home and furniture of her own. "Will I have a kitchen like Melly has? And a hearth? Will we have a porch to sit on and watch the sun rise or set? Will Adam have his own room?"

Samuel smiled down at her. "You may have whatever you want. And Adam certainly can have a room with us if you want him to. But I've given it some thought, and I would advise against moving Adam in with us. I spoke to him and gave him a choice between staying with the Grants or moving in with us. He's content to stay with the Grants, especially now that he has a puppy to keep him company. He needs stability in his life, and the Grants are both growing terribly close to him."

"I think the feeling is mutual."

"I'm sure you don't know," Samuel said with a lowered voice, "but Baldy and Melly's only daughter died. Hopefully, since they have no other children of their own, they will come to think of Adam as a son. A son God sent to them."

She did know about their loss. Melly had told her that first day they were together. Louisa nodded, a mixture of sorrow and joy filling her. Sadness for the tragedy the Grants had experienced and joyfulness that Adam would have a home with Melly and Baldy. A home where he would be close to her and she would be able to see him every day. She glanced over at the Grants. They were both petting the puppy with Adam. As the two gazed down at Adam, the lines of sorrow etched on both their faces seemed to fade. "Adam loves both of them. And he's learning so much from the good doctor. Baldy makes him study something every day."

"They are good people," he said. "I'm so thankful the two of them decided to make the journey to the Province of Texas with us. My uncles and my sisters were all beside themselves with worry about my father coming here with four young sons. When Baldy and Melly, who were even then my father's closest friends, decided to go along to help protect and care for us, it thrilled everyone, including me."

"Someday, I hope to meet the rest of your family, especially your sisters."

"You will, and Martha and Polly are going to love you. You'll also meet Captain Sam and Catherine, William and Kelly, Bear and Artis, and Edward and Dora. And all their children and grandchildren. Not this Christmas, but next Christmas Father promises we will all return for a visit."

"That sounds so exciting. Adam and I have never really had a Christmas celebration."

"Aunt Catherine makes Christmas a merry, festive affair with lots of presents while Captain Sam makes sure we remember why we're celebrating."

"I can't wait! Speaking of presents, thank you for finding a pup for Adam. Sometimes you astound me with how kind you are. You are so good to both of us."

"I've only just begun to be good to you. Come with me." He took her hand and hurried toward the horse shed. Just outside of it he said, "Wait here and close your eyes."

She did as he told her and waited, wondering what on earth he was up to. Surely he didn't intend to go for a ride during their wedding celebration. Or maybe he had another pup hidden in the shed.

"Open your eyes," he said. She could hear the excitement in his voice.

She opened her eyes and right in front of her was the prettiest little filly she had ever seen. The horse's chestnut coat glowed, and her eyes looked kind. "Is she…"

"Yes, she's yours. All yours."

"Truly? Oh, Samuel. I didn't think I could ever be any happier. But you just keep making me happier." Her voice broke on the last few words.

"Get used to it, my darling."

She first let the filly smell her hand and then Louisa hugged the mare's neck. "I will cherish her. Thank you, Samuel."

"She's extremely well-trained already. You can ride her into the settlement tomorrow and you'll see."

"Oh Samuel, I can't wait," she said. "I'll have to think of a good name for her."

He led the mare back inside to her stall.

While he was gone, Louisa stood there shaking her head in amazement. Her life seemed so perfect now. A peace she'd never known filled her. And she would swear her heart was smiling. Would it always be like this?

Samuel hurried out of the shed and took her hand. "Let's join the others and toast to our future."

"I've never toasted before." There were so many things she'd never experienced before.

He gave her that roguish look that always made her heart flutter. "Tonight, you'll do something else you've never done before."

CHAPTER 24

ᘒ☙

WITH THEIR HEADS STILL ON their pillows, Samuel turned toward Louisa the next morning and smiled at her. He'd shaved just before the wedding, but now a dark shadow of whiskers covered his strong jaw giving him a rugged, roguish look.

Having slept better than she could ever remember, she sighed contentedly and marveled at how much her life had changed for the better.

"Good morning, Mrs. Wyllie." He breathed her name into the sensitive spot behind her ear.

"Good morning, husband."

"You know, love is a grand thing. But making love is a magnificent thing." He pressed his mouth to hers and kissed her.

She had to agree. She couldn't get enough of kissing his soft, warm lips and caressing his hard, muscular body. When he finished the long, deep kiss, she grinned happily and entwined a hand in his.

Samuel sat up and drew her head against his chest. "Love inspires musicians to compose and sing songs. Love moves the quills of poets, playwrights, and novelists. And love inspires the paint strokes of artists. And nearly everyone else hopes love will find them. But you and I, Mrs. Wyllie, we have found love."

"I feel as though I am feasting on love," she said.

Samuel moved a strand of hair out of her eyes. "We are so fortunate to find such pleasure in each other's arms. And I will never take that love for granted or the amazing feeling of joining with you."

"It's almost a sacred act of sharing. Like giving yourself wholly and completely to the other person. We became two bodies linked by one soul."

"I know what you mean," Samuel said. "It's an expression of absolute trust and devotion. A special gift."

"And sometimes we get a gift back. Sometimes life is created," she said. Even now she could have a life growing inside of her. The beautiful thought made her heart skip a beat. She looked forward to being a mother. A *good* mother.

He kissed her again. "Yes, though I hope not too soon. I want sons and daughters, but I want you all to myself for a while." He playfully nuzzled her neck.

It tickled and made her giggle. Life with Samuel was going to be so much fun. And passionate. And loving. Last night, a surging tide of passion raced through both of them the first time they joined. They'd made love at a gallop, a thrilling ride that she would remember forever. Later, the second time, it was more of a slow, gentle lope, touchingly tender and unhurried. They'd learned, and explored, and caressed. But most of all, they'd loved.

Both times, though, it was utterly exquisite.

Her body still craved him, but it was time to begin preparations for their married life together. She'd come awake earlier than Samuel and lain there thinking about the layout of the home they would soon build. Samuel had said they would work on the plans for the cabin this morning and she wanted to be ready with her ideas. She would like the view from their kitchen window to be of the sunrise so she could see morning's dawn spread across the sky as she began her day. And she wanted the view from their front porch to be of the sunset so they could sit together at the end of each day and watch the sun go down. There was something so special about the last light at day's end. As though God saved the best for last.

Below them, she heard the high-pitched nickering and neighing of hungry horses that seemed to be saying, get in here and feed me now! Steve, who usually fed and cared for the horses, must be approaching. He would give them some grain and then let them out to graze.

"We need to dress and then, after breakfast, sketch out the house plans," Samuel said, sitting up.

"I already have some ideas," she said.

"Good. I'll get ready first and meet you outside. We can sketch it out in the mud with a stick first. Then we have a desk with paper and quill in the upstairs loft."

"I'll join you as soon as I wash up a bit and fix my hair."

"Here's how I fix my hair." Smiling broadly, he combed his fingers through his hair and plopped his hat on his head.

Louisa shook her head. "Men have it so much easier than women."

⁊☙

Samuel and Louisa glanced up from their house plans when they heard the drumming of hoofbeats approaching at a rapid gait. Samuel stood and glanced down over the loft rail.

Everyone, including Old Bill, had been having a second cup of coffee at the table. At the sound of the riders drawing near they all stood at once and went to the front portals.

"What is it?" he asked them. "Who's coming?"

His father and Baldy peered out the two left front portholes. His brothers jostled for positions in front of the other slits on the right side of the front wall.

"Spanish soldiers, riding at a gallop," his father said. "About twenty of them. Arm yourselves!"

Samuel's heart raced. Spanish soldiers often meant trouble for settlers. In San Antonio de Bexar, Arredondo's forces arrested three hundred of the townspeople suspected of being revolutionaries. They were crowded into a single adobe building on a hot August night and then shot the next morning without trial.

He hurried down the stairs, followed by Louisa. He peered out the portal where his father stood.

The soldiers rode two across until they neared the cabin. Then, with a hand signal from their leader, the troops spread out and formed a semi-circle in front of the cabin before bringing their horses to an abrupt halt.

Samuel swiftly loaded his flintlock weapons with fresh powder. Then he loaded a pistol for Louisa and gave it to her. "If the need arises, use it."

She nodded. "Take care, Samuel. I can't lose you."

"Let me talk to them," Old Bill said. "I speak Spanish."

Father nodded. "We'll be right behind you."

Old Bill stepped out onto the porch, and the rest of the men stood behind him, just inside the door.

The trapper cheerfully greeted the soldiers in Spanish, but their demeanor remained unfriendly.

The heavily armed soldiers held bayonet-tipped rifles. The bayonets glinted menacingly in the bright early morning sun. The primary benefit of bayonets was often its impact on morale, a clear signal to a foe of a willingness to kill brutally at close quarters. Long swords also hung from their sides. They wore fine blue uniforms trimmed with red. White shoulder straps crisscrossed the front of their uniforms, and large feathered hats sat upon their heads.

Despite their splendid uniforms, they all appeared to be men who had not stepped across the line of gallantry. He suspected some wouldn't even know the meaning of the word much less live by it. They were just about the roughest looking bunch of men he'd seen anywhere. They looked more like bandits than soldiers. He wouldn't doubt that many of them chose service in the Spanish army over imprisonment or were poorly trained peasants. Even so, they presented two extremely real threats—weapons and numbers.

Their leader spoke up and Old Bill translated, speaking loudly so they could all hear.

"We have just come from Nacogdoches. We are here investigating the treachery of one Herman H. Long, Commander of insurgent forces at Camp Freeman at Nacogdoches. He is an agent of political discord and illicit trade. His insurgents in Nacogdoches just suffered a disastrous defeat and we, of course, were victorious. And now, we want to bring Commander Long to justice as well."

Justice! Samuel sneered. Their idea of justice was a firing squad without benefit of a trial.

Old Bill translated and then paused to allow the leader to speak again.

"Commander Long was seen recently in this settlement, often in the company of a man named Pate. They were both committing treason by seeking to recruit followers to their cause of revolution."

Samuel glanced at Louisa whose face had gone pale.

He wondered who in the settlement had informed on Pate and Long to the Spanish Royalist officials. Likely it was someone they bribed to be their informant.

After Old Bill translated, the Spaniard asked, "Where is Commander Long?" The man's horse stomped a front hoof into the mud.

"I have never spoken to or seen Commander Long," Old Bill said, "although I have heard of his harassment of this family."

Clever answer, Samuel thought. It was the truth, after all.

The Spaniard, however, seemed displeased with that answer. His face grew angry and his voice grew hotter as he said, "We are told Mr. Pate's daughter and son live here and he may be here as well."

Old Bill said, "Mr. Pate was killed by a Caddo Indian brave two days ago. We can show you his fresh grave. It is about an hour away. His daughter and young son are here. But they had nothing to do with their father's activities. They have been working here at the Wyllie ranchero for some time."

"I will see to Señorita Pate later."

Old Bill said, "She's a Señora now. Mrs. Wyllie."

The leader shrugged dismissively after Old Bill translated. "We are also here to question a man by the name of Dr. Grant. We have been informed that he is preaching the protestant faith on Spanish soil. Again, that is treasonous, and it is also sacrilegious."

Behind him, Samuel heard Melly gasp.

"Dear God," she said.

Baldy's eyes grew wide. "I feared this day might come."

"You're not going out there," Father said. "Without a second thought, they will put you up against a wall and shoot you."

"Stephen, I won't put you and all of your sons at risk to protect me," Baldy declared. "I'm going out to face them and defend my faith. I won't be the first Christian or the last to be persecuted for my beliefs. Or to die for them."

"No!" Melly cried, and grabbed ahold of Baldy's arms. "No! You can't go out there. I won't let you!"

Adam frowned and grabbed ahold of Baldy's pant leg. "I won't let you either," he said. "I need you to teach me. We all need you to take care of us."

"That's right," Louisa said. "There must be another way."

"Steve, keep Baldy inside this house. That's an order. You three with me," his father said and then stepped outside, leaving the door open. He took a bold stance, feet wide apart and hands resting on his pistols.

Samuel, Thomas, and Cornelius, all holding longrifles, stood slightly behind their father.

"Old Bill, please translate for me," his father said.

Old Bill nodded.

"My name is Stephen Wyllie. These are my sons."

"I am Capitán Tomás Fernández of the Royalist Army of the Kingdom of Spain."

The Spaniard's eyes reminded Samuel of a rattlesnake already coiled up and ready to fight.

Could his father induce the Capitán to uncoil?

"Sir, my sons and I and those we associate with did not support Commander Long. In fact, we told him several times that his plans were foolish and treasonous to the United States. As far as Dr. Grant is concerned, he is a family friend and makes his living as the settlement's physician, not as a preacher. He does not hold church services or conduct any type of religious ceremonies."

That was true. Baldy looked upon the whole earth as his alter and all living things as his flock—man and animal. But would funerals and weddings be considered religious ceremonies? Samuel wondered.

Father continued, "You have my word that although he is indeed a man of God, he does not preach against the Catholic faith or attempt to convert those who practice Catholicism. Unlike your Spanish government, Americans believe in the right to religious freedom for all faiths and the right to practice that faith as we see fit."

"I'm going out there before he gets himself shot," Samuel heard Baldy say behind him.

Samuel glanced back. Steve, although only sixteen was already taller than Baldy. He stood in front of the doctor with his hand on Baldy's chest. Samuel could tell that Baldy was not getting past him. Melly, her eyes wide and frightened, was also helping to hold her husband back. Samuel's gaze returned to his father.

His father took a step forward. "Dr. Grant is one of the many settlers who have come here to settle this land. Spain has encouraged our settlement here so that we might fight the Indians for you and bring prosperity to this remote area between our two countries. We have done both of those things. Last week, we killed Indians right where your horses stand now. And behind us, our cattle graze over many acres. These are cattle that could feed Spanish soldiers as well as American soldiers."

"Spain claims all the land to the Red River," the Capitán shot back as soon as Old Bill translated.

"And the United States bought land stretching from here to Canada from France," his father countered. "Can we not agree that boundary lines should be left to the politicians?"

"Politicians like Commander Long you mean?"

"Certainly not. He is a filibuster acting on his own. He does not represent me, my sons, or Dr. Grant. Our politicians are in Washington."

Capitán Fernández's lips pursed and his dark eyes bored into Samuel's father. "Mr. Long is but one of a succession of filibusters and zealots. These men—Mexican revolutionists, American land seekers, and democratic crusaders—are disloyal to Spain and the Royalist Army. They continue to challenge us because they have the clandestine support of men like you, Mr. Wyllie."

"Respectfully, Capitán, I am a mere cattleman. I raised cattle in Kentucky before coming here, and my sons and I are raising beef here to sell to the forts in Arkansas and the Missouri Territory. If the Spanish army is interested, we could also sell to them as well. You'll find no better beef in the Province."

"Mr. Wyllie, I am not here to discuss your filthy cows," Fernández said with a sneer. "I am here to arrest enemies of Spain."

After he heard the translation, Father took another step forward. "Spain has no enemies here. Dr. Grant and I have no interest in politics. We would be happy to treat you and your men to a beefsteak. And should any of your men require medical attention, I am certain Dr. Grant would be happy to treat them. His clinic and apothecary are right over there," he said and pointed. "But first, we must have your assurance that Dr. Grant will be allowed to continue practicing medicine and may live here peacefully with his wife."

Fernández cocked his head to the side and narrowed his eyes.

"As a matter of fact, one of my men has a hand that's being poisoned by a thorn."

"Do I have your word that Dr. Grant will be left alone to practice medicine here at the settlement?"

The leader shrugged. "Oh, but of course. We have no desire to rob this community of a good doctor."

Something in the man's voice and the glint of his eyes made Samuel suspicious.

His father said, "One moment." Then he stepped back inside and Old Bill, Samuel, Thomas, and Cornelius followed.

"It's up to you, Baldy," his father said quietly. "We can fight them now if you don't want to take the risk of going out there to treat the soldier. You know we will all stand with you."

"I'm with you," Old Bill said.

Father nodded thanks at the trapper. "That means we have seven men. Melly and Louisa can reload for us."

"You know you can count on my rifle," Samuel said. "And my pistols. If it comes to a fight, though, since there are twenty of them, this will likely end in a fight to the knife."

"And the knife to the hilt," his father agreed with a fierce look on his face.

Samuel knew what that meant. It would be a bloody, vicious battle. Only by fighting savagely would they stand a chance against brutal, experienced soldiers. He snatched a hatchet off the wall and stuck it in his belt.

His brothers did the same.

Adam, who was holding Louisa's hand, said, "I'll fight too."

"Make that seven men and one feisty little boy," Samuel said. But he hated the thought of the child getting mixed up in this battle.

With a glance at Adam, Louisa shook her head. "No. Fighting them will be far too dangerous. We must find a way to reason with them. They are after Long and my father. Not us. Perhaps if we treat them with kindness, they will see that we are no threat to them or to Spain."

"I agree," Baldy said. "But for a different reason. If we fight them, that's an even bigger risk than my going out there to face their accusations. One or more of you could be killed. We are outnumbered more than two to one."

"I don't trust Capitán Fernández," Samuel said. "Or his men."

"Neither do I," his father said. "I fear it's a ruse. The capture of a protestant preacher would be a feather in his cap. A way to impress his superiors. But it's Baldy's decision."

Baldy exhaled deeply. "I can't risk Adam's, Louisa's, or your sons' lives. I have to do this."

Melly collapsed into a chair and sobbed into her hands.

Louisa gripped Melly's shoulders sympathetically. "Don't worry. We'll stop this...somehow."

Baldy went to his wife, took her face in his hands, and kissed her. "I love you. Remember, whatever happens, I will *always* love you."

Baldy strode to the door. Holding his head high, he stepped onto the porch. "I'm Dr. Grant. Which soldier's hand needs attention?"

Before Samuel could stop her, Louisa also slipped out and spoke up saying, "I'm Louisa, Dr. Grant's assistant. I will help him treat the soldier. Then we will prepare a nice meal for all of your men."

Samuel stood beside her as she smiled at the Capitán. He understood what she was doing. But Fernández wasn't interested in a peaceful solution to this situation.

"Mrs. Grant is a fabulous cook," she said. "Why don't you all rest under that oak while we prepare a feast for you. My husband's brothers can slaughter a cow and you can enjoy the best beef you've ever tasted."

As Old Bill quickly translated, the Spaniard smiled back at Louisa admiringly. The hungry look in his eyes wasn't for food.

She turned her head toward Samuel. "Will you and your brothers go slaughter a cow? Melly, can start cooking vegetables. I'll be in to help shortly. I'm going to go assist Dr. Grant now."

Naïve and guileless, Louisa didn't understand that she was playing with fire. She marched off without waiting for Baldy toward the apothecary and clinic.

Stunned, Samuel called after her. "Louisa, come back here!"

"Louisa, go back inside. I don't require help," Baldy called to her, but she ignored him too and kept walking.

Samuel hurdled off the porch to run after her.

"Seize the doctor and the girl!" the Capitán shouted.

Louisa gasped and turned around. Her eyes widened with astonishment and then panic.

Baldy grabbed Samuel's arm and whispered, "Stay here. You will only inflame the situation if you fight them and maybe get Louisa shot. Come for us later. Timing is everything."

The soldiers seized first Louisa and then Baldy.

They tied Louisa's hands in front of her and tossed her onto a spare horse. Her luminous eyes were wide with fear as she glanced back at Samuel.

"Capitán, don't do this. Louisa and Dr. Grant have done nothing wrong," Samuel pleaded. "Louisa is my wife now. Leave them both and I will go with you to help you find Commander Long. He is the only one who is guilty of anything."

The shrewd Capitán narrowed his eyes and asked, "Of what is he guilty?"

"Mostly of being an idiot," Samuel said, his patience growing threadbare.

The Capitán cackled and then his dark eyes turned cold. He nodded toward Baldy.

The two soldiers that held Baldy shoved him to the ground and kicked him.

"No!" he heard Melly cry out from the porch. "Please, stop!"

"Stop!" Samuel yelled as he attempted to pull one of the soldiers away from Baldy. Two more soldiers yanked him off to the side. He gritted his teeth as he struggled to suppress his mounting anger. "For Christ's sake, he's a man of God!"

The soldiers ignored their pleas and continued to boot Baldy viciously while Old Bill rapidly translated.

Stoically, Baldy accepted the blows from their boots without even grunting. The doctor wouldn't give them the satisfaction, Samuel thought.

"Capitán," his father shouted out, his voice full of authority and simmering anger. "The Almighty's angels will shower retribution upon you for this injustice. We are not peasants to be bullied."

A glimmer of unease shown on the Capitán's face. "Suficiente."

Enough. Enough to cause Samuel's thoughts to race dangerously. This man would pay for his actions. Not now, but soon. Very soon.

The soldiers picked Baldy up, hauled him toward another spare horse, and tied him on the mount.

Samuel's heart wrestled with his mind as he tried to figure out what to do. Baldy was right, to resist now would only light the fuse of this powder keg. And if it blew, they might all die in the process. He could risk his own life, but not Louisa's or his family. But the sight of those soldiers touching his wife and beating Baldy made every muscle on his body clench with anger and rage surge through his veins. He was seconds away from doing something, anything, to stop this madness when he felt his father and brothers dragging him back inside.

"No!" Samuel shouted as the soldiers turned to leave.

His father slammed the door and threw down the bar.

CHAPTER 25

ॐ

"DAMN THAT DOUBLE-CROSSING, TREACHEROUS MAN to hell!" Samuel shouted. "They're riding away with Louisa and Baldy." Anger boiled inside him, but he couldn't afford to be rash. He had to keep his head if he was going to successfully rescue the two.

"Oh, God, please help us," Melly cried.

"They took my sister! And Dr. Grant too," Adam wailed and started sobbing in earnest.

"I'm going to follow them," Samuel said. "When they stop for the night, I'll sneak in while they're sleeping and get them out."

"That's too risky for you," Thomas said.

"And it may be too late for Louisa," Melly said. "By then, that captain may have…" she hesitated. "You know."

Samuel seethed with anger, clenching his teeth. "No!" he shot back. "That's *not* going to happen."

"Let me follow them," Old Bill offered. "They don't see me as a threat. Only as a trapper and translator, which they value. Samuel can follow behind me at a distance."

"I don't expect you to get tangled up in this," Samuel said. "This isn't your problem."

"Friends don't desert friends in time of need," Old Bill said with a look of implacable determination. "So, I'm here for the duration of this trouble."

"Our deepest thanks, Old Bill," his father said. "In case the worst happens, and we pray it doesn't, do you have family somewhere that we should know about?"

At his father's invitation, Old Bill had made himself a comfortable campsite behind the main cabin. But other than the stories the trapper had told, they knew little about this uncommon man.

"No, the great trapper in the sky took my family many years ago. You're the closest I've come to having a family in many years."

Stephen nodded. "When this is over, you're welcome to share our hearth fire for as long as you like or just when your travels take you this way."

Old Bill's eyes filled with gratitude. "I thank you for that."

His father turned to Samuel. "You should both go. When you determine where they've camped, Old Bill can come back for the rest of us. We'll follow a mile or so behind the two of you."

"I agree," Thomas said. "But if they somehow discover they've been followed, Samuel and Old Bill will need our help sooner rather than later. A mile is too far away."

"You're right, Thomas. You two go first," his father told Samuel and Old Bill. "Thomas, Cornelius, Steve, and I will follow a short distance behind you."

Samuel nodded. "It won't be hard for us to follow the tracks of twenty horses."

"Melly, I must ask you to stay here with Adam," Samuel told her.

"Stay here in our cabin, it's more secure. And be sure you have enough water so you won't have to go outside for anything," his father told her. "If we're not back by tonight, and Indians come to steal your and Louisa's horse, just let them take them."

"All right. I'll get some food sacked up for you to take with you. No telling how long you'll be gone." She turned toward the kitchen. "Come on, Adam, take that bucket and we'll get fresh water from the spring house."

"After you get the food together," Samuel told Melly, "teach Adam how to reload your weapons."

"I already know how," Adam said and swiped at the tears on his face. He snatched up the water bucket and headed to the door. "Louisa taught me." He paused in front of Samuel and stared up at him. Despite his youth, the boy put steel in his gaze. "I'm countin' on you to bring my sister back. And Dr. Grant too."

"I will," Samuel told him. He would rescue his wife if he had to die to do it. Married only a day and they were already facing the troubles Wetmore had talked about. Well, the Capitán wouldn't get far with his wife. And he would pay for mistreating the good doctor.

Samuel, his father, and brothers all quickly gathered up additional weapons that hung on both sides of their front door, leaving Melly and Adam with two loaded rifles and two pistols. Beneath the mounted weapons, two side tables held large containers of powder and shot. A half-dozen extra powder horns, crafted from cow or buffalo horn, hung on a peg. Horn was naturally waterproof and already hollow inside, so it made a perfect vessel for frontiersmen, who were often outdoors or traversing rivers, to carry their powder. They each grabbed an extra powder horn and filled it. They also stuffed pouches with ball and buckshot. Next, they snatched up the bedrolls stored beneath their beds and filled their canteens with the fresh water that Melly and Adam just carried in.

After clipping a knife inside his boot, and giving Adam a quick hug, Samuel bolted for his horse.

Old Bill's horse was already saddled since he had expected to be leaving right after that now cold cup of coffee.

As soon as Samson was saddled, he sheathed his longrifle. There was no inaccuracy in the rifle, and she always shot true as long as he could hold his hands steady. He prayed he would be able to. Normally, that wasn't a problem for him. But now, both Louisa's and Baldy's lives were at stake.

As he led Samson out of the barn, his father and brothers hurried toward the horse shed.

His father handed him a saddle pack. "Baldy's pistols are in there. They're loaded. We'll stay about a quarter mile back. If you need us, send Old Bill back to me."

"I will," Samuel said and tied the pack to Samson's saddle.

His father's square jaw tensed visibly. "Be careful, son. I don't say it often, but I love you and I'm proud of you."

"I feel the same." He hugged his father and then glanced toward his brothers. "All of you *youngsters* be careful as well." Losing any one of them would be like losing a part of him. "I'll need *all* of you to get our new home built before winter."

"Don't worry," Thomas said. "We'll all be there."

"You're gonna need me to be sure you don't cut logs as crooked as the Red," Cornelius said.

Steve grinned and flexed his arm, "And me to do your heavy lifting."

Samuel swallowed the lump clogging his throat. Moments later, he leaned forward on Samson, urging the horse to a fast trot. Old Bill followed.

Once they neared the soldiers, they would fall back into the cover of the woods. The soldiers weren't heading into the settlement, as Samuel had suspected. Instead, they were headed south to Trammel's Trace—the road to Nacogdoches. Trammel's Trace from Pecan Point crossed the Sulphur River. The road eventually met the Camino Real de los Tejas, the road to San Antonio, commonly known as the King's Highway.

Samuel slowed his horse as soon as he caught the first glimpse of the Spanish soldiers, riding two across in the distance. Motioning to Old Bill to follow him, he ducked Samson into a stand of pines. The soft needles would soften the sound of their horses' hooves and the thick pine boughs would provide cover. He suspected the captain would have some of his men keeping an eye on the trail behind them to determine if they were being followed. If he and Old Bill were spotted, it would almost certainly mean the soldiers would be ordered to fire upon them. With twenty rifle shots to two, their odds would be exceedingly poor. And he didn't want his father and brothers to come racing to their rescue only to face certain peril.

For now, all he could do was stay well-hidden and follow them as he waited for the right moment to take action. Baldy was right, timing was everything. Especially with an enemy.

Louisa and Baldy rode directly behind Capitán Fernández. Louisa's yellow hair glistened in the sun, and she held her head high. He couldn't see Baldy's face, but he suspected the doctor's normally kind eyes would be sending daggers into Fernández's back.

They trailed behind the troops all day, their journey becoming more hazardous every mile they advanced. Fugitives, highwaymen, cowardly deserters, ruffians, and Indians roamed the desolate land. The soldiers stopped only twice to water their horses and relieve themselves.

At dusk, when they reached a nicely flowing creek, Fernández finally held an arm up and yelled, "Alto." The Capitán dismounted and then, smiling warmly, helped Louisa down.

The sight of another man touching his wife made Samuel's blood boil. The man would pay dearly.

As soon as she was on her feet, Louisa yanked her hands out of the Capitán's and snarled something at him.

"I'll be back shortly," Old Bill whispered.

"Hurry," Samuel hissed through gritted teeth.

In the twilight, he watched the soldiers make camp, taking careful note of their layout. Several soldiers quickly threw up a large tent that a pack mule had carried on its back. The soldiers made Baldy and Louisa sit near the tent. Baldy moved slower than normal but otherwise appeared to be all right.

Samuel carefully surveyed the woods surrounding the tent. A dense stand of pines grew to the rear of the tent.

The soldiers soon had their horses watered, unsaddled, and tied. Wood was gathered and two cook fires started. After spreading their bedrolls out, several men began cooking while others passed out jugs of whiskey as night fell.

Louisa's beautiful face glowed in the light of the fire's flames, but she appeared nervous, her eyes darting between one soldier or another. When the Capitán passed by her, Louisa opened her mouth to speak to him but then stopped. She must have realized that without a translator it was pointless for her or Baldy to try to argue with Fernández.

As the soldiers settled in, many of them walked past Louisa and glanced down at her with lecherous eyes. Undoubtedly, they were hoping their leader would toss Louisa to them when he finished with her. Samuel's jaw clenched.

It wasn't long before his father rode up beside him. The others stayed back a bit further.

"What's your plan?" his father asked, speaking softly.

"They cut the ropes off of both Louisa and Baldy and gave them water. So their hands and feet are free. Fernández just went inside the tent. The reprobate probably wants to freshen up before he brings Louisa in there. The men seem to be relaxed. Most of them have set aside their rifles and removed the straps that hold their pistols and swords. They are already passing around jugs of whiskey."

"All that is favorable for us."

"I think the six of us need to encircle the camp. We'll wait until Fernández takes Louisa inside his tent. I'm certain that's his intention. When he shoves her inside, we'll fire our rifles at his men, and then attack, pistols drawn, with the force of the Almighty. Then I'll kill Fernández."

His father sighed. "It's a good plan. But…"

"What is it?" Samuel asked. "Are you worried about bringing the force of Spain's army down on us if we kill Spanish soldiers? I thought about that. But I think Long was right about one thing. The Spaniards are losing control of Texas. With high-handed acts like this—taking a man's wife and arresting an innocent preacher—their days in Texas are numbered. And now, with their empire facing Napoleon and uprisings in Mexico, they are withdrawing troops back to Mexico and Spain."

"All true, but if Mexico takes control of Texas, I'm not sure that we'll be any better off. It may be even worse. But that's another battle to fight another day. Let's just get on with this battle. I don't think we have any choice in the matter, we have to fight them."

Samuel nodded. "Agreed."

"Give me Baldy's weapons. I'll toss them to him. Then I'll use my second pistol to take a shot at Fernández in case you miss the Capitán."

"I won't miss."

"Good. Let's tell the others what your plan is."

They both slowly and quietly turned their mounts around and rode back to the others. In a hushed voice, Samuel explained the situation and his plan. Lastly, he said, "Be sure none of your shots are aimed toward the tent. I don't want Louisa or Baldy accidentally shot in all the commotion."

Everyone nodded their understanding.

"Our rifle shots should take down six," Samuel said. "That leaves fourteen men. When Fernández comes running out, I'll kill him. So we'll have thirteen others to kill or take prisoner with our pistols. Old Bill, shout the Spanish word for surrender as we ride in with our pistols. Hopefully, some or all will simply drop their weapons and hold up their hands and we'll be able to spare their lives."

"Don't count on that," Old Bill said.

"If they don't yield, we'll have to shoot them. Don't hesitate. They brought this on themselves by abducting my wife and our friend," Samuel said.

"Indeed. We are well within our rights to fight them," Steve said with the confidence of youth.

Samuel worried the most about his youngest brother. To his knowledge, Steve had never been in a serious fight before, much less one of this magnitude. "Steve, be careful. Don't take any chances. Promise me you won't!"

His brother, soon to be a man, drew himself up with determination and dignity. "I promise. And you watch your back."

"Yup, Samuel," Cornelius said. "Your hide's pretty darn thick, but lead balls won't glance off you just 'cause you're the oldest."

"Let's quit jawing and get on with this business," Thomas said.

"I'd recommend buck and ball," their father said. Buck and ball combined a rifle ball with three or six buckshot.

Samuel drew out his rifle and loaded it with loose buck. The others did the same. It would make their rifle shots even more lethal and give them a greater chance of hitting their targets.

"All right," he said. "I'll take a position behind and slightly to the right of the tent, so I can shoot Fernández when he comes out without risking shooting Louisa. The rest of you quietly spread out around the camp, staying far enough away so we don't alert them. Dismount so your rifle shot will be more accurate."

"How will we know when to fire our rifles?" Cornelius asked.

"Keep your eyes on the tent. Fernández is not going to let a beautiful woman sit outside his tent without violating her. When you see him dragging Louisa into his tent," Samuel said, "count to ten, then fire your rifle at the soldier closest to you. Then mount up and charge in on your horse, pistols drawn."

"The sound of six Red River rifles firing at once should startle the beans out of them," Cornelius said.

Samuel gave him a half grin. "Let's hope so."

With a faith that allowed him to not fear dying and a conviction that they would succeed, Samuel wound Samson through the woods toward the Capitán's tent.

CHAPTER 26

ैक

L OUISA COULD NOT BELIEVE SHE was once again paying for her father's sins. It was his greed and arrogance that
brought these Spanish soldiers down upon her. And his fool-
ishness. Her father had unwisely allied himself to a man these
soldiers considered a traitor. Even in death, her father caused her
pain. Yet again, she would be subjected to the whims of a man.

She had thought she was helping the situation by offering to
help the doctor and extending an invitation to the Capitán and his
men to stay for a good meal. She believed it would be a peaceful
solution. But Fernández repaid her kindness with treachery. And
from the looks the Capitán gave her, the worst was yet to come.

And poor Dr. Grant. A man of God whose only crime was to
try to cure body and soul of his fellow man. Baldy was the kind-
est, most helpful man she'd ever met. The doctor had become so
important to her brother. Adam nearly worshipped the man. Her
brother was probably crying right now. And poor Melly must be
sick with worry.

"Are you all right?" she whispered to Baldy. The doctor had
taken quite a beating.

"Some bruised ribs and a few painful spots," he said, keeping
his voice low. "Nothing that won't heal."

She had no doubt Samuel and the others would come for her
and Baldy. How many would die in the battle with these soldiers? They would be hopelessly outnumbered. She glanced over
at the sharp bayonet on the rifle of the soldier closest to her. The
deadly point sparkled in the firelight. Her breath froze, and a chill
made her shiver despite the fire's warmth. Would that blade draw

the blood of one of the family she'd grown to love? A whimper escaped her throat at the thought.

Baldy leaned closer and whispered, "Don't look at that. Look to the heavens. With God's help, it won't matter that Samuel and the others are outnumbered. You must believe that God will guide their every shot. Have no doubt. He will see justice done. He always does."

Louisa gave him a single nod. She reached deep inside and drew on her recently reawakened faith reminding herself that with God all things are possible. "I will believe," she whispered back.

"Good, that's all God asks of you."

"What should I do if that Capitán drags me into that tent before they get here?"

"They're already here."

Her eyes widened. "Are you sure?"

"Yes, but they're staying well outside the circle of the encampment. I caught a flash of Samson's red coat in the pines. Then he disappeared. They've probably been following us all day."

"Why doesn't the Capitán seem worried and watchful? None of his men are paying attention to the forest."

"Arrogance and perhaps stupidity. They think their numbers will protect them."

Louisa had to agree. Fernández didn't seem like a particularly smart man. His family must have purchased his post, or he'd known someone he could bribe to secure him the rank of Capitán. Or perhaps he'd found favor with his superiors by bringing them captured women like her.

"When the fighting starts, Louisa, lay down on the ground, wherever you are, here or in the tent. And stay down until the fighting is over."

"You too. Please don't let them hurt you. Adam has grown to love you. He needs you."

Baldy appeared thoughtful. "You know, I need him too. So does Melly."

The soldier closest to them glanced over at her. He was the same one that had been leering at Louisa every now and then. This time his eyes did not focus on Louisa's face.

Embarrassment and anger made her face feel flushed. She narrowed her eyes and glared at the man.

Baldy leaned even closer to her. "I have a knife in my boot meant for that one."

"He deserves punishment for what he did to you." The soldier was one of the two men who beat Baldy so viciously.

The soldier glared back at them. "Silencio!" Then the man took a long swig of the whiskey jug and handed it to another soldier.

They spoke no more and listened to the Capitán puttering around in his tent behind them. An oil lamp cast a sliver of light between the tent's front flaps.

A soldier soon brought a platter into the tent that held a jug and two pewter goblets. He left the platter and then returned to the other soldiers.

Louisa glanced behind her and could see the Capitán's shadow against the tent's canvas as he poured the jug.

Another man soon brought in a platter heaped with food.

She heard Baldy's stomach growl. They hadn't eaten all day, but Louisa's stomach only knotted further. Every minute brought her closer to being violated. A silent scream filled her throat.

The thought of a man other than Samuel touching her filled her with disgust. For Adam's sake, she had never fought back against her father's punishments, but now she intended to defend herself. Her fists clenched as she resolved to fight Fernández with all she had and then some.

She steeled herself for the inevitable. As soon as the Capitán finished his meal, the vile man would likely come for her. Her skin crawled at the thought of his touch. It made her wish Samuel would hurry and that he and the others could rescue them before the Capitán attacked her.

Just as quickly, she dreaded the violence and danger that was to come.

Samuel must be waiting for the right moment. Waiting until Fernández and the others were drunk. She'd noticed that all the soldiers were sharing whiskey jugs. The more they drank, the louder their conversations in Spanish became. They seemed to be amused and kept pointing and laughing at her. One even made a lewd gesture that made a hot flush of anger race up her neck as she quickly glanced away.

While two soldiers prepared food, three others produced harmonicas and started playing. She guessed the tunes were bawdy because the men laughed and guffawed at certain parts as they all sang along.

Soon, the shirtless Capitán stepped out. For a few minutes, he just stood there, singing and laughing along with his men.

When the song ended, the Capitán stepped toward Louisa and grasped her wrist. His men all whooped uproariously. Some even clapped and shouted something as the musicians started to play another song.

"Muy bella dama, eh?" Fernández told his men, holding her hand up and gesturing to her breasts. Then to her horror, Fernández yanked out his knife and sliced through the fabric of her dress between her breasts.

The soldiers all erupted in vulgar, boorish noises as they ogled her.

She glanced down at her exposed chest. To her horror, most of her breasts were revealed to the leering men. With her free hand, Louisa hastily pushed the fabric back and held it in place.

"You bloody bastard," Baldy spat and stood, fists clenched.

Eyes bulging and jaw clenched, Fernández shoved his blade against Baldy's throat drawing a line of bright red beads of blood.

"Don't!" Louisa cried and tried to push the man away from Baldy.

The Capitán ignored her and spoke to Baldy through clenched teeth. "Tu eres el bastardo!" He narrowed his dark eyes and pointed to the ground with his knife.

Relief filled her when Baldy wisely sank down to the ground.

Fernández took a step toward the tent entrance and tugged her along.

She resisted, but his tight grip on her wrist forced her to follow him. As they passed next to Baldy, she glanced down and saw the doctor slip his hand inside his boot.

Fernández dragged her the remaining distance to the tent and shoved her inside.

The moment he released her, Louisa whirled around and faced him.

He pointed first at her and then back at himself. "Eres mío!"

"No!" The force of her voice surprised even her. "I am not yours!"

"Sí!" he said with a lascivious smile.

She didn't have to protest further. The air erupted with an explosion that sounded like the blast of multiple black-powder rifles being fired at once. The blast shook her and startled, she instinctively dropped to the ground. But her heart lifted with hope.

Samuel was here!

Outside the tent, pandemonium broke out and men started screaming and shouting in Spanish. The Capitán grabbed his rifle and charged out the tent.

She heard Old Bill shout in a strong voice, "Rendición!"

"No! Muerte a ellos!" Fernández shouted.

What did that mean? she wondered. Did Old Bill call in Spanish for them to surrender? Whatever the trapper said, the Capitán had refused. Did he order his men to kill?

As soon as he'd killed their leader, and fired his two pistols, Samuel raced Samson around the campsite to the other side of the woods and sought out Steve. His brother, pinned down by rifle fire, crouched down behind a tree. Samuel tied Samson and plopped down next to him.

Beads of sweat covered Steve's forehead and upper lip. Breathing hard, his brother cleared his throat but didn't speak.

"Are you all right?" Samuel asked him.

Steve nodded. "Yes...I did just as you said. Shot one of the soldiers with my rifle. I didn't think I could, but I did. But then, when I saw how many of them there were and they started firing back, I spooked. I never fired my pistols. I came back here."

"You did well, Steve. I'd much rather have you alive and well than your pistols fired."

"The five remaining soldiers have each found cover behind their wagons," he said, still breathing rapidly. "They're keeping us all pinned down. We don't have a shot without exposing ourselves."

After their initial shots, the others had been forced to withdraw to the cover of the forest to reload.

Samuel reloaded his own weapons and then studied the situation. He had to agree. They couldn't get a good shot at the Spanish soldiers.

"What are we going to do?" Steve asked.

"I'll have to sneak around and come up behind them," Samuel said.

"Where's Father? Maybe he's already doing that."

Samuel searched the tree line hoping to spot their father or one of the others. Hidden in the woods, he didn't see any of them.

Louisa heard more shots. Then another and another in rapid succession. Shots rang out over and over. Men and horses shrieked again and again. She squeezed her eyes shut, but it didn't keep out the appalling sound of men dying or the acrid scent of black powder.

What was happening? She doubted that she could withstand the agony of not knowing much longer. Suspense squeezed her heart and stole her breath. She wanted to help. Still flat on the ground, she glanced around the tent frantically looking for a weapon but found none.

Suddenly, to the left of the tent, she heard arrows, one after another, hum through the air. Their ghastly, swift tune ended in thwacks as arrows collided with flesh.

Indians!

Men were dying out there.

Were any of them Samuel? Or his brothers? Father Wyllie? Baldy?

God, save them. Save them all!

CHAPTER 27

❦

"**L**OOK!" STEVE SAID AND POINTED.
Samuel couldn't believe his eyes.

Kuukuh appeared from nowhere. From the woods and perched on his magnificent horse next to the tent, the brave fired one arrow after another into the five remaining Spanish soldiers. Like lightning, the shafts slashed through the air with blinding speed raining a quick death upon the soldiers. Not one of the brave's arrows, fired in astoundingly rapid succession, missed their target. With arrows through the middle of their chests, the soldiers all fell dead before they could react.

In another moment, the campsite grew quiet. It was over.

"Stay here," he told Steve. Samuel leaped upon Samson and cautiously approached the campsite. With Samson's reins in his mouth, he held both pistols at the ready. Guiding Samson with his knees, he took it slow, watchfully moving toward the tent. None of the soldiers moaned or moved. They all appeared to be dead.

"Louisa!" he shouted when he neared the tent. He sheathed one of his pistols and then bounded from the saddle, praying she was unharmed.

She flung open the tent flaps. "Samuel!"

In a blink of tears, they were in each other's arms fiercely hugging each other. "Oh, my darling, are you all right? Did he hurt you?"

"No, you came just in time!" she said, with tears of joy spilling from her beautiful eyes. "Oh, Samuel, I was so frightened for you."

"Frightened for me?"

"Yes. I wasn't frightened for me. I knew you would come for me. I never doubted that."

Relief washed over him as he kissed her tears away and then hugged her tightly to his chest before releasing her.

She held a blanket over her shoulders as she glanced around and took in the carnage. "Lord, have mercy." Then her eyes widened at the sight of a soldier nearby with a knife in his chest.

Samuel recognized it as Baldy's knife. Beside the dead man lay the Capitán with a sizeable hole in his head from Samuel's longrifle.

"Don't look. It's over. You're safe," he said.

Louisa's eyes darted around them. "What about Father Wyllie and your brothers? Where's Baldy?"

"I only caught a glimpse of some of them in the woods," he said. Worried himself, he looked for them but only saw his father standing next to Baldy. Then Thomas emerged on his horse and Cornelius stepped out leading his mount. He didn't see Steve, but since they'd just been together, he wasn't too worried about him.

"The Capitán cut my gown with his knife," she cried. "In front of all his men."

"I saw, from the woods." When Samuel saw the man point his knife at Louisa and then rip her clothing apart in front of the other soldiers, he'd nearly jumped out, guns blazing. If he had, it would have ruined their plan, and he'd be a dead man. So he'd clenched his jaw so tight it still hurt.

"It made me doubly glad to shoot him," Samuel hissed. He tied the blanket in front of her and then hugged her until they heard the sound of the others coming toward them. Remembering Kuukuh, he turned around and searched for the brave.

"Where did the arrows come from?" Louisa asked him. "I was terrified that you were fighting Indians too."

"Kuukuh."

"Kuukuh came to help? Where is he?" she asked. "We should thank him for helping you."

"I don't know," he said. "He was there next to the tent one minute and then gone the next. He killed five of the soldiers." He searched the woods again for some sign of the brave.

Kuukuh was nowhere to be seen.

His father, leading George, and Baldy both strode over to them.

Their expressions were grim.

"Is everyone okay?" Louisa asked them.

Baldy glanced over his shoulder. Thomas, Cornelius, and Steve were coming toward them. The doctor waited until the three were there before he spoke. "With extreme regret, I must say Old Bill is dead. He took a shot to the heart. There was nothing I could do." He shook his head and sighed. "A waste of a fine man."

Shock and grief ripped through Samuel like a knife. "This wasn't even his fight."

"You're wrong, son," his father said. "On the frontier, we all fight for one another. Any one of us would have fought for him if he needed our help."

"Kuukuh came to help us too," Samuel said.

"I saw Kuukuh kneel next to Old Bill," Thomas said. "He put his hand on Old Bill's wound and then the Indian touched his temples with Old Bill's blood. Strangest thing I ever saw. Then he mounted that big white horse of his and rode off without a word."

Their father nodded. "It's an ancient ritual to pay homage to a man or animal who nobly sacrifices his life."

"He's some sort of uncanny spirit," Cornelius said.

Samuel thought Cornelius might be right. The brave's timely help saved not only Louisa but also the rest of them.

Steve remained quiet, and his face wore a detached look. Understandably, his brother seemed to be shaken by all the killing. Samuel suspected Old Bill's death hit Steve particularly hard.

"Listen, all of you," his father said. "As we have learned the hard way, we do not live in a place where the rule of law prevails. Here we must, as we have today, defend ourselves and those we love against evil men who would do us harm. Their motives may be greed, power, lust, or just plain meanness. Here on the frontier, though it is a hard thing for a man to do, killing is sometimes the only path to justice or safety. You did well."

His eyes downcast, Steve still appeared to be numb with shock.

"Steve, I am particularly proud of you," his father said.

Steve glanced up. Those few words made his eyes brighten.

Their father continued addressing his youngest son. "You became a man today, Steve. This was your first real battle. But you must realize, there will be others and you should steel yourself to that hard fact."

"Indeed," Baldy said. "Earthy battles are a part of life. And they come in many forms. But when they come, always remember to look up before you fight them."

Samuel knew that Steve would certainly face future trying battles, but he'd seen his brother become a man right before his eyes. For a man must recognize a time to fight with courage and a time when danger tells you to wait. With this threat, he'd had to learn that lesson himself. Although Steve's journey into manhood had only just begun, Samuel vowed to stand beside his brother, and Thomas and Cornelius, whenever he could in the years to come.

"I want to thank each of you for rescuing us," Baldy said. "I'm certain execution awaited me in Nacogdoches. Someone in the settlement must have informed them of my humble efforts to spread God's word and love.

"We can't stay here any longer," his father said. "I don't want any of us found with twenty dead members of the Spanish army."

"I'm going to check these soldiers to be sure they are all actually dead. I won't leave a wounded man to suffer," Baldy said and, with pistol drawn to be sure he wasn't shot, he began going from one body to another.

"With the arrows in some of them, perhaps their deaths will be blamed on the Indians," Cornelius suggested.

"I don't like the idea of Indians being blamed for this," Samuel said.

"You're right," their father said. "It might cause the Spanish army to retaliate and cause an Indian war."

"I'm going to remove Kuukuh's arrows and keep them," Samuel said.

He found the five men Kuukuh had killed, the last soldiers to die here. While he collected the arrows, he remembered that Indian arrows and butchery had killed his friend Billy. He'd flung those arrows away in anger. But now, he stared down at the arrows with gratitude. An Indian's arrows had helped to save his wife and perhaps the life of one of his family. Kuukuh's arrows would serve as a powerful reminder that he should always judge the worth of a man not by his skin but by his heart.

"Steve, knock out those fires," his father ordered. "Thomas and Cornelius, wrap Old Bill's body in a blanket and then load and tie him on his horse."

"Be certain you've reloaded," Samuel said. "Then let's get out of here straightaway. At night, we're likely to meet more enemies than friends on the road going home."

"Just let me get my knife," Baldy said.

CHAPTER 28

WITH A GLOWING FULL MOON and a starlit sky, they were able to ride all night toward home. Since their horses were weary from being ridden all day, they could only proceed at a slow walk and had to stop often to rest and water their mounts. And their efforts to hide their tracks also slowed them. Several times, they rode well up the path of streams hiding their horses' hoof prints beneath flowing water. And twice, they separated into small groups and rode off in different directions before rejoining down the well-traveled trail.

None of them spoke because they wanted to be able to hear any threat. The hours of silence certainly made the trip seem slower and the darkness more foreboding.

Still wearing the blanket on her shoulders, Louisa rode in front of Samuel on Samson. When she'd shivered with chill and fatigue, he'd given her his coat too. With her head resting against his chest, she was able to find a few hours' sleep. But her sleep was fitful, and she moaned aloud every so often. It would take her a while to fully recover from this ordeal and the other terrors that had filled her life.

Baldy rode with Stephen on George. The powerful stallion was big enough to carry them both for a good part of the night. Then Baldy switched over to Thomas' horse and finally to Steve's for the last leg of their journey home. They hadn't taken one of the soldiers' horses for him to ride because they didn't want to be found with a horse that belonged to the Spanish army. That could get a man hanged.

Thankfully, they'd met no enemies on the ride home. Although, a pack of wolves trailed them for a while. And Samuel heard the growl of a cougar once. The sound sent a shiver racing down his spine and made goosebumps on his still scratched arms.

By the time they finally reached the cabins, Samuel's eyes burned from sleeplessness and his muscles screamed from the long hours in the saddle. When they stopped, Louisa woke and she smiled up at him. The warmth of her smile was enough to refresh him.

Wisps of sweet-smelling smoke from oak wood burning in the hearth welcomed them home. And the dim lights inside told them that Melly was still awake. She'd probably paced and prayed all night long.

Samuel and the others stayed on their weary horses while Baldy dashed inside briefly to let Melly know he was home and safe but that Old Bill had died in the battle and needed burying. Melly stayed behind with Adam who was sound asleep. As soon as Adam woke up, she would let him know that his sister was safe.

Baldy remounted and then by moonlight, they searched for a site to bury Old Bill. They selected a nice high spot, about a hundred yards from the cabins, surrounded by towering pines and oaks.

Since they were all exhausted, the brothers each took a turn digging the earth. While each one dug, the others stood by wearily, listening to the occasional hoot of an owl and every now and then, the yap of coyotes in the distance.

When they were ready to lower the body into the grave, Samuel knelt down next to Old Bill. He unwrapped the blanket that covered the body and removed the bear claw necklace that Old Bill wore. Blood from the wound in the trapper's heart stained a few of the claws. Samuel would keep the necklace and let the stains remind him of a man who gave his life's blood to help new friends.

Respectfully, he rewrapped the blanket. "Farewell friend. And thank you."

"Goodbye, Old Bill," Steve said.

Although Samuel had only known the trapper a short time, the man felt like family to him and reminded Samuel a great deal of his Uncle Bear. Perhaps, in the end, Old Bill was family. For he'd fought for them as though he was. Not only had he saved Louisa from the three Osage braves that pursued her, but he'd also killed three Spanish soldiers before dying himself. He'd literally given his heart for his friends.

Baldy began saying a few words, but given the late hour and their exhaustion, he soon concluded, "May the good Lord welcome Old Bill into the lush forests of heaven. And may those in heaven enjoy his company and stories as much as we did."

Samuel and his brothers were learning that the Texas frontier was a rock hard place. A place where good collided with evil. Sometimes, it was man against nature. At times, it was man against beast. And far too often, it was man against his fellow man. There was no rule of law—only the rule of honor, virtue, and righteousness. And since there were no sheriffs, no courts, or even a recognized government, those values were defended with the rifle. And reliable pistols and sharp knives.

Even more than good weapons, the defense of the frontier required a man's courage. It wasn't just pluck or guts, it was bravery that never faltered. The kind of valor that stood by family and friends no matter what. The same courage Old Bill had shown.

The same courage his father had always shown.

Samuel hoped that in the battle with the Spaniards he'd shown that same kind of courage.

The others left for the cabins to get a couple of hours sleep. Only he and Louisa remained by the grave, standing beneath the moon-splashed trees. He waited, sensing that she had something to say before they could leave.

"I feel so bad," Louisa said as she gazed down at the fresh mound of earth and rock. "Did I cause this by going out and letting the soldiers see me? Did I do something to cause them to abduct me?"

"No, Louisa, of course not. I'm sure someone told the captain that Pate had a beautiful daughter. In another minute or two, he would probably have demanded that you come out. Then I would have had to challenge him because I wouldn't have let you go out there."

"I don't doubt that. And you would have been killed if you did so."

"That would have been likely," he agreed. "I only stopped myself when I did because Baldy whispered to me that I should keep my head and come after you later."

"Old Bill's death wasn't my fault then?" She sounded guilt-stricken and nibbled on her bottom lip. "I keep thinking that if I hadn't invited them to a nice meal, none of this would have happened."

"No, that wasn't what caused this. Long's blatant calls for rebellion raised someone's ire and that someone notified the Spanish authorities. Either that or someone in the settlement is an informant for the Spanish. And, don't forget, they were after Baldy too. The Spanish have little mercy for Protestant preachers. Even if they hadn't taken you, we would have had to go after Baldy to rescue him."

"It's so wrong to want to kill a man because he doesn't worship God as you do."

"It is. It's a terrible injustice. Unfortunately, there's a lot of unfairness and ignorance in this world."

Her eyes glistened under the light of the stars. "Sometimes too just being a woman is unfair. Women are harassed, dominated, and denied rights simply because of our sex."

"Only some men do that to women. The same ones who treat slaves, Indians, and others with little forbearance or even cruelty. Other more honorable men, respect and value women, treat them as equals. As I do you. And as my father did with my mother. As Baldy does with Melly."

She nodded, but her voice broke as she said, "You're right, Samuel. You've always only treated me with kindness and respect. And your father is as different from my father as day is from night. My father was…"

Abruptly, tears began to stream down her face. Samuel could almost see the bitterness within the teardrops. He was actually glad to see them for they were tears she'd been holding inside for far too long. He took her in his arms. As his brave little wife sobbed against his chest, she released the resentment, the anger, the hurt that festered inside her.

"My father is dead," she choked out, as though the realization finally hit her. "I feel guilty because I'm…"

"Glad?" he asked.

She nodded. "I shouldn't be, but I am. I'm relieved."

"He's the one who made you feel that way, Louisa. Not you."

Great, racking sobs poured out of her. She tried to speak, but couldn't. He felt her shudder against his chest. He let her cry a while and then gave her his handkerchief. He would wait until she could speak of the inner torment that was gnawing at her.

She blew her nose and then said, "When I told Adam he was dead, he said we wouldn't have to be afraid anymore. That's how I felt too. I don't fear my father now. Nevertheless, and I know it doesn't make sense, the memories of him still scare me sometimes. They cause me to want to put my guard up again." She glanced down at the grave. "Old Bill told me that if your heart and mind are free, your spirit is free. My heart is free now, but my mind still tries to run from those memories."

"Your father may be gone, but his hurt remains. You have to accept that you and Adam were abused. And you were betrayed. The important thing is despite what your life was like, you now have a better life. You must have the courage to learn from the past. But you can't dwell there, or your hurt will become hate. Focus on the present. Someday, you may even be able to forgive."

"I hope so. Despite everything, the man was my father." She started crying again in earnest as she let loose denied grief. When her tears slowed, she said, "I truly wish I could remember something about him with fondness. But I just can't."

He reached for her hand. "The memories are still too fresh. But, Louisa, I promise we'll make new, good memories to replace the bad ones."

She sniffled and then smiled a little. "Yes, we will! I know we will!"

"Remember, you have a new father now. And my brothers are now your brothers. You can let that guard down because we will be your guard. A safeguard that will always protect you and Adam with our lives. You also have Baldy and Melly. You and Adam have a big, new family."

"A peaceful, normal, happy family," she said. Her face brightened, but moisture still made her eyes sparkle brilliantly. "It's what I've always wanted. What I always dreamed of having. You and your family brought my life out of unhappiness and into happiness. Until I met you, I had almost given up hope of ever being happy...of ever finding my own life."

He lifted her chin with his finger and gazed intently at her. "A person should never give up, especially on hope."

She swallowed. "Especially on love."

He nodded. "You're so right. If there's anything worth hoping for, it's love."

"It takes courage to hope for love."

"And it takes courage to embrace love," he said.

"Once found, though, nothing can give you more courage than love. Or more happiness. Now I don't have to pretend to be happy. I truly am happy. That's why I wanted to marry you, Samuel. I know I'll be content and happy as long as I'm married to you."

He slipped her gold curls back behind her ears and wiped a finger across her tear-streaked face. "You know, I've always thought you were exceedingly smart. Now, you've gone and proved it. And we've only been married a day. Or is it two days?"

"It doesn't matter as long as it's the beginning of forever."

EPILOGUE

❧

"LET'S GO HOME," SAMUEL SAID.

Louisa nodded and they turned away from Old Bill's grave. In the distance, he could hear the Red River flowing strongly once more after the heavy rains. The soothing sound somehow allowed his inner thoughts to be heard more clearly.

As they strolled, the moon and the night's stars disappeared from the heavens and the light of a new dawn spread across the land before him, bringing the world to life.

Bringing the West to life.

A wilderness dawning.

Like a summons, the dawn's light called to them. He and Louisa both stopped and turned toward the eastern horizon with quiet expectancy. Like a messenger from God, the dawn offered them the gift of a future. Not just for that one day. For the rest of their lives.

Samuel knew the gift required courage to see it fully.

And now, he understood the future also required love for it to be all it could be.

Hand in hand, they both turned and strode toward their temporary home. It was merely a small, cozy room above a horse shed. But one day, they would have a spacious home to share with a family.

Counting the Indian thieves, Billy and his wife, Mr. Pate, and Old Bill, they'd buried seven people. Samuel sincerely hoped they would be the last for a long while. He had things he wanted to do—a house to build, cattle to buy and sell, and most importantly, a wife to love.

And maybe someday, a herd of children to raise.

Samuel glanced down at his new wife. A wife made even more beautiful by her smile and the soft glow of the rising sun—a 'smiling morn,' as the song said.

A feathery breeze, as though made from the waft of angels' wings, lifted strands of her golden hair. Louisa was a true treasure. Yes, she was a woman, but that didn't make her weak. It made her strong. Yes, she'd led a life of neglect and abuse, but that didn't defeat her. It inspired her determination to make a better life for her brother and herself. And yes, in a place like the West, she might face hardships or setbacks in the future. But with her courage, she would not falter.

He had so much faith in her.

And in them.

"Tomorrow morning you can ride your wedding present into the settlement to order what we need for our home. Then we can ride out and check on our cattle," he said. He emphasized the word our.

Her face filled with gratitude. "I thought of the perfect name for the mare."

"What's that?"

"Texana."

Together, here in this beautiful new land, they could dream big and never give up as they shared a future as wide open at the Texas prairies.

Texas stretched far and wide, but not just east, west, north, and south.

It reached up and into their full hearts.

THE END

FACTS AND INSPIRATIONS BEHIND THE STORY

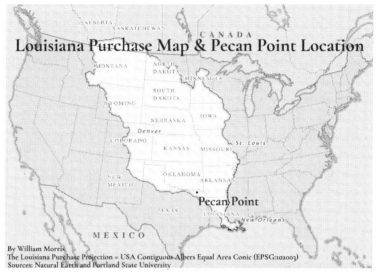

Louisiana Purchase Map & Pecan Point Location

By William Morris
The Louisiana Purchase Projection = USA Contiguous Albers Equal Area Conic (EPSG:102003)
Sources: Natural Earth and Portland State University

BELIEVE IT OR NOT, IN south-central Texas, about 400 miles from the setting of this story, my husband and I live on a cattle ranch in a small country community called *Caddo*. With a population of somewhere around one-hundred, we have only a few homes and ranches and no stores, but the area has been called Caddo for as long as anyone can remember. I like to believe Caddo was named by my husband's ancestors who settled in the area in the 1850s. Perhaps they had known a Caddo Indian, maybe one or several, that had helped them when they were living in North Texas. And, when they moved here, maybe they wanted to honor them by naming their community Caddo.

The origin of the community's name is only a theory or possibly my active imagination. The truth is lost to time, but that theory is what inspired the character of Kuukuh, the Caddo brave. It also inspired me to write Louisa's promise to herself to be sure future generations knew of the help the brave had been to her.

The Caddo Nation is now a confederacy of several southeast-ern Native American tribes. Their ancestors historically inhabited much of what is now east Texas, Louisiana, and portions of southern Arkansas and Oklahoma. They called the confederacy the Tejas...yup, Texas is a Caddoian word. It means "those who are friends." In the 17th century, the Spanish knew the western-most Caddo peoples as "the great kingdom of Tejas" and the name lived on to become the name of the 28th state of the United States—Texas.

Historical geography is an important element of this book. Just as the French had disputed Spain's claim to the Red River area, so also did American settlers, who rightly believed the land to be part of the Louisiana Purchase, as shown on the map at the beginning of this section.

According to the Texas State Historical Association (https://tshaonline.org/handbook/online/articles/hcr05),American hunters and traders were active in the north Texas area by 1815. By 1818, permanent settlement was underway at Burkham's Settlement, Jonesboro, and Pecan Point when the real-life Stephen Wiley (my husband's 4th great grandfather) and his sons joined other actual settlers like Claiborne Wright, George and Alex Wetmore, and William Mabbitt, all of which inspired minor characters in this book.

By the mid-1820s, these first-wave settlers began to move out onto the Texas prairies. When the United States government refused to issue land titles to these settlers, many of them turned first to the Mexican government and then to Benjamin Milam in an attempt to obtain valid land titles. These efforts were unsuccessful for the real-life Stephen Wiley and his sons.

Louisa was my husband's third great-grandmother, but her father's character is entirely fictitious. Unfortunately, we know nothing about him. But the concept of arranged marriages on the frontier is based on fact. Frontier marriages were often practical unions characterized by strong patriarchal authority, and marriage was frequently viewed as a business transaction. Parents could control their children's ability to marry before the age of twenty-one. And until the first half of the 20th century, arranged marriages were common in migrant families.

Herman H. Long's character was, in part, inspired by James Long (ca. 1793–1822) who led an actual filibustering campaign, the Long Expedition, an early attempt by Anglo-Americans to wrest Texas from Spain. On his return to Nacogdoches, Long found the settlement nearly deserted. In his absence, the Spanish soundly defeated his forces, killed his brother, and captured most of the settlers. Long's wife, child, and a few other survivors fled to Louisiana. Long was forced to cross back over the Sabine into safety and rejoin his family. His efforts to take Texas from Spain met with one setback after another. Long remained convinced, however, that the paradise that was Texas was there for the taking. (https://tshaonline.org/handbook/online/articles/qyl01)

The character of Old Bill Williams was based on the trader William Williams (1747 – 1849) a noted mountain man and frontiersman who was fluent in several Native American languages. He served as an interpreter for the government and guided several expeditions to the West. The real Williams died at age 62 when ambushed and killed by Ute warriors.

The song sung and played at the tavern by Claude O'Neil, a man who was too fond of the bottle, was composed by my husband Larry and is about a long lost relative.

To learn more about the old song sung by Cornelius, 'Hail Smiling Morn,' go to https://en.wikipedia.org/wiki/Hail_Smiling_Morn. You can also listen to several versions on YouTube. The song was composed in 1810 by Reginald Spofforth, an English musician and composer.

This is the second time a cougar has appeared in one of my books. Also called a mountain lion, panther, catamount, or puma, they were a definite threat to early settlers and lived throughout Texas. In 2018, a 200-pound cougar was killed just west of Fort Worth. And just recently, Colorado wildlife officials were forced to trap and kill five mountain lions after aggressive behavior by the predators. Unfortunately, capture is not always an option. Capturing a wild cougar that is accustomed to traveling great distances and then confining it to a small enclosure is not a humane option.

According to Texas State Historical Association Trammel's Trace, the road the Spanish soldiers took was an early road into Texas that ran from the Red River to Nacogdoches where it met the Camino Real de los Tejas, the Old San Antonio Road. The trace had two points of origin—one at Pecan Point, Texas, and another at Fulton, Arkansas, where it connected with the Southwest Trail from Memphis. The trail began as a series of Caddo trails which were first used by Anglos in the early 1800s for illegally smuggling horses from the Red River prairies in Spanish Texas. Trammel's Trace was the first road to Texas from the northern boundary with the United States and was used for migration from Arkansas, Missouri, and Tennessee before Texas became a republic.

Regarding the Spanish Army soldiers, when war broke out with France in 1808, the Spanish Army was ill-prepared and deeply unpopular with citizens in Spain, Mexico, and the Province of Texas. Leading generals were assassinated, and the army proved incompetent to handle command-and-control. The officer corps was selected primarily on the basis of royal patronage, rather than merit and junior officers often received no formal military training. Some officers from peasant families deserted and went over to the insurgents, both in Mexico and Spain, and later in Texas.

In Baldy's apothecary, he kept a supply of malaria pills containing quinine. The pills were not actually available for another fourteen years. In 1832, John S. Sappington developed a pill, using quinine taken from cinchona bark, to cure a variety of fevers, such as scarlet fever, yellow fever, and influenza. He sold "Dr. Sappington's Anti-Fever Pills" across Missouri. Demand became so great that within three years Dr. Sappington founded a new company known as Sappington and Sons to sell his anti-fever pills nationwide. The anti-fever pills were popular in Arkansas, Louisiana, Mississippi, and Texas. Although Dr. John Sappington's successful creation of an anti-malaria pill did not eradicate malaria, it did help save thousands, if not hundreds of thousands, of lives. The cause of malaria, mosquito bites, would not be discovered until 1897. Quinine is still one of the most effective antimalarial drugs available today.

In this book, the Wyllie's best bull was a Longhorn. According to the Texas State Historical Association, the Longhorn is a hybrid breed resulting from a mix of Spanish stock and English Longhorn Hereford cattle that American frontiersmen brought to Texas from southern and midwestern states in the 1820s and 1830s. Spanish cattle had roamed free in Texas probably before the eighteenth century. We have no idea if the real-life Samuel Wiley bred one of his family's bulls to a Spanish cow and created a Longhorn, but I like to think that he did.

Finally, I chose the title RED RIVER RIFLES for this book,

because Americans should appreciate and remember the impor-
tance of guns in our history. The Revolutionary War, the War of
1812, and the settlement of the West were influenced by the gun
in ways most people don't recognize. Then, as now, real freedom
must be won and defended. That does not mean that as a nation
we can afford to be careless or irresponsible with our guns or gun
laws. As with all our other freedoms, we must guard the freedom
to own guns with wisdom.

D EAR READER
A million thanks for reading my novel! If you are interested in reading my other novels, they are listed on the next
pages. The first series—AMERICAN WILDERNESS SERIES
ROMANCES—are novels about each of the Wyllie brothers,
starting with Samuel's father, Stephen. And the second series—
WILDERNESS HEARTS—are stories about their grown
children, though the Wyllie brothers are also major characters in
each of the second series books.

I hope you will long remember **RED RIVER RIFLES**, Wilderness Dawning Series – Book One. If you enjoyed reading this
story, I would be honored if you would share your thoughts with
your friends. Regardless of whether you are reading print or elec-
tronic versions, I'd be truly grateful if you posted a short review
on the book's page on Amazon.com. Reviews are so helpful to
both authors and readers. It helps the works of authors to stay vis-
ible on Amazon and it helps readers find books they will enjoy.

If you would like to contact me directly, please send me a note
through my website *www.dorothywiley.com* under the 'Contact' tab.
Under that same tab, you can also sign up for my Newsletter to
receive special offers for free or discounted books.

To receive notifications of my new releases follow me on Amazon at *www.amazon.com/author/dorothywiley*.

Thanks for your support and your review!

Blessings,

TITLES BY DOROTHY WILEY

All of Wiley's novels, in her closely related series, are available in both print and eBook, and many in audiobooks at www.amazon.com/author/dorothywiley

AMERICAN WILDERNESS SERIES
Book One — the story of Stephen and Jane:
WILDERNESS TRAIL OF LOVE

Book Two — the story of Sam and Catherine:
NEW FRONTIER OF LOVE

Book Three — the story of William and Kelly:
WHISPERING HILLS OF LOVE

Book Four — the story of Bear and Artis:
FRONTIER HIGHLANDER VOW OF LOVE

Book Five — A story of Sam and Catherine and the entire family:
FRONTIER GIFT OF LOVE

Book Six — the story of Edward and Dora:
THE BEAUTY OF LOVE

The story of the Wyllie family continues in the second and third series—
WILDERNESS HEARTS SERIES

Book One — the story of Daniel and Ann:
LOVE'S NEW BEGINNING

Book Two — the story of Gabe and Martha:
LOVE'S SUNRISE

Book Three —the story of Little John and Allison

LOVE'S GLORY

Book Four—the story of Liam and Polly
LOVE'S WHISPER

WILDERNESS DAWNING SERIES
Book One—the story of Samuel and Louisa
RED RIVER RIFLES

ABOUT THE AUTHOR

AMAZON BESTSELLING NOVELIST DOROTHY WILEY is an award-winning, multi-published author of Historical Romance and Western Romance. Her first two series, the *American Wilderness Series* and *Wilderness Hearts Series*, are set on the American frontier when Kentucky was the West. Her third series, *Wilderness Dawning—the Texas Wyllie Brothers*, continues the highly-acclaimed Wyllie family saga but brings some of the family to the new edge of the West—the Province of Texas. All of her novels blend thrilling action with the romance of a moving love story to create exceedingly engaging page-turners.

Like Wiley's compelling heroes, who from the onset make it clear they will not fail despite the adversities they face, this author is likewise destined for success. Her novels have won numerous awards, notably a RONE Award Finalist, a Laramie Award Finalist, a Chatelaine Finalist for Romantic Fiction, an Amazon Breakthrough Novel Award Quarter-finalist, a Readers' Favorite Gold Medal, a USA Best Book Awards Finalist, and a Historical Novel Society Editor's Choice. And Wiley's books continue to earn five-star ratings from readers and high praise from reviewers, including several Crowned Heart reviews from InD'Tale Magazine.

Wiley's extraordinary historical and western romances, inspired by history, teem with action and cliff-edge tension. Her books' timeless messages of family and loyalty are both raw and honest. In all her novels, the author's complex characters come alive and are joined by a memorable ensemble of friends and family. And, as she skillfully unravels a compelling tale, Wiley includes rich historical elements to create a vivid colonial world that celebrates the heritage of the frontier.

Wiley attended college at The University of Texas in Austin. She graduated with honors, receiving a Bachelor of Journalism, and grew to dearly love both Texas and a 7th-generation Texan, her husband Larry. Her husband's courageous ancestors, early pioneers of Kentucky and Texas, provided the inspiration for her novels. After a distinguished career in corporate marketing and public relations, Wiley is living her dream—writing novels that touch the hearts of her readers.

YOU'RE INVITED TO CONNECT
WITH THE AUTHOR

Amazon – Follow Dorothy Wiley on Amazon
www.amazon.com/author/dorothywiley

YouTube – Enter Dorothy Wiley in YouTube's search box to
see beautiful book trailers

Author's Website and Newsletter Signup
www.dorothywiley.com

Facebook – *www.facebook.com/DorothyWileyAuthor*
and *www.facebook.com/DorothyMayWiley*

Twitter – *@WileyDorothy*

Goodreads – *www.goodreads.com*

Pinterest – Follow *dorothymwiley* to see inspiration boards for
each book

ACKNOWLEDGMENTS & THANKS

WITH EACH BOOK I RELEASE, my gratitude to my loyal readers grows. I am enormously appreciative for all your kind reviews, thoughtful notes sent to me through my website, and caring Facebook comments. Believe me, you are the primary reason I keep writing!

As always, I want to thank my real life courageous hero, my husband of forty-three years, a 7th generation Texan! Thank you for showing me what forever and ever love is and for being the kind of man who treats women with respect and kindness. I would never have been able to write about love without experiencing it so richly with you all these years. I pray that God will give us many more years together.

Many thanks to the beta readers of this novel, including award-winning historical romance author Amanda Hughes, reviewer JoAnne Weiss with Romancing the Book, Marlene Larsen, and Lori Ratterman, for their helpful suggestions and proofreading. Your help and encouragement were invaluable.

And my thanks my talented cover designer, Kimberly Killion, and the interior designer, Jennifer Jakes, both with the Killion Group, www.theKillionGroupInc.com.

I honestly don't know where the series will go from here. If there will be books about Samuel's brothers Thomas, Cornelius, and Steve or more books about Samuel and Louisa. Or maybe the characters return to Kentucky. Please let me know what you'd like to read about in future books! Send me a note through my website http://www.dorothywiley.com under the 'Contact' tab.

Blessings,

Dorothy

P.S. Don't forget to write a short review, please! You can find this novel and all of my other books on my Amazon author page at *www.amazon.com/author/dorothywiley*

Made in the USA
Lexington, KY
14 November 2019

56975395R00146